"Some things just don't have a price."

Nick turned the steering wheel sharply as he spoke, swinging Brooke toward him. It was as if the Dusenberg held his power, his worth, his confidence.

"Was the relative who left you this car rich?" she asked.

Nick laughed. "Not by any stretch of the imagination. My grandfather was a shoemaker."

"Then how could he afford a Dusenberg?"

"He didn't buy it. One of his best customers did. When he died, he left the car to Grandpa. He wrote in his will that Grandpa was the only man he'd known who understood the meaning of the word *quality*. So the car came to represent everything my grandfather stood for. It was his most prized possession."

"And he left it to you."

"Yes. He told me, 'You put care and love into everything you do, Nicky, that's quality. It doesn't matter about money. You love what you do, you'll be a rich man.'"

Brooke's heart swelled at the look of love on Nick's face, and she told herself that if he ever looked at her that way, she'd abandon everything else to be with him. This time around, she would have no other choice.

ABOUT THE AUTHOR

Tracy Hughes is a pseudonym for prolific
romance novelist Terri Herrington. Winner of
the 1987 RWA Golden Medallion Award, she's
written books that have drawn rave reviews
from critics and fans alike. Set in Terri's
adopted state, Florida, *Emerald Windows* deals
with a subject close to every writer's heart:
the business of making a living as a creative
artist. Terri, her husband and their two small
children make their home near Tampa.

Books by Tracy Hughes

HARLEQUIN SUPERROMANCE
304–ABOVE THE CLOUDS
342–JO

Emerald Windows

TRACY HUGHES

Harlequin Books

TORONTO • NEW YORK • LONDON
AMSTERDAM • PARIS • SYDNEY • HAMBURG
STOCKHOLM • ATHENS • TOKYO • MILAN

Published November 1989

First printing September 1989

ISBN 0-373-70381-3

CHAPTER ONE

THE WINDOWS OF THE Hayden Museum were caked with dust, and from outside Brooke Martin could see web-shaped cracks that had been evident ten years earlier, when she'd last seen the place. It surprised her that the town of Hayden, Florida—usually much tighter with their purse strings than they were with their gossip—had decided to allocate funds for renovations. What surprised her even more, however, was the fact that they had hired her to design the stained-glass windows that would replace the relics she saw now. There had been a time when the town of Hayden wouldn't have hired her to mop their floors. But things had changed, she supposed. And it was about time.

She rounded the building to the small employee parking lot in the rear, skirted by palm trees and one sprawling oak that shaded the pavement from the early-spring sun. Only one car occupied a space there, and her heart jolted at the sight of it. She stopped as her breath caught in her lungs, and for a split second gave serious thought to running back to her own car and out of Hayden in the time it would take to say "Not again...."

It was a 1931 Duesenberg Model J coupe...and she knew, without a doubt, that there couldn't be two such vehicles in Hayden, Florida. She also knew that the man who had once owned the luxury car still did. No amount of money nor persuasion had ever convinced him to part with it. Which meant that he was here, inside the museum, waiting for her....

Brooke's heart staggered in her chest, and she felt her face burning as red as the loose crimson blouse she wore. Her hands began to tremble, and she dropped her portfolio to her side, letting her five gold bracelets jangle around her wrist. Inhaling deeply, she let her troubled gaze drift to the door, straightened her posture and made herself take a step forward. So he was in there...what of it? A lot had happened since that night...since that kiss....

A March breeze whispered through the long golden strands of her hair, touching the earrings that dangled like mute wind chimes. Fingering the chains adorning her throat and chest, she paused at the door and told herself that it wasn't facing him now that bothered her so. It was that she hadn't faced him before. She had run away, but what else could she have done? The town had the juiciest piece of gossip they'd ever had...that the high school art teacher, Nick Marcello, had been sleeping with one of his students. It didn't matter how much of it was true—or how much wasn't. All that mattered was that she had gotten out of town as fast as she could, hoping to spare her family any more shame.

But now, Brooke reminded herself with a grim lift of her chin, she had made a pact with herself. She had sworn that when she came back to take this job, she would face the town with dignity and integrity, and somehow, by creating a work of art that would send them all reeling, she would redeem herself. Part of that process, she had known, would be facing him again. She just hadn't expected to do it so soon, before she'd had her job to act as a crutch.

She opened the door and stepped into the musty old building. The door creaked behind her, then slammed with an echoing thud. She stood there quietly for a moment, listening, looking....

"I've been waiting for you." His voice came from just inside the darkened corridor, and she saw him leaning against the wall in a pair of tight faded jeans, an old flannel shirt rolled up to the elbows and a pair of new sneakers. He stepped toward her, a tentative smile tugging at those full lips she had often fantasized about in class. A fan overhead blew his black hair away from his face in quiet disarray, and she noted that it was longer than before, when his job had dictated his image. He seemed younger than he had when she was in high school, she realized instantly. But maybe it was just that she was older. She recalled the dress shirts and ties he'd always worn, the freshly pressed trousers, the shiny loafers. Only he didn't work as a teacher anymore. He'd been fired as soon as the scandal hit the papers.

Brooke tried to smile, but the effort was too much for her. "I . . . I didn't know you would be here. Mr. Anderson said—"

"If you'd known, you wouldn't have come," Nick cut in softly. "That's why I asked him to call for me. Truth is, he's the chairman of the renovation committee, but he's on leave of absence from his job here until the renovation is finished."

Her emerald eyes grew round in consternation. "So, you're going to be working here?" she asked.

He heard the trepidation in her voice, and his smile faltered as his eyes swept over her, from the full waves in her gold and chestnut hair, to the bare, tanned legs revealed beneath her skirt, to her sandal-clad feet. Even in the dimness of the room she could see the sparkling clarity in the opaque onyx of his eyes. She realized they were even darker than all the charcoal sketches she had made of him from memory then torn to pieces before anyone could see them. "I'm in charge of artistic development in the renovation," he said. "But to be perfectly honest, that consists mainly of those windows. I'm going to be helping you design them. The town is counting on them being a new point of interest in the museum. *I'm* counting on them being a master-piece."

Brooke's head clouded at the onslaught of information. It contradicted what she'd expected, and she stepped back and leaned against a table. "Oh," she said, issuing the word as a long breath. "I don't know. I just don't know."

Nick took another step toward her, and she caught the scent that had tantalized her so long ago—the unique, un-tainted scent of him. She brought her eyes up to his, saw the gentleness that had always been there, the openness that had once enabled him to see in her work what no one else had seen. "You don't know what, Brooke?" he asked qui-etly. "If you can create a masterpiece, or if you can work with me?"

"Both." She tried to control the quiver at the corners of her lips. "It's just...I didn't expect to see you so soon. And if we're working together, I just...Nick, what will people say?"

He smiled sadly then and touched her cheek with a hand she had long ago memorized and cherished and adored. "Nothing they haven't already said," he whispered.

She dropped her eyes, but he kept his hand on her cheek and inclined his head in order to see her face. "It's so silly," she whispered, knowing that a fine mist was coming to her eyes, and that if she didn't hold tightly to her tenuous emotions, she would start to cry. "I know I shouldn't let it bother me. Especially when nothing ever really hap-pened."

His fingers touched her chin lightly, and he urged her face up to his. Her eyes met his, and she saw the frown cutting between his dark brows. "Oh, something happened, Brooke," he whispered. "You know it did."

She moved away from the table, breaking contact, trying to gain some semblance of control over her feelings. Why couldn't she have looked at him and told her heart that her memories of him had been exaggerated? Why couldn't the intensity of emotion connected with him have faded the slightest degree? "So I had a crush on you," she admitted, making too light of a memory that had plagued her for years. "Lots of girls get crushes on their teachers. I feel silly about it now. I let my infatuation with you carry me away, and I did something stupid."

"Stupid?" he asked quickly, as if her recollection of that night didn't match his. "Is that really how you feel about what happened?"

She shrugged, but the gesture didn't look as nonchalant as she'd intended. "What do you want me to say, Nick?"

Nick stiffened then and moved back, as if to offer her the distance from him she so obviously needed. "Nothing," he said quietly. He studied the floor for a moment, his frown engraving his forehead more deeply than it had ten years earlier, and finally he brought his eyes back to hers. "Look, I didn't hire you for this job because of any of that. I hired you because you're talented. I've kept up with your work since you left."

"You have?" she asked.

He nodded. "I saw the windows in the church you did in Tallahassee. And the door you did at that restaurant in Pensacola. I heard your business is doing really well, but you could do so much more. My decision was purely a business one."

Brooke peered at the old glass that skirted the circumference of the ceiling. "I've never done anything of this caliber, though."

"You've done plenty of this caliber," he said. "Maybe just not this size."

She regarded him with questioning—almost suspicious—eyes. It wasn't often that she was praised for her body of work. Most people viewed her as an interior decorator of sorts, someone who added life to dull rooms.

"I've always wanted to work with you," Nick said quietly. "Ever since you were in high school and I saw the talent you had. We always had compatible visions, Brooke. I know we could do something really special together."

She shook her head, wondering if that "something special" could be limited to those windows. She doubted it. There was too much at stake—her heart, her mind, her soul. "I just don't know," she said. "This is the first time I've been back to Hayden since—" she glanced up at him, steadied her voice "—since I graduated. The gossip has had ten years to die down. I don't know if I can stand to have it start back up again, just because we're working together. My family has had enough embarrassment, and so have we."

Nick crossed his arms, and she saw him stiffen visibly, as if the subject was growing tedious. "Brooke, I asked you here to take an assignment, not to have an affair with me. Ten years is a long time. A lot of water has passed under the bridge." He clenched his jaw, then shrugged. "Job changes, experience, marriage..."

Brooke recognized the hostility in his tone at the word *marriage*, and she diverted her eyes. Her marriage to Skip Nelson, the town's football quarterback, had been a mistake from the beginning. At the time, however, four short months after the scandal erupted, it had seemed a welcome escape and a way to restore her pride. But it hadn't worked, and she didn't want to dwell on the experience now.

"I need time to think about this," Brooke said. "I don't know if I can go through with it."

He turned away from her, slid his fingers into his front pockets and seemed to consider a yellowed document set on exhibit in a box of glass. "How much time do you need?" he asked. "I wanted to get started this week. It'll take months to do this job right, and we haven't got a day to waste."

Brooke looked up at the windows again and thought how much she had pinned her hopes on them. They were the means by which she'd turn her life around and set things right once and for all. She had almost seen them as symbolic windows through which she could assume her old life—the one she had as an innocent, before labels were pinned on her and opinions were formed of her. She had temporarily closed her business in Tallahassee for this project, and now...

"I don't know," she said again. "Maybe I can give you an answer tomorrow."

For a moment Nick didn't respond, but finally he lifted his shoulders grudgingly. "All right."

She started back to the door, feeling as if the weight of the town had been set on her chest once again, limiting her breath. She reached for the tarnished doorknob, turned it.

"Brooke?" Nick's voice filled the building.

Brooke turned around and saw that the hardness in his expression was gone, and in its place was that old smile that used to turn her heart inside out. "Uh-huh?"

"It was good to see you," he said.

"Yeah," she whispered, for she could barely make her voice function. "It was good to see you, too, Nick."

NICK WILTED AGAINST the table the moment the door closed behind her and kicked himself for confronting her the way he had. Maybe he should have given her more time to get used to the idea, he thought. Maybe he should have asked Horace Anderson to be here today, to break the news to her. . . .

Then, at once, Nick berated himself again for even entertaining the idea. It had been best to face Brooke the moment she came to town. That way the thing she dreaded the most was behind her. It was all downhill from here.

He stood up and went back to the curator's office, which he was using for the duration of the renovation. Nick tried not to think about the fact that she looked even better than she had when she was eighteen, nor about the unique, creative style of dressing she retained, with the chains and bracelets that added an artist's flare to her thrift-shop clothes. He'd watched the rich girls clamor to imitate Brooke in high school, and wealthy women probably envied her panache now. He tried not to dwell on the fact that her hair was a little darker, as if an artist's brush had painted it in different shades of gold, with just a subtle trace of brown for substance. He tried to forget that her shamrock-green eyes looked exactly as they had years ago when she had looked at him—round and innocent and secretively pensive. But that was her look, he told himself. It didn't denote adoration, any more than it did love. It never had.

He dropped down into the chair behind his desk and propped his chin on his hand, staring at the peeling wallpaper and seeing Brooke's face, instead. Back then, when she'd looked at him, making his heart twist in guilty yearning, he could have sworn there was something there...

She was seventeen when he'd first seen her, sitting in the front row of his class, working on the sketch of the mangled bicycle he'd placed at the front of the room. The project had been deliberately difficult, and he'd used it to test the students' talents and abilities. Slowly he had walked up and down the aisles between work stations, commenting on each student's crude progress . . . when he had come to her.

It was her work that caught his attention first. The lines of her sketch had been so precise, so accurate, that he doubted he could have captured the bicycle better himself. But something about the drawing had reached out to him. It was the shiny newness, the uniqueness of the image...the vision of something fresh in something so used up. . . .

He remembered the way she had looked up at him, embarrassed that he'd been watching her, and he had instantly melted at the sight of those round, innocent green eyes full of expectation. Her hair, strands ranging from silky blond to tawny brown, feathered into her eyes and shimmered around her shoulders, tangling with the chains she wore even then.

"It's not finished," she had said, and he'd recognized the apology in her voice.

"It's very good," he'd told her. "Have you been studying art for long?"

"Just two years," she'd said, meeting his eyes directly. "Mr. Jasper taught me last year, but he didn't let us get very creative."

Nick's smile had reached up from his heart, and suddenly he was glad he'd become a teacher. "You can get as creative as you want in my class."

Brooke had laughed under her breath, and he remembered thinking that he'd never seen a more light-up-the-abyss smile. It had warmed something deep within him, something that had lain cold and dormant for too long. "Yeah, I kind of thought you'd feel that way when I saw you," she'd said. Then she'd caught herself, as if she'd given too much away, and qualified her statement with, "I mean, most stuffed shirts don't drive antique hot rods."

If there was anything that made a friend of Nick, it was complimenting his Duesenberg. "You saw my car outside?"

"Who could miss it?" she asked. "You parked it on the football field."

He had laughed then, not really caring that others in the room were beginning to listen in. "I'm real protective of my car," he'd said. "My grandfather left it to me, and there aren't many like it. It's a real work of art."

"Yeah, it is," Brooke had agreed, with genuine sincerity that most women he'd known couldn't duplicate. "And you've taken good care of it. That's how I knew I'd like your class."

There had been a lot of pretty young students in his classes that year he'd taught at Hayden High School, and not all had been there because of a burning interest in art. Some of them saw art as an "easy A." Others competed for the interest of the handsome young teacher who seemed so aloof outside the classroom. But Brooke had been different. Her passion for art had been evident in every assignment she'd completed for him, and that passion excited him.

It wasn't long before he found himself watching her from his desk as the other students worked. He'd found it pleasant to watch her eyes glaze over with the unique vision he somehow understood on each project she tackled. He had enjoyed watching the long, sensuous strokes of her hands as they moved across the page, had loved wondering what special insight she would put into her work this time.

But as the year progressed, Nick found his interest in Brooke growing into something that disturbed him.

To combat his plaguing feelings, he had deliberately tried to avoid her on anything more than a teacher-student level. When he worked with her, he tried not to lean too close, so that he could avoid her enticing scent, which made his fantasies run wild. He tried not to brush her hand with his when he taught her a new technique. And he tried not to look directly into her compelling eyes unless he had to.

It had worked for a while. He had managed to convince himself that she was just another student, that she wasn't occupying too many of his thoughts, that he was handling his job appropriately.

Until she had started her final project for the year.

The sculpture she began to create intrigued him so much that he found himself abandoning all his promises to himself, and watching, mesmerized, as the piece took form. It was the sculpture of two hands—a man's and a woman's—joining in a gentle embrace. There was something so sensual about the tender touch that, once again, Nick found himself powerless to keep his distance. Continually he offered her extra advice, extra lessons, extra help. When they reached the final term of the year, he urged her to begin staying after school to work on the project, so that he could be there to watch her progress and help her finish in time to enter the sculpture in the statewide competition for an art scholarship at Florida State.

It was during those hours after school that Nick finally had to admit to himself that he had fallen irrevocably in love...and that there wasn't a damn thing he could do about it. Somewhere along the line he had told her to call him Nick, rather than Mr. Marcello, when they were alone. And each time she had uttered his name, he had felt his emotions quiver like the melodic strings of a violin. As difficult as it had been, he had acted only in the most appropriate manner, in the capacity of a teacher guiding a student into taking her talent as far as it could go. But sometimes, when the afternoon hours rolled into early evening, it became a real struggle.

It was on one of those days that Brooke had looked up at him with forlorn defeat in her eyes. "I can't do it," she'd said. "It's too ambitious. I should have tried something easier."

"What do you mean you can't do it?" he asked. "You're halfway there already."

"With the woman's hand," she'd said. "But I can't get the man's hand right. It's too smooth. I don't know how to capture the texture...the strength."

Before he'd realized what he was doing, Nick had sat down beside her and offered her his hand. "Here," he'd said quietly. "Study mine."

Brooke's hand had trembled as she'd taken his, and she had looked at it as if it were a fragile piece of china that she had no right to touch. Finally, when he realized she couldn't take the initiative on her own, he had lifted her other hand, and set her fingertips on his knuckles. "Feel the texture," he'd said quietly, willing his heart to stop urging him into making a mistake. "Feel the bone structure. The veins. The imperfections."

Slowly Brooke had begun to study his hand with the most exciting, maddeningly tentative touch he'd ever experienced. He had held his breath as she ran her fingertips over each knuckle, exploring the height of the bones and the cracks in the skin. Her touch had grown less tentative as she'd followed the line of one swollen vein down to his wrist, then turned the hand over and studied the creviced palm. Her fingernail had tickled across the lines there, making something deep in the pit of his stomach tighten. His fingers had relaxed and curled inward.

His eyes had drifted away from their hands to her eyes, and he had wondered how much of a crime it would be to lean over—just a few inches—and kiss her. And then, as if Brooke had read his thoughts, her gaze had risen from their hands, still entwined, and met his.

They looked at each other for a moment—a moment in which all the rights and wrongs in Nick's life passed before his eyes. But finally good judgment had forced him to make a choice, and he had withdrawn his hand. "Now see if that helps," he'd whispered.

Brooke had looked back at the sculpture, deep disappointment etched in her eyes, and he'd wished he could have taken one of his oil paint brushes, and erased those somber lines with a few delicate strokes.

Rumors began to fly around the school after that, stories that one of the cheerleaders had come into the class after cheerleading practice to get something she'd left in her desk, and seen Mr. Marcello and Brooke Martin "holding hands." The rumors grew, and embellishments thrived, until there was speculation that Nick and Brooke were having an affair, that they were secretly married, that she was pregnant with his child. Nick had assured the principal that there was nothing going on, and that Brooke was a very gifted student working on the most poignant piece of sculpture he'd seen by an amateur, and that as her teacher, it was his job to guide and encourage her so that she could win the state competition.

But at night, it had been so difficult to find sleep, when she kept drifting in and out of his dreams, fulfilling the elemental fantasies he would never have dared entertain in his waking hours. In her eyes, he could see that Brooke felt the same way about him, and thankfully she didn't act on her desires, either. But one night near the end of the year, when her sculpture was almost finished, Nick finally made a decision.

He couldn't do anything about his feelings now, while she was his student, but there was no law that said he had to keep his distance after she turned eighteen and graduated. And so he had counted the days until that would happen, waiting for the moment that he could hold her in his arms, kiss her with the passion that had fueled him all these months....

When the night of graduation finally came, Nick had sat through the agonizingly long graduation ceremony, then had gone to stand in the lobby to congratulate his other students. He had watched for her with bated breath, his heart pounding in anticipation, as one by one, graduates filed out of the school's auditorium.

And finally Brooke had come out, holding her cap in her hand and unzipping her robe as if she couldn't shed that phase of her life fast enough. But just as their eyes had met, she'd been encircled by her family, swallowed into their hugs and congratulations, and ordered to put her robe back on and pose for an eternity of pictures. Finally, their gazes collided again, and he could have sworn he saw fire dancing in her eyes—a fire that consumed the innocence and shyness that had been there before, a fire that ignited a stirring heat in his heart.

"Enjoy the party," her father was saying. "We need to get Roxy to bed."

Nick saw her bend over to trap her little sister in a strong hug, and at the seven-year-old's delightful giggle, he smiled.

She waited until her family was out of sight, before looking at him again. Finally, she had come toward him. "I was looking for you before," she'd admitted with a soft smile. "I thought you hadn't come."

"You didn't think I'd miss your graduation, did you?" he'd asked. "Not when you were getting the art scholarship."

She had blushed then, the prettiest shade of pink he had ever seen. "Thank you for that. I couldn't have done it without you."

He would have said more, but he'd felt his throat constricting. After all those months of holding back, he'd found it difficult to follow his feelings. "Are you going to the graduation party?" he'd asked, lowering his voice to an intimate pitch.

"Are you?" she'd asked.

Nick's face had grown hot, and he'd tugged slightly on his tie. "I was invited. But to tell you the truth..." His gaze had dropped to her lips, where her tongue was wetting the cherry lipstick that had a soft, seductive scent. "I was hoping...that you and I could...maybe go somewhere and...talk."

He'd watched her pupils enlarge to the size of her irises, darkening the green in evidence of her vulnerability. The pink blush climbed her cheekbones as she'd nodded. "I was hoping that, too. In fact, I have something for you. Something I want to give you."

In spite of the tension pulsing through him, Nick had managed to smile. "Hey, it's your graduation. I'm supposed to give *you* something."

"You already have," she'd whispered.

Before he'd had the chance to ask what she meant, she had started through the crowd, shedding her graduation gown as she went. She'd tossed the robe over her arm, revealing a periwinkle dress that hugged her body in a way that made his mouth go dry. Heart tripping, he had followed her through the dark halls of the school, where no one had reason to be, and into the art room that seemed to be their private, shared domain.

He had stepped inside and watched, quietly, as she'd turned on one of the easel lights, leaving the rest of the room dim. Brooke had taken the sculpture that he'd kept displayed on his desk since she'd won the competition, planning for her to pick it up after school was out, and she had held it out to him. "I've named it *Infinity*" she'd said quietly. "It's for you. I want you to have it."

Nick had caught his breath and told himself she didn't really understand the significance of her gesture. "But Brooke," he'd said, his voice cracking. "It's the best thing you've ever done. You should keep it . . . or sell it . . ."

"I could never sell this," she'd whispered, setting the sculpture in his hands. "It means too much." Then, with a touch that had almost sent him over the edge of control, she had traced his hand with her fingertips again. "It's your hand . . . and mine."

Slowly Nick had reached out and cupped the back of her neck and, with a gentle touch, drawn her closer to him. Their lips met, and months of simmering emotion came to full boil, robbing each of them of control. She had tasted like the most exquisite wine but the potency of her kiss was more intoxicating than one-hundred-proof whiskey. His heart had bashed against his rib cage as he'd held her, warning him that the feelings were more powerful than he'd counted on, more devastatingly precious. Nick wasn't sure how he'd managed to set the sculpture down without breaking it, but suddenly both arms were around her, and he was crushing her to him, vividly aware that even the ultimate closeness, the absolute intimacy, would still not satiate the hunger she'd created in his soul. The kiss deepened rhythmically, and he'd buried one hand in her hair, while the other roamed recklessly over her hips, pressing her tightly against him. His rugged breath mingled and merged with hers, and he'd felt her breasts tantalizing his chest as her hands slid over his back, as if she, too, had fantasized about the moment and had choreographed each touch in her mind.

Suddenly the lights had flashed on, flooding the room in cruel white. Nick and Brooke had jumped apart and turned to the door. There stood the principal, Gerald Hemphill, and his wife, Abby, gaping at them in horror and condemnation, as if they'd caught a teacher raping a child.

Nick's first thought had been that he didn't owe them an explanation. He had only kissed Brooke—a legal adult—and she had now graduated, after all. But the Hemphills perceived things differently.

For the rest of his life, Nick was sure he would never forget the look of mortified humiliation that had passed over Brooke's face as the principal had warned her to "get her clothes and go home," referring to the graduation gown she'd draped over a chair.

Before Nick had the chance to stop her, she had fled out the door...and out of his life.

It hadn't mattered to him that night that Mr. Hemphill had fired him on the spot, or that the school board threatened to take punitive action. The thought that kept running through his mind was that Brooke was hurting. He'd wasted no time getting to a telephone to call her, and when she'd answered the phone, there were sobbing undulations in her voice.

"It's going to be all right," he'd assured her in a voice that had almost calmed her. "You have to trust me. Promise you'll trust me."

She had promised, but the next morning the headlines in the paper read, "Teacher Fired for Affair with Student," and the article exaggerated details of how rumors had abounded for weeks about the teacher and the student, their full names spelled out for all to see. It also stated how Mr. and Mrs. Hemphill had finally "caught them in the act."

When it came right down to it, Brooke had not been able to trust him. She had left town that day, and as far as Nick knew, she had never returned until today. Oh, he had considered going after her, once he was able to locate her at Florida State University, where she had enrolled in summer school. But something had told him to give her time. The scandal needed a while to die down, and she needed to recover.

But he supposed he had given her too much time, because the following October, a short four months after the kiss that had changed their lives, he'd heard that Brooke had married Skip Nelson. Skip, the town's football hero, had also attended Florida State. The news had sent Nick into a depression he hadn't shaken for nearly a year. Had it all been just a foolish dream on his part? Just a passing crush on hers?

He'd gotten over the pain years ago, and there were times when he would have sworn he'd gotten over her as well. Memories had a way of fading. But once a lesson was learned, it was hard to forget. And Brooke had taught him plenty of lessons... many more than he had taught her.

"So I had a crush on you... infatuation... stupid..." She had said it herself today, and for the life of him Nick wished he had only seen it years ago instead of pretending that there was more between them.

There wasn't more. There was only Brooke and himself and the windows that needed an artist's touch. He hoped she wouldn't turn down the project, and swore that if she accepted the job, nothing would happen between them.

Brooke had made her position to him clear a long time ago when she'd married. And even though she was divorced now, he wouldn't let himself hurt like that again. Some lessons were never forgotten, he thought. Especially when one learned them the hard way.

CHAPTER TWO

BROOKE PULLED HER CAR out of the museum's parking lot and into the main street that ran through Hayden, past the old building that housed J.C. Penneys, the Phillips 66 gas station owned by Jarrett Plumer and his son and the Our Lady Catholic Church where Father Jessup had baptized her. Everything was the same as when she'd left it. And yet everything was different.

She'd had her down moments since she'd left Hayden, and Brooke was quite certain she'd have a few more in her life. But there hadn't been a day since that night of graduation that she hadn't felt the abysmal humiliation and shame that Mr. and Mrs. Hemphill had dredged up in her. A day hadn't gone by since then that she hadn't closed her eyes in remembrance of that kiss and wondered how something so beautiful could have had such ugly consequences.

"Trust me," Nick had said. And she had promised. But that was before her parents had been disgraced and the newspaper had made the kiss a front-page story.

Now, as she drove through the blue-collar section of town on her way to her family's home, she recalled the anger in her father's face the night Mrs. Hemphill had called and told him what they'd allegedly caught his daughter doing. For the first time in her life Brooke had seen the capability in George Martin's eyes for doing harm to another human being. As long as she lived, she would never forget his huge frame bolting across the floor as he'd carried his broken pride like a weapon that would exact the only revenge he understood.

"Daddy, where are you going?" she had shouted.

"I'm going to find that bastard and kill him!" George Martin's voice had shaken the frame house and shattered every ounce of security Brooke had known in her life.

She had turned to her mother, desperately seeking her aid. "Mom, stop him!"

"No!" her mother had screamed. "If he doesn't kill him, I'll do it myself."

The horror of their quick belief in the things the Hemphills had said had driven Brooke over the edge. "But it wasn't him!" she cried. "It was me! He kissed me because I wanted him to. *I* led *him* to that room tonight!"

George Martin had turned slowly around, his eyes two blazing sapphires that had singed her very soul. "You *what*?"

The condemnation in his question had cut into her like a snakebite, shooting venom into Brooke's dying heart. "We just kissed, Daddy. What's so wrong with that?"

"He's a grown man, and you're a child," her father had roared. He had grabbed her before she could flinch and shook her with a force so great she thought he would break her in two. "He's a teacher!"

"But...he's only five years older than me," she'd cried. "You're that much older than Mom."

"I wasn't her *teacher*!" he shouted again. "And she wasn't a kid when we met!"

"I'm not a kid," Brooke sobbed, but she knew that nothing she said would ever make things right in their eyes. "Nick didn't take advantage of me."

"That's not the way Abby Hemphill tells it!" her mother had said, hysteria cracking her voice. "We've worked all our lives in this town to be known as good people with good children, and it wasn't easy with an income that makes people look down on you, anyway. But now, in one night, it's all ruined. We're reduced to trash, because whatever happened, Abby Hemphill's word is the only word that matters!''

And her mother had been right. As long as she lived, Brooke would never forget the headlines the next morning, the words that implied she and Nick had been having a secret affair during school. When she read that he had been fired for something that he hadn't done, it had been too much to endure.

She had packed her suitcases that morning, withdrawn all the money she'd worked at the local theater box office to save, and driven her little third-hand car she'd bought months earlier out of town before her parents even knew what hit them. The only person who had seen her leave was her little sister Roxy, only seven years old at the time. Roxy had sat on the porch and waved goodbye, a look of complete confusion on her face as she tried to understand the events that had changed her family forever.

The summer that followed was one of the loneliest and most miserable of Brooke's life. Throughout it all she never gave up hoping that Nick would find her and come after her, so that they could continue what they had started in a place where no one would care if or how they were involved. But he didn't come, and with each passing day, she'd realized more fully that he had given up much too much for what had happened between them. The loss of her pride had been nothing compared with the loss of his livelihood. She doubted he would ever forgive her, and so Brooke never forgave herself.

She had found an apartment in Tallahassee, and had taken a job as a hotel clerk to support herself until she received her scholarship, enabling her to enroll in Florida

State University the second session that summer. It was then, after she had moved into the dormitory, that she'd run into Skip Nelson, a football quarterback who'd been her close friend in high school until he'd graduated a year earlier.

Skip hadn't condemned her for the scandal, as he knew her well enough to know that she wasn't the type to make love with her teacher in a janitorial closet after school. He had also witnessed the powers of Abby Hemphill's gossip firsthand, when his parents had divorced years earlier. It had been a profound relief to find someone who sympathized and understood. When Skip's college football career was halted by an injured knee, it seemed that Skip began to depend on her, as well. They were two wounded spirits, bound by loneliness and disappointment.

And as the months wore on and the scandal mushroomed and thrived in the form of a history professor who'd heard she "liked teachers," and the girls in her dorm who whispered about the way they supposed she "earned her grades," Skip had taken the role of her protector, as well.

Brooke would never forget the night she'd left the library after cramming with Skip for a history test. She was determined to pass, despite her professor's threats to "withhold from her if she withheld from him," when J. J. Harper, one of the basketball players she had repeatedly refused to date, had cornered her in the darkness.

"Come on, Brooke," he'd said, his breathing hard and anxious as he clamped a hand around her elbow. "We all know you're no lily-white saint. The guys in the locker room say you're hot."

"What guys?" Brooke had asked, horrified, for she had dated no one since she'd left Hayden.

"The ones you've shared your talents with," he'd said with a cold chuckle, dragging her against him.

Fury greater than fear had risen up inside her as Brooke tried to jerk loose, and she had dropped her books and watched her papers disperse in the wind. "Let go of me," she'd hissed, almost wrenching free and shoving him with all her strength. "If anyone said that about me they were lying! Get your hands off me!"

Her wrestling seemed only to excite him more, and with a wicked grin that sent a shiver rippling through her veins, he had pulled her into an inconspicuous cluster of trees. "Come on, babe," he'd said, rough hands groping at her clothes as he'd flung her against the trunk of the tree and pinned her with his body. "It'll be so good out here...with the wind on our skin..."

Brooke had tried to scream, but his hard, wet mouth covered hers, muffling her horror.

Then, suddenly, someone had pulled him off her. She had fallen away from the tree at the sudden impact of freedom, and she'd seen Skip's fist crashing into J.J.'s jaw. She'd watched his large frame fall to the ground, seen the blood trickling down his chin.

"Don't you *ever* go near her again!" Skip had warned him. "Or I'll knock out every tooth in your head."

Gasping in order to catch her breath and still trembling, Brooke had clung to Skip as he'd taken her back to where her books were scattered on the ground, gathered them up for her and insisted on walking her back to her dorm.

It was that night, at the lowest point in both their young lives, that Skip had had an idea.

"End the scandal, Brooke," he'd told her, his blue eyes as serious and sincere as she had ever seen them. "Marry me, and it'll all end."

"I can't marry you," she'd argued. "I love you, Skip, but not in that way. Not in the way..."

"Not in the way you love Nick Marcello," he'd finished for her. He had sat back on the dorm steps and scraped his fingers through his short-cropped blond hair. "I know that. But don't you think if something was going to happen with you two, it would have happened by now?"

Brooke hadn't been able to deny that grim fact, and Skip had continued trying to persuade her. "You'll come to love me in time," he'd assured her. "You need me, Brooke. And I need you. Most people don't have that much to start a marriage with."

She wasn't sure what argument had finally convinced her, but one night, not long after his proposal, when her nerves had been strung taut as bowstrings and her emotions were as high and low as a roller coaster out of control, she had surrendered and eloped with him. With no delusions of how their life together would be, and no expectations that could fall short, Brooke had stood before the judge and agreed to become Skip's wife. Though she hadn't planned it when she'd set out, she remembered thinking that night that she had redeemed herself with Hayden and purified herself in the eyes of those determined to believe the worst of her...that marriage to the hometown's football hero would bring her respect once again.

But the next day, when she called and told her parents, she learned that the town was already abuzz with the news, and that a small article in the newspaper had even appeared, in which she was described as "eighteen-year-old Brooke Martin, who left town abruptly in June after the scandal concerning herself and the art teacher with whom she was involved."

And Brooke knew then that nothing she ever did would clear her name.

She had given the marriage a good try, and so had Skip. But as the need for each other wore off and the reality of marriage seeped in, they both realized that the important things in a union just weren't there. Skip's mood swings over his aborted career had gotten under her skin, as her long hours alone with her art got under his.

On the rare occasions when they made love, he never failed to accuse her of thinking of Nick, and of holding back what he felt she "owed" him as his wife. After two years of drifting apart they had both more or less reconciled themselves to the idea that they were happier apart. Three more years of various separations followed, during which Skip began to sleep with every pretty girl who smiled at him, until at last they both agreed to file for divorce, and Brooke had taken back her maiden name.

The town had jumped on their divorce as if it were one more disgraceful thing Brooke Martin had done to embarrass her family. No one could imagine that the town darling, Skip Nelson, had done anything to deserve a broken marriage.

The tragedy of it all, in Brooke's mind, was that she and Skip had ruined a perfect friendship by trying to make their relationship more than it was. Just as she and Nick had ruined the perfect romance.

She thought of the way Nick had uttered the word "marriage" today, as if it made him angry even now. But why, she asked herself, when he'd had every opportunity to come after her and hadn't? What difference had her marrying Skip made to Nick?

She took a deep, quivering breath and told herself that she would never heal from her wounds until she learned to stop pushing things past their natural limitations. Some people were meant to stand back and observe relationships, she thought. People like that had no business developing their own.

She pulled into the driveway of her family home and sat there for a moment, staring at the little house in which she had grown up before she'd known what cruel games adulthood played on people. What would her parents say, now that the black sheep of the family was finally back in town? Would they count the days until she left, fearing that the longer she stayed, the more gossip she would provoke? And when they learned she would be working with Nick...

She reeled the thought back in and told herself just to face what came and not to dwell on the unknown. Slaps in the face were easier to endure when they came as a surprise, she told herself. Dread and anticipation were wasted energy.

Brooke grabbed her suitcase from the back seat and got out of the car. For a moment she peered up at the small house that clearly represented the Martins' lack of wealth, but revealed the stoic pride in what little they had. The house was freshly painted in blue, she noted, though it had been white the last time she'd seen it. And they had changed the color of the front door. A large awning hung over the picture window, a new addition in the last few years. Funny that her parents had never mentioned it when they'd visited her in Tallahassee, Brooke thought, and then she told herself that it was such a little thing...not the kind of thing families talked about when they got together only once or twice each year.

Brooke went up the steps to the porch, set her suitcase down and shook her key chain around until her old house key was in her hand. It jammed in the knob, as if it didn't fit, and she stepped back, frowning. Had they changed the locks?

The door opened from the inside, and her mother smiled at her, as she had when Brooke was a little girl—long before she had become the family albatross. Alice Martin's expression gave Brooke's heart a nostalgic twist, making her ache for the simple childhood days when her parents' approval was so easily earned. For a moment, as Brooke smiled at her mother, who still wore her hair in the same frosted bob she'd worn for fifteen years, Brooke believed that things hadn't changed all that much, after all. "Brooke, we've been waiting for hours! Where have you been?"

"I got tied up." Brooke hugged her mother and stepped over the threshold, dropping her keys back into her purse. "The key...it didn't fit...."

"We had the locks changed a few years ago," her mother explained, taking her suitcase out of her hand and setting it against the wall. "Roxy lost her purse, and we were afraid whoever found it would break in." Her mother saw the distraught look on her daughter's face and gently touched Brooke's hair. "I'm sorry, honey. It never occurred to me to tell you. It's been so long since you were here...I guess I thought you'd never come through that door again."

Brooke sighed, and her gaze panned the living room. Her mother had covered the warped hardwood floors with an inexpensive wall-to-wall carpet, and new furniture filled the room. The old recliner she remembered with its split seams where the stuffing oozed out was gone, as was the old couch with the leg that fell off if you sat on the wrong end. The unfamiliarity and newness made her want to step back outside and focus on her mother's face a little longer, before more changes assaulted her senses. "Everything looks...different," she whispered.

Her mother took her hand and drew her toward the kitchen. "Don't look so surprised, Brooke. When you decide to stay away for ten years, you have to expect a few changes."

Brooke rallied and forced a smile, determined not to reveal how difficult this homecoming was. She should have come home sooner, she told herself, when there was still time to break the proverbial ice and put the past behind her. But somehow, before today, she hadn't been able to do it.

The swinging door to the kitchen burst open, and her father hurried out, his leather-tanned face sporting the same smile he'd worn when she was his "little princess." "There you are!" He swept her up into his arms and swung her around, as if she weighed fifty pounds again. "I took off work early today to see you, but we were beginning to think you'd never show up."

"I'm sorry, Dad," Brooke said, her delight at seeing him fading as he set her down, waiting for an explanation. "I had something to do before I could come home."

"Well, it'd better be good to keep your old man waiting," he said.

Tell them now, Brooke told herself. *Get it over with, so you can relax and enjoy the rest of the night.* Brooke's throat constricted suddenly, and she opened her mouth to tell them about the renovation and the windows and Nick...
"I had to—"

The sound of footsteps cut her off, and she glanced around to see her sister Roxy leaning in the doorway, watching the homecoming with an expressionless face. Her baby-blond hair was pulled up in a banana clasp, and loose curls trailed down her back. Her eyes, an almost bronze color that Brooke had never seen on anyone else, seemed distant and guarded. Brooke had begun to notice a change in her sister over a year ago, just before Roxy had stopped making the trips to Tallahassee with their parents.

"She's just busy with her job at city hall," her mother had said, trying to explain Roxy's aloofness. Or, "She's just preoccupied with school." But now Brooke could feel that there was something more in the strain etched on her sister's face and the distance she'd put between them.

"Roxy." Brooke reached for her sister and pulled the stiff young woman into a one-sided hug. Roxy's subtle resistance instantly confirmed that all was not well. Brooke released her and saw that while Roxy did smile the gesture didn't appear to be without effort. "Hi, Brooke," she said quietly.

Brooke peered into her eyes, searching for a clue as to what was wrong. "Are you okay?" she asked.

"Sure," Roxy said. "Fine."

Brooke dropped her hands, allowing them to hang at her sides.

Her mother stepped between them before Brooke could analyze her sister's mood further, shoving them both into the kitchen. "I've kept dinner warm for you, Brooke," she said. "I wouldn't let anyone touch a thing. So, tell us. What in the world finally convinced you that you wouldn't turn into a pillar of salt if you came home?"

Brooke looked at her mother, who bustled around the stove filling the plates, at her father, who sat down at his designated place at the head of the table, at her sister, who still stood slightly away from the table, waiting with grudging interest for an answer.

"It's a job," Brooke said. "I had an offer to do the stained glass windows in the museum. They're renovating it, you know, and—"

Her mother swung around, astounded as she regarded her daughter. "You mean, the town council asked *you* to do it?" A slow smile spread across her face as she met her husband's eyes.

"Of course they asked," George replied with a characteristic chuckle, puffing up as if the town council assigned his daughter to every important job that came along. "Our little girl designs the best windows in the hemisphere. Who else would they have asked?"

"Well, the town council members aren't really the ones who asked me," Brooke corrected them tentatively.

Her mother brought two of the plates to the table and set them on their place mats, still listening intently.

"In fact," Brooke went on, "I'm not even sure they know that I was chosen."

Her mother went back for the other two plates, and Roxy sat down. "Then who hired you?" her mother asked.

Brooke stared down at her plate, wishing some miracle would occur to wipe the subject from their minds. They hadn't discussed Nick Marcello in all these years. Why did it have to happen now? She took a deep breath and told herself there was no way to avoid it. "Nick asked me," she whispered.

Her mother dropped the fork she had just lifted, and it landed on her plate with a loud clatter. Her father didn't move a muscle, but his face hardened over to a colorless granite. Even Roxy's eyes seemed to dull in consternation as she stared at the iced tea beside her plate.

"What in the hell has Nick Marcello got to do with it?" her father bit out in a voice as quiet as a volcano before its eruption.

Brooke met her father's eyes and swallowed hard. "He's in charge of artistic development for the renovation." She turned to her mother, saw that the same expression had altered her face, as well, as intense as if she'd broken the news that she was next month's centerfold for *Playboy*. "Mom, I haven't agreed to take the job, yet. I didn't know he was involved, and when I saw him this afternoon, I told him that I'd have to think about it."

"Think about it?" her mother repeated. "You actually have to *think* about it? After all that's happened? After all he's put us through?"

"What about Skip?" her father cut in, his voice barely suppressing a quivering rage. "He lives in this town now, you know. The divorce was enough of an embarrassment to him, without *this* mess starting up again."

Brooke took a deep breath and warned herself that losing her temper would serve no purpose. "Dad, nothing is starting up again. I'm not going to embarrass anybody. I was interested in the job because it's a fantastic career opportunity. That's absolutely the only reason. Don't you think it's time I came back here and faced up to everything that's happened? I'm getting tired of running."

Her mother leaned toward her at the table, gaping at her in disbelief. "You *can't* be considering taking this job, Brooke." The statement sounded too much like an order, and Brooke's white-knuckled fingers clamped more tightly over the edges of her chair.

"Mom, I closed my business down in Tallahassee for the duration of this assignment. Most of my work comes from building contractors who want my windows in their new construction. I channeled all of that business to my competitor. If I go back, I don't know if I can get the business back. There are things like that that have to be considered."

"She's going to take the job," her mother uttered, shooting a glance back to her father. "She's going to work with him, and it'll all start up again."

"*Nothing* is going to start up!" Brooke said. "I'm a grown woman now, and he's not my teacher anymore. And we aren't involved or even interested in each other. Don't you think after ten years that I ought to have the chance to work in my home town, holding my head up? Haven't I earned that?''

"That's not something you can earn," her father said. "Once respect is taken away from you, you can't get it back."

"Dad, that isn't—"

"Just eat," her mother blurted out, her eyes misting with anger. "It's been sitting long enough. We'll talk about this later."

Roxy's chair scraped back from the table and the girl got to her feet. "I'm not hungry," she said. And before anyone could protest, she had left the table.

IT'S GOING TO HAPPEN AGAIN. Pain rose in Roxy's heart as she closed her bedroom door and sat down on her bed, hugging her knees to her chest. *She's going to come back, start another scandal, then leave me to deal with it.*

A tear fell and she smeared it across her face, wondering why Brooke always made her into that weepy-eyed little seven year old she'd left sitting on the porch steps. Maybe it was because there was a hole somewhere in the lives they'd had since then. A hole that Roxy had never figured out how to fill.

She slid off of her bed and went to the window, and tried not to remember the pain she had felt when it had finally occurred to her, years ago, that Brooke wasn't ever coming home. Suddenly, she had been like an only child, with a ghost of a sister people talked around instead of about, for fear of reviving the embarrassment they had all suffered. Because her parents had never told Roxy directly, she had learned the truth from snickering classmates, gossiping teachers, curious neighbors.

How could Brooke put her through that again?

Roxy closed her eyes, and told herself not to cry anymore. She'd suffered Brooke's reputation for ten years, she thought. What was one more indiscretion?

But it wasn't that easy to accept. Brooke's indiscretions had altered Roxy's life. But Brooke hadn't been around enough to know that.

Maybe it was time she found out. Maybe this time Roxy would tell her.

THE REMAINDER OF THE MEAL was short and stressfully quiet, and Brooke managed to choke down at least half of the dinner that had once been her favorite. She told herself she wouldn't cry, and she wouldn't engage herself in a screaming argument with her father and mother, like the one she'd had when she was eighteen.

Without a word she helped her mother clear the table, then went to look for Roxy, to see just what was bothering her sister. *Surely not the thing with Nick*, Brooke thought. Roxy had been too young to understand when the scandal erupted. Still, Roxy's quietness and coolness were bothersome.

She knocked on her sister's bedroom door, and at Roxy's uttered "What?" opened it and stepped inside. Roxy was sitting on the wide bench in front of her window, hugging her knees to her chest.

Brooke looked around the small room that revealed the stages of Roxy's growth: a tattered teddy bear on a shelf next to a ballet trophy, a framed photo of the boys on the soccer team, a stack of books on a table ranging from Shakespeare to Rod McKuen, a pair of toe shoes hanging from a hook on the wall. She looked at her sister, wishing that words came more easily and that she knew how to dispense with the awkwardness between them. "Sorry about the scene at the table," Brooke said.

Roxy's gaze drifted out the window. "What did you expect?"

Brooke set a hand on the bedpost. "I don't know. I guess I hoped that after ten years it would die down a little. At least among my family. I keep thinking enough time has passed. That we could talk about it . . . make some sense of it all."

Roxy didn't answer. Instead she kept her eyes transfixed on some invisible object outside the window.

Brooke sighed. "I like your room," she said, trying to find some common ground. "The last time I was in here, you were mostly into Mickey Mouse and Snow White, instead of Bruce Springsteen and Kenny Loggins." She smiled and stepped over to the stereo system, sitting on a cabinet in the corner. "You had this little plastic record player with a picture of Donald Duck on the top, and you listened to Sesame Street records all the time and made up little dances to them."

"I don't dance anymore," Roxy said belligerently.

Brooke turned back to her. "Why? You were good, weren't you?"

Roxy laughed mirthlessly. "How would you know? You never saw me dance. Not since I was seven."

"No, but Mom told me you were the soloist in the ballet company, and that—"

"Not anymore." Roxy left the window and lifted her toe shoes off their hook. She looked down at them, holding them with a reverence that didn't match the lack of interest in her words.

Brooke knew she was pushing too hard, but she couldn't keep from asking, "Well, why not?"

Roxy spun around, vexation coloring her cheekbones. "Because I got tired of it," she said. "Why the sudden interest?"

Brooke's quiet laugh held much more pain than mirth. "Because you're my sister."

Roxy brought her eyes to Brooke's, disgust and resentment narrowing them. "I graduate from high school in June, Brooke. But you probably didn't know that, either, did you?"

Brooke's forced smile faded, and she braced herself for whatever was coming. "Of course I know. What are you talking about?"

"I'm talking about the fact that I grew up while you were off burying your head in the sand."

Brooke lowered herself to her sister's bed, and settled her eyes on Roxy, suddenly aware that the coolness Roxy had displayed earlier had roots much deeper than awkward shyness. "What's the matter, Roxy?" she asked quietly. "Why are you mad at me? Is it Nick?"

Roxy laughed, a sound so cold and mirthless that it made Brook shiver. "Is it Nick?" she repeated harshly. "Hasn't it always been Nick, Brooke? For you, for our family, for me?"

Brooke's patience stretched taut at the vague accusation. She hadn't expected this from Roxy. Emotion welled in her throat, making her voice wobble. "It didn't happen to you, Roxy. It happened to me. You were little, and you probably have no idea what I went through back then. But don't judge me for staying away when I had no choice...."

Roxy's eyes were two golden flames dancing with fury as she faced her sister. "You've got a lot of nerve, you know that? Do you think it only affected you? You made headlines in the newspaper, Brooke! I may have been seven years old, but I could read! And if I hadn't, it wouldn't have mattered because everyone else in town was there to tell me about it!"

The outburst made Brooke's face burn. "I'm sorry that you were hurt by it," she said, tears coming to her eyes though she spoke through clenched teeth. "It hurt all of us."

"It didn't hurt you," Roxy charged. "You didn't have to face it. You disappeared, remember? *I'm* the one who had to sit in class and listen to my teachers whisper about you when they thought I didn't know what they were talking about. *I'm* the one who got in fights with the kids at school because they made fun of me for being your sister. For over half my life, I've been known as the sister of that girl who slept with her teacher!"

Anger pulsated through Brooke's veins, and one hot tear fell onto her cheek. "I didn't sleep with him, Roxy," she said, clipping each word. "It was a lie."

"Not according to the Hemphills," Roxy reminded her. "They set the truths in this town, and they're still here. He's still running the school, and she's still on the town council. And now their children are grown and all over town, following in the family tradition. And when they hear that you've come back here to work with *him* . . . it's going to start all over!"

Brooke lifted her chin defiantly, and her words came slowly, quietly, through her teeth. "I won't let them dictate my life anymore, Roxy. I'm tired of trying to redeem myself for a bunch of lies."

"Redeem yourself?" Roxy cried. "What have you done to redeem yourself? Stayed away for ten years? Divorced the nicest guy in town? I'm the one who's spent my life trying to make up for the shame you brought to this family. I'm the one who's tried to redeem you!"

Brooke's tears stole down her face, but she held her posture defiantly stiff, determined not to collapse under the weight being set upon her shoulders. "I'm sorry I hurt you," she whispered.

"It's too late for apologies," Roxy said, the finality in her tone bolting the door to whatever relationship they might have had. "About ten years too late."

Brooke bit her quivering lip, for there was nothing left to say. Finally she pulled herself together enough to leave the room. Roxy sat alone with the bitter anger that overshadowed the sweet little girl who had followed her older sister around as a child. The loss hit Brooke like a death of someone she had cherished, but she managed to keep the pain from her face until she was hidden in her room, where no one else could see.

For Brooke had learned long ago to deal with her pain alone.

CHAPTER THREE

BROOKE LAY IN BED later that night, in the bedroom that had been converted into a cold, impersonal guest room, and wondered if, indeed, this had once been her home. The basic structure of the place was unaltered, but nothing looked the same...and in her soul she could feel the difference, as if she'd been transported back into the wrong family.

She rolled onto her back and looked at the ceiling, where long ago she had painted a blue sky and clouds so vivid that one would have sworn she was sleeping outside. Roxy used to sneak into her bed at night after their parents were asleep, swearing that she couldn't sleep in her own room because there were no clouds. But the clouds were gone now, and in their place was white latex paint that fit the new practical decor of the room.

Tears rolled down her temples and soaked the roots of her hair. Why did some things change so much, when other things—things like feelings and fantasies and aches that throbbed in the night—never changed at all? It all boiled down to those stubborn feelings...and Nick Marcello.

She turned onto her stomach and fluffed the pillow, then buried her face in it in order to stop the agony from venting itself audibly. When was she supposed to heal? Brooke wondered. When would she ever be forgiven?

It was out of the question, of course, to take the job he'd offered. She would have to tell him no, because she couldn't stand the looks on her parents' faces, or the pain on her sister's. It was too much for one person to endure, and yet she had carried the burden for ten long years. She'd simply carry it ten more...or twenty...or however long it took for the feelings to fade. And someday they would, she was certain, if she fought them hard enough and stayed far enough away.

Oh, Nick, Brooke cried into the pillow, weeping out years of misery and heartache. *Why couldn't you have left me where I was? Alone, quiet, functioning...secure in the knowledge that I wasn't hurting anyone?*

Her tears flowed into the night, under the cover of darkness. The saddest thing of all was that no one was there to stop them. And she was soul-weary of battling them alone.

THE DARKNESS FILLED Nick's Duesenberg like a comfortable scent, making his own ghosts more vivid as they waged fresh battle. He felt more lonely tonight than he had in some time, and he found that fact disturbing. Wasn't his aloneness one of the most valuable assets in his life? Wasn't it something he cherished?

Tonight the answer came as a cold aching in his hollow soul. No, tonight the solitude was a plague, and the loneliness was a punishment. For what, he wasn't sure.

The headlights of the antique car lit up his front lawn as Nick approached it. Behind the house he could see moonlight playing off the surface of the canal that threaded behind his yard, a parking lot of sorts for the boats his neighbors kept there. On any other night his artist's eye would have absorbed the gentle scene, and he might have rushed into his studio, leaving the house dark and captured the picture from the massive window that looked out over the water. Dark colors and shadows had always fascinated him. Tonight they only made him feel more alone.

Some unconscious decision compelled him to drive on when he reached his driveway, and without a second thought, he headed back out of his neighborhood. He needed somebody tonight, he thought. Somebody... even if it couldn't be Brooke.

As if it needed no directing, the antique car laced through town, and in moments idled in the driveway of an older two-story home, full of light spilling out from the first floor and dim nightlights lending faint hues to the rooms upstairs. He parked the coupe carefully to the side of the drive, so that no one pulling in behind him could sideswipe it or nick it with a car door. When he got out, he walked around it, stroking his hand along the polished black finish, carefully making certain no nearby shrub would scratch the paint if a strong wind stirred.

"Nick? What are you doing here?" a woman's voice from the open garage called out into the darkness. "For heaven's sake, leave the stupid car and go in the house. I swear, nothin's gonna hurt the thing."

Nick grinned as the woman came out of the garage and into his sight, hoisting a curly-haired baby on one hip and carrying a basket of laundry on the other. "How's it going Anna?"

"Not too bad," she said.

Nick took the baby and pressed a kiss on her fat cheek. She beamed up at him. "What's this kid doing up so late?"

"She's spoiled rotten, that's what," Anna said, as if that answered the question. "Controls the whole house. Me, Ma, Vinnie, everybody."

"How is Ma?" he asked as they started up the steps to the porch.

"Ask her yourself," his sister said. "She's watching some Bogart movie and chomping on popcorn like a little kid. And here I am trying to get 'her little highness' to bed, and instead of a bottle she wants popcorn. Do you know what one popcorn husk can do to a baby? Do you have any idea?''

Nick grinned as they stepped into the house, and his mother got off the couch, worry animating her face at the sight of her son. ''Nicholas! What's the matter? You never come over here this late!''

Nick planted a kiss on his mother's cheek and offered a wave to his brother-in-law, who sat at the dining room table with a calculator and a stack of bills. ''Nothing's the matter, Ma. Can't a guy come by to see how his ma's doing once in a while?''

''You need money,'' she said with absolute certainty, then turned back to Vinnie. ''He needs money. I knew it! A man can't make a living drawing pictures! Sooner or later he has to hold his hand out.''

Nick dropped his hands helplessly and began to remember why he limited his visits here. ''Ma, I'm not here for money. I have never asked you for money, have I?''

''There's always a first time.'' She grabbed her big purse and dug for her checkbook. ''It's nothing to be ashamed of to ask for help, if you learn from it,'' she babbled. ''It's not too late to help yourself.''

Nick's frustration vented itself in half laughter. ''Ma, I'm not taking your money! I'm doing fine. I sold three paintings last month. The IRS loves me!''

His mother closed her purse and glared up at him, indictment all over her wrinkled little face. ''Did you hear yourself?'' she asked accusingly. ''You sold three paintings last month. Is that all you did? Vinnie there works his fingers to the bone, day after day, wiring people's houses, *helping* people. Your father, God rest his soul, worked around the clock, day and night, making shoes for people who wouldn't think of buying them anyplace else, because of the quality of business that your grandfather founded with his own sweat. And you sold three paintings?"

Nick's smile was strained. "That's what I do, Ma. I'm an artist."

His mother made a sound that was half grunt, half disgust, and all derision. "He's an *artist*," she said, sarcastically.

Nick took a deep breath, expelled it slowly, and told himself that a response wasn't worth an argument tonight. He looked through the door into the dark kitchen, hoping for some sign of his nineteen-year-old nephew. "So where's Sonny?"

"In his room over the garage," Anna said, flopping the baby down on the floor and beginning to change her diaper.

"He's working on some project for his shop class at Vo-Tech," Vinnie said. "Kid's great with his hands."

"I think I'll go up and say hello," Nick said, then turned back to his mother. "And Ma, when I come back, I want to see a smile, okay? No more tongue lashings? And no more talk about money?"

"You can watch Bogie with me," his mother said grudgingly, settling back down on the couch.

Nick left the house through the back door and climbed the stairs to the garage apartment Sonny had moved into when the baby—number five in his sister's family—was born. He knocked on the door and heard something in the room fall. Then, in a voice a little too loud, Sonny called, "Just a minute!"

"Hey, Sonny," Nick said through the door. "What are you doing in there? You hiding a girl or something?"

The door opened, and his nephew, every bit as tall as Nick with the same black hair, faced him with a mischievous grin. "Picasso!" he said, waving Nick into a room that looked as if it had been fruitlessly ransacked by a gang of thieves. "I thought you were Pop."

"So you had to stash the evidence before you could open the door?" Nick asked, looking around for a sign of the culprit. "Where is she?"

Sonny laughed and cleared off a chair for Nick to sit down. "No girl. I was just working on something. A...project for school."

"Oh, yeah?" Nick asked, still suspicious. The strong scent of oil paints wafted through the air, and he saw a palette lying on a table, blotted with various colors of fresh paint. "I didn't know they did home projects in electrician school."

Still wearing a wry smile, Sonny straddled a chair backward and propped his hands on the back. He evaluated Nick with a critical eye, then sighed. "All right. If I tell you something, do you swear to God that you won't tell nobody? Pop would bust a gut, and Grandma would fake a heart attack or something. Ma would just mope around like Joan of Arc..."

Nick laughed. "Come on, I can't stand the suspense."

Sonny took a deep breath, apparently struggling with some monumental confession. "Well, I've been...sort of...playing around with paints and stuff...."

The confession was uttered with as much shame and guilt as if he'd admitted to playing around with a dangerous drug. "You mean, you've been painting? Like I do?"

Sonny stood up, running his fingers, blotched with dried paint, through his hair. "Yeah, just like you, Picasso. Only not as good. Not anywhere near as good."

A glint of pleasure and surprise illuminated Nick's eyes, and he sat up straighter and scanned the room for the evidence. "Well, let me see."

"No, I can't," Sonny said, suddenly wilting. "It's pretty terrible, really. I don't know why I bother...."

"Sonny, let me see," Nick told him. "I'm not a critic."

A self-conscious smile tugged at Sonny's lips, and he crossed his arms and stared at Nick for a long moment. Finally he went to his bed, got down on one knee and pulled a wet canvas out from under it, along with the collapsible easel he'd hidden there. Mechanically he set it up.

In vivid color, Sonny had captured the house he lived in, stroking its character and history in every line and hue, from the crooked mailbox on the front corner to the laundry line strung up on the side. Nick set his chin on two fingers, studying the painting with a lump of emotion in his throat, then turned back to his nephew. "Why didn't you tell me you could do this?"

Sonny gave a half laugh. "Guess I thought if I didn't tell anybody, I'd get tired of it after a while and lose interest."

Nick knew that feeling. "It doesn't go away, though, does it?"

Sonny sank back down to his chair. "Pop thinks I'm going to finish Vo-Tech and keep working with him as an electrician. His pride's all caught up in my doing that. I don't really have a choice, you know?"

"No," Nick said. "I *don't* know. Everybody has choices."

"Aw, man, that's easy for you to say. You're already doing it. Nobody's ridin' you about it."

Nick's laughter came as a surprise to them both, for nothing about the subject was funny. "You think my pop liked what I did? When I went to college to study art, he swore I was just loafing. I was supposed to work in the shoe store with him. The family business. He was going to rename it Marcello and Son Shoes, just for me. To this day, Ma says she's glad he didn't live to see what I've done with

my life. Like I've gone to work for the Mob or something.''

"No," Sonny said with a wicked grin. "That would even
be a little more respectable than being an artist.''

"You're right." Nick looked back at the painting, wondering at the raw talent smoldering just below his nephew's leather-and-tough-guy facade. "Look, have you had
lessons or anything? Any kind of training?''

"Just what I learn from books," Sonny said. "But what
I wouldn't give to learn more." His eyes lit up, as if sharing his secret with Nick had set him free, and he'd just discovered the power to ask for help. "Nick, you could teach
me, couldn't you? I mean, you were a teacher...."

"You got it," Nick said without hesitation. "Only
problem is, I'm about to be working some long hours for a
while at the museum. But if you want, you can use my studio anytime you want. I'll give you a key to my house."

"You mean it?" Sonny asked, his eyes as wide as a kid's
half his age.

"Yeah. And I'll tell you something else. I could use your
talent on the windows. If Brooke agrees to work with me,
she and I are needed for the most complicated part of designing. There're a lot of things that we need creative people to help us with."

Sonny's eyes sparkled with surprise and a touch of
amusement. "Brooke? Not the one..."

Nick swallowed and held out a hand to stem Sonny's
question. "She's an artist, too, Sonny. The best I've run
across in stained glass. It's strictly business."

"I know. I didn't mean nothin'." Sonny's voice faded
and he dropped his gaze to the floor. "Stained glass," he
whispered with awe. "Man, if you think you can use me,
I'll be there. I work for Pop in the afternoons, but I could
help at night."

"All right," Nick said with a grin. "I'll let you know when we need you. Now, you get back to work on that. I have to go watch Bogart with Ma."

Sonny smiled with a new sparkle of excitement in his eyes that Nick hadn't seen before. "Thanks, Picasso. I won't let you down."

"Yeah, well," Nick muttered as he started out the door. "You're not the one I'm worried about."

IT WAS EARLY MORNING when Brooke loaded her suitcase into her car and left the house without saying good-bye. A strange feeling of déjà vu crept over her, but she told herself there was no other way. She was leaving for good this time, and they would all know from the note she'd written that she wouldn't be coming back. There was no point in dragging it out.

She drove through a take-out window at a fast-food restaurant and got a cup of coffee and sat in her car to sip it until the cup was empty. Then, because it had to be done, she drove to the museum, planning to wait there for Nick.

But as she pulled into the back parking lot, she saw that his car was already there, along with several pickup trucks, a cement truck and various other commercial vehicles, indicating that the renovation was already underway and that the crews were taking advantage of the early morning hours before the heat set in. Gathering all her courage, she got out of the car and slid her hands into the pockets of her jeans. It had seemed a waste of time to dress up today, Brooke had decided. The drive back to Tallahassee didn't require special attire.

She stepped into the museum and saw the activity already beginning. Men were up on ladders removing the old windows and replacing them with temporary boards covered with plastic in case of rain. Others were stripping the walls, while still others worked on pulling up the old floor-ing. The activity would have been exciting had Brooke been a part of it all.

Ignoring the catcalls from some of the workers as she walked through, Brooke stepped over some thick electrical cords and around some machinery and headed for Nick's office in the back of the museum. The light was on, and she knew that he was there, waiting for her to bring him an an-swer . . . expecting it to be the one he wanted. Dragging in a shaky breath, she forced herself to step through the door-way.

Nick looked up, and the smile on his face took her back to those awkward high school days when her heart had belly flopped each time their eyes had met. "Brooke, you're early." His voice, once again, held a tentative note, as though he held back for fear of frightening her away. She hated seeming so fragile.

His eyes swept the length of her, then rose back to her hair, long and neglectfully straight, falling around her shoulders. "And you're dressed for a hard day's work," he said. "Does that mean you've decided to—?"

"I'm not taking the job, Nick," she cut in quietly. "I'm going back to Tallahassee today."

Nick's face fell. At first he registered disappointment, then, benign nothingness. It was almost as if he'd re-hearsed the response he would give if she let him down. "I see."

"I think it's best for everyone," she said, feeling the ache of tears stinging behind her eyes, no matter how wide she held them.

"Everyone?" he asked. "Who is 'everyone'?"

She sighed and lifted her shoulders. "My parents. My sister. You."

"Me?" he asked, raising his brows with the question. "Why is it better for me?"

She dipped her head, letting her hair fall around her face. Her bracelets jangled as she raised her hand to pull the tresses back. "You can find someone else to do the windows. Someone who won't bring a dark cloud to the project. Someone who won't start everyone in town talking."

Nick stood up slowly. "Do I look as if I care what anyone says?" he asked. "I'm the one who stayed in town, remember? I'm still here, Brooke. They haven't sent me running, yet."

She lifted her head and leaned back against the door's casing and exhaled a breath that revealed the depth of her pain. But the numb expression he had worn gave way to deep-seated pain of his own. "You don't understand," she whispered. "It wasn't just you and I who were hurt ten years ago. There were other lives affected."

Nick came around his desk and took her shoulders, his eyes trapping her with such force that she couldn't look away. "Listen to me, Brooke. We didn't do anything. We kissed. I wasn't some dirty old man taking advantage of a child. Neither one of us deserved the catastrophic changes they put us through. And if anyone was hurt, it wasn't our fault."

Those tears that had badgered her all night rushed forward again, and she caught her breath on a sob. "It doesn't matter whose fault it was," she said. "What matters is that it has to stop. And my working here with you isn't going to stop it."

"Wrong, Brooke," he said, not allowing her to look away from him. "Running away won't stop it."

Her tears overtook her, and Brooke closed her eyes, letting them run down her face in warm rivulets. She didn't make a sound as she cried, but her shoulders shook with the fierceness of her pain.

Nick's touch grew more tender, and he pulled her against him and held her, the way he'd never had the chance to do before. It felt so good—too good—and she was too weak to resist. "Think of yourself for a change, Brooke," he whispered against her hair. "You'll never find peace as long as you let other people dictate your life."

She opened her eyes, which were glimmering with tears, and looked up at him, wishing with every fiber of her being that things didn't have to be this way. "I'll never find peace as long as I keep making the same mistakes," she corrected.

"Maybe you're right," he said softly. He pushed a strand of hair away from her wet cheek. "But be sure you know what the mistakes really were. If you don't take the time to figure that out, then you can't help but repeat them. I don't think the mistake was what we did...maybe it was what we didn't do. Or maybe it was listening to what everyone said."

Brooke stepped out of his embrace and turned away from him, shaking her head helplessly. "Maybe the mistake was wanting," she whispered, so softly that he almost couldn't hear. "Maybe it was knowing that what they said about us was something that *could* have happened. I wanted it to. If you'd made the first move, there's no telling where it would have stopped. It's knowing that that scares me, Nick. That's what's made the gossip so hard to take." She turned back to him and faced him, her eyes red with her tears. "See, I could never look my father in the eye and tell him that it was innocent. I knew what I was doing that night."

"And I knew what I was doing," he said. "And whether we've deserved to or not, we've paid and paid and paid. Why can't we put it behind us and go on with our lives? We shared something important back then, Brooke. A love of art. Together we can create something that people will come from miles around to see. It's too big to pass up."

She turned away again and tried not to let his tone sway her. Anguished, she ran her fingers through her hair. She felt his hands at her shoulders, felt his fingers cutting into her rigid muscles, balled so tight and hard that she doubted anything would loosen them up. He began a slow massage, and his breath fanned her hair.

"Come on, Brooke," he whispered. "Say yes. There doesn't have to be any intense involvement between us. I'm not asking you to pick up where we left off. Too much has happened. But we can be friends and partners. And we can show them all what we're made of."

She couldn't answer, for the desire in her rose to her head, swimming around with all the reasons why she had to leave. It wouldn't work. It could never work. And yet...

Sensing her hesitation, Nick brought his mouth closer to her ear. "Come on, Brooke. Say yes."

Suddenly, someone in the doorway cleared her throat, and Nick and Brooke turned to see Mrs. Hemphill, standing before them just as she had done ten years earlier, smiling with I-might-have-known smugness. Her permed hair was styled in a short bob, and the roots were a slightly yellower shade of platinum than the rest, as if they had recently been touched up. Mrs. Hemphill might have been pretty, Brooke had thought before, if not for the guarded, ready-to-pounce expression she always seemed to wear, or the shrewd arch of her pencil-thin brows. Her body was in good shape, though the suit she wore—too severe and authoritative—distracted from her appeal. She smiled now, though Brooke couldn't remember ever seeing a smile so lacking in grace or amusement. It almost seemed like a sad smile, as if seeing them together affected her, somehow…as if Mrs. Hemphill had some stake in both of their lives.

Nick released Brooke's shoulders and crossed his arms. "Well, well," he said. "If it isn't Abby Hemphill. Speak of the devil."

Mrs. Hemphill pursed her lips and stepped into the small office. "I doubt you were speaking of me," she said, her silver eyes sweeping critically over Brooke and lingering with distaste on the collection of bracelets on her wrist, the chains of various lengths around her neck and the long gold hoops hanging from her earlobes. "You seem to have something else on your mind at the moment."

"Is that why you came here?" Nick asked, startling Brooke with his nonchalance. "To read our minds?"

Mrs. Hemphill settled her eyes on Nick, and for a second Brooke could have sworn that the aggressive expression flitted away in favor of a deep pensiveness. But then the woman turned her attention to Brooke, who stood in the office waiting for the inevitable verbal blow, and her bitterness returned. "I heard you were back in town," she said. "And that you were going to be working here… together." She regarded a long, acrylic fingernail, then brought her eyes back to Brooke. "I thought it was only fair to warn you that I don't intend to let the town pay for your little rendezvous. I intend to oppose their commissioning you for this project."

"It's too late," Nick said. "They've already done it. They hired me and gave me carte blanche to hire anyone I chose."

Mrs. Hemphill laughed…a cold, hollow sound, and she leaned back against the doorway and regarded Nick again. "They may have hired you, Mr. Marcello, but they haven't allocated the funds for your particular job, yet. That's where I come in. I happen to chair the finance committee, and I can assure you that when I get finished with the museum's budget, there won't be a penny left for 'artistic development.'"

Brooke flashed a furious look to Nick—silently asking if Mrs. Hemphill's threats could be carried out—but Nick only smiled at the woman, undaunted. "Do what you have to do, Abby," he said. "Go ahead and vote according to your smutty little conscience. I don't think you'll find the other members of the council on your side."

Her smile was a threat in itself...a promise that things would not go as smoothly as he thought. "We'll see about that, won't we?" she asked, then pivoted on her heel and made her exit, leaving Brooke gaping after her, eyes blazing with fury, and Nick only shaking his head in disgust.

Brooke spun around. "You see? I told you! I haven't even taken the job, and already it's started."

Nick dropped to the corner of his desk. "We're damned if we do, and damned if we don't." He gave a helpless shrug. "The way I see it, if it doesn't make any difference *what* we do, we might as well do what we want."

"That's not the answer!" Brooke cried. "You know it."

Nick looked down at the desk, cluttered with papers and blueprints and measurements for the windows. He picked up some of the papers, tossed them up haphazardly and watched them flutter back down to his desk. "What I know is that I can't afford to lose another job. I was counting on this, Brooke. And it's not likely that I'm going to find anyone else to come in here and work under Abby Hemphill's threats to pull the money. I can't do it by myself because stained glass isn't my specialty. I guess if you decide to walk away from this, it's over for me, too."

The words shattered Brooke's resolve, and she knew that if he lost this job, it would be the second he'd lost because of her. A painful fissure cracked through her soul, leaving the two halves heavily laden with guilt. On one side there was her family, who regarded her with disgust and shame. And on the other was Nick, as innocent as she in a scandal bigger than either of them. Between them both was a haunting cry in her heart that told her, unequivocally, what she really wanted. She wanted to take the job and create this masterpiece with Nick and show Mrs. Hemphill and the whole damn town that they could knock her down but they couldn't walk on her. It was time she got back up. Suddenly her decision seemed clear.

"You won't lose your job," she told Nick finally, glaring out through the door where the woman had stood only moments before. "She won't get away with this again. We're going to fight her tooth and nail this time. And I'm going to tell her that right now."

Without saying good-bye to Nick, Brooke stormed out of the office, determined to confront Mrs. Hemphill once and for all.

NICK WATCHED BROOKE LEAVE and leaned back against the door, smiling in relief. *Damn,* he thought. He should have used the job thing earlier. It had turned her around so fast she hadn't known what hit her.

Conscience assailed him for a moment, and he told himself that it wasn't right to heap more guilt on her shoulders, when Brooke was carrying so much already.

But a man did what a man had to do. And she was going to stay.

It was the right thing to do, he told himself. Once she began to work on the project, she would be glad she had stayed. None of the gossip would matter once the windows began taking shape. None of their history would interfere. None of their past feelings would intrude.

If they did, he'd keep his emotions to himself. He wasn't about to give her regrets a second time.

HAYDEN CITY HALL smelled of mildew and old dust, and if she could have sketched those smells, Brooke would have drawn them in the very shape of this building. She walked down the hall, the heels of her loafers clicking on the cold Formica floor. A small sign on one corner directed her toward the left wing to the offices of the town council's committee chairpersons.

As she passed the office marked Records, she wondered if her sister Roxy was working today, since school was out for term break. If so, she hoped Roxy wouldn't see her. It would be a shame to let her sister down, after her note had indicated that she was leaving town again. A small surge of pride shot through her, however, that they were wrong this time. She had changed her mind.

Just as she feared, Roxy spotted her as she passed her office, and her sister stepped out into the hall. "What are you doing here?" she asked, her voice echoing in the wide hall. "I thought you had left."

"You thought wrong," Brooke said, not slowing her step. "Where is Mrs. Hemphill's office?"

"Over there," Roxy said, breaking into a trot to keep up with her. "But, Brooke, you can't go in there. You're asking for it if you do."

"Asking for what, Roxy?" Brooke asked. "Gossip? Lies? I get those no matter what I do."

Roxy fell behind as Brooke pushed into the cubiclelike office with Mrs. Hemphill's name on the door. The woman, sitting behind her desk with the phone to her ear, gasped when Brooke burst in. She dropped the phone and shoved back her chair.

"No need to get up, Mrs. Hemphill," Brooke said, leaning over the woman's desk. "I won't be here long. I just came to tell you that it's open season on Brooke Martin. So go ahead. Take your best shots. I have to warn you, though. It won't be quite as much fun sparring with a grown woman as it was with a high school senior. I'm not as easily intimidated now."

"Now, wait a minute, young lady!" the woman spat out, bolting out of her chair.

"No," Brooke said. "I'm going to design the windows for the museum because I'm good at what I do, and because I need the recognition it will bring me in the art world. And no thanks to you, this town will have something to be proud of when I get through. Whether or not they deserve it is another story. Whether or not Nick and I do is without question. So I'll be seeing you around, Mrs. Hemphill. The next few months should be interesting."

And before Mrs. Hemphill could catch her breath to reply, Brooke had turned on her heel and left the woman in the office, pushing past Roxy, who stood stunned and speechless. But Brooke could have sworn as she passed her that the tiniest sparkle of admiration shone in her eyes.

And for the first time in ten years Brooke felt good about herself.

ABBY HEMPHILL SAT PARALYZED for a moment after Brooke had gone, trying to contain the raging emotions Brooke had incited. But the job was too big, and suddenly her last thread of control snapped, and her arm swept across her desk, knocking off her telephone, her can of pencils, her calendar, her calculator.

"That slithering little...tramp!" she bit out through her teeth. She set her face in her hands, felt the heat seething there and knew that she had to get out of the office before something inside her exploded.

Grabbing her purse, she went to her car, then drove like a maniac to the high school, where her husband was still principal. There were few cars in the parking lot, for it was a school holiday, and only teachers were present to tally the grades for the report cards to be issued the next day. Slamming her car door, Abby walked as fast as she could in her high heels, the color in her face rising.

Dashing past the secretary in the school office, Abby stormed into her husband's office, noting that he was on the phone. "I have to talk to you," she whispered harshly.

Gerald Hemphill raised his hand to silence her, and continued in his conversation.

Abby crossed her arms and began to pace back and forth across his floor, back and forth, back and forth, like an inmate waiting to be released from confinement.

When her husband finally hung up, she braced both hands on his desk and leaned over. "She's back," she said.

"Who's back?"

"That Brooke Martin. Nick Marcello hired her to work on those windows for the museum, and they're over there doing...doing God knows what."

Gerald Hemphill distractedly flipped through his Rolodex as his wife railed on, and without looking up at her, he muttered, "Sit down, Abby. I have to make another call."

Abby grabbed his hand to stop him from dialing and forced him to look up at her. "She came to *my* office and chewed me out, Gerald!"

Gerald grinned as he began dialing again. "Mmmm. That sounds interesting."

"Would you listen to me?" Abby raged. "I have to stop this. It isn't right that our taxpayers are going to be paying those two for having their little daily orgy. If they did that right here in this school under your very nose, what do you think they'll do over there?''

"Yes, is Mr. Hartford in?" Gerald asked, flipping through some papers on his desk. "Bob, hi. Gerald here. I have those transfer papers you were asking about . . ."

Abby stood back, flabbergasted, as impotent tears sprang to her eyes. "Gerald!" she whispered, but he didn't seem to hear. Instead he lifted one index finger and pointed to the chair.

Abby dropped into it, crossed her legs and began swinging her foot. The phone call dragged on, and finally she couldn't contain herself any longer. She jumped up and began pacing again.

Gerald hung up and reached for another file, as if he had forgotten his wife was in the room.

"Gerald, I came in here to talk to you!" she shouted.

"It's not a good time, dear. I'm really swamped today."

"You're always swamped!" she said. "I'm swamped, too. But I'm upset about this! It's my job to see that our taxpayers' money is spent well, and I—"

"Could you hand me that book on the table behind you, dear?" he cut in, pointing to the tome in question.

Abby stopped midsentence and gaped at him. At times like these, she thought miserably, tears would be a welcome release. But she hadn't been able to cry in years. Anger was the most vivid emotion she knew these days. "You know, Gerald," she said finally, in a voice as dull as her metallic eyes, "sometimes I wonder what it was that possessed me to marry you!"

With that, she left his office.

"Good-bye, dear," Gerald replied. "I'll be home for dinner."

ABBY STOPPED IN THE SCHOOL corridor and leaned back against the wall. Her eyes misted over, but no tears flowed. She had learned long ago to curb the weakness that led to life-altering mistakes. Perhaps she had learned too well. The hard shell she'd built around herself was efficiently defensive . . . but it also kept her distanced from those she sometimes needed.

Slowly she began to stroll up the corridor, where teachers sat hard at work in their classrooms, evaluating the performance of each of their students for their third-term grades. There were few familiar faces. It wasn't as easy to get to know the teachers in Gerald's school as it had once been. She was so busy now that she rarely came here, and when he took her to faculty parties these days, she found it harder and harder to laugh and smile and listen.

She found herself in the liberal arts wing and strolled further to the classroom at the end of the hall, the one that smelled of paint and mineral spirits. She looked inside the door, noting that the teacher wasn't there.

Slowly Abby stepped inside and looked around at the simplistic drawings on the walls, the crude representations of life. Hayden hadn't had an art teacher in years who really had talent, she thought, or one who was able to inspire latent creativity in his students. Not since Nick Marcello.

It was too bad he had taken that inspiration one step too far.

She sat down at one of the desks and remembered vividly that night when she and Gerald had seen the light on and had stumbled onto Nick's little affair with that girl. The price for propriety was high. The cost for impropriety, by rights, should be far greater.

And indeed it was. His affair had been nipped in the bud, and Nick Marcello had lost his job. What cut Abby to the quick now was that it hadn't seemed to matter. Over the years he'd thrived despite what he'd lost. And now...

Abby searched her heart, honestly seeking the reason why Brooke grated on her senses so much. Perhaps it was the long, flowing mane of hair, the trim little hips that fit into a glove-tight pair of jeans, the bright eyes that always seemed to see things no one else saw. Perhaps it was the defiance of status, apparent in the unaffected way she dressed, or the confidence in her own carriage, or her ability to savor life despite its mistreatment of her. Perhaps it was because Brooke reminded Abby of everything she herself had once been...everything she had exchanged for the sake of appearances.

She got up and went to the desk at the front of the room, staring sightlessly down at it. It wasn't right that some chose the correct path with great sacrifice, while others thumbed their noses at the world and went on.

Brooke and Nick had deserved everything they'd gotten so far, she told herself, letting her eyes sweep the room again. He had deserved to lose the job he had and the respect and the reputation. What he didn't deserve was the opportunity to continue his fling when he began designing those windows.

After all, the renovation had been *her* idea to begin with. *She* was the one who had suggested redoing it. But then someone had suggested the windows, and Horace had hired Nick, who'd hired that girl, and everything had gotten out of control.

Well, Abby was going to get back in control now, if it killed her, she decided. No bracelet-jangling tramp was going to treat her the way she had been treated this morning and get away with it. If she had anything to say about it, Brooke Martin would be out of this town by week's end.

CHAPTER FOUR

NICK TRIED NOT TO LOOK as if he was waiting for her, when Brooke pulled back into the museum parking lot. He wasn't after all, he told himself. He'd merely come outside to pull the cloth cover over his car, for fear that the dust and gravel kicked up by the trucks filling the parking lot would nick or scratch the finish. So what if it took him longer than he'd planned, or if he'd spent more time watching the road for her car than protecting the Duesenberg?

Well, she was here now, he thought as he walked toward her, analyzing her face for a sign of her mood. And for the life of him, he couldn't tell from her expression if she was staying or going.

Brooke got out of her car, tossed her silken hair back with a flip and faced him squarely. Even in jeans and a T-shirt she looked fresh and stylish. Chains hung delicately around her throat, and some teased the tops of her breasts, lending a note of extravagance to the simple, genderless shirt. And those earrings mingled with the strands of her hair and moved against her face like golden feathers touching her ivory skin. "I told Mrs. Hemphill that I was taking the job," she said. "So you win. I'm staying."

A subtle smile gleamed in Nick's eyes, but he didn't let it reach his lips. "I think we both won."

"Not yet, we haven't," she said. She started to speak, stopped and took a deep breath. The breeze swept her hair back into her face. She pushed it away with one finger and struggled to organize the right choice of words. "Look, Nick, I think if we're going to be working together, we should lay down some ground rules. Otherwise I might just be a nervous wreck the whole time, and that won't be productive at all."

Nick leaned back against her car and inclined his head solemnly as he slid his fingertips into the top pockets of his jeans. "What do you have in mind?"

Brooke looked down at the concrete beneath her feet. Her hair feathered into her face once again. Shoving it back, she met his eyes. Her tone was matter-of-fact when she answered. "It's strictly business, Nick. I don't want this to turn into some kind of...second chance. That part of our lives is over, and I'm not up to starting it again."

Nick nodded as if in agreement, but something in his eyes lacked conviction. "We're going to be partners, not lovers," he said quietly. "What we're going to create together will be very special and very personal. But it's also strictly business."

Brooke nodded and set her hand on her small hip, and for a second Nick thought she was struggling to speak. Instead she fidgeted with the bracelets on her left wrist. "Okay," she said, her voice a decibel quieter than it had been before. "Then let's get started."

His smile reached his lips, then, and he stood up fully, a head taller than she. And as he looked into her eyes and gestured toward the museum door, he wondered if it was disappointment he saw in her emerald eyes, because he had accepted her ground rules so readily. When it came right down to it, he thought, following Brooke in, all the rules in the world might not be worth a damn in light of this chemistry that still pulled like a gravitational force between them.

Brooke went into the museum and at once saw that a new group of people were milling around, dodging the carpenters and contractors. A group of women were dragging boxes into the back rooms of the museum with strained expressions on their faces, as if they couldn't get away from the contractors fast enough.

"The Historical Society is in charge of preserving all of the museum pieces," Nick said, closing the door behind them and stepping over a cord. He grabbed Brooke's hand. "Watch your step."

Brooke caught her balance and withdrew her hand at once. She jammed it into her pocket, as if to assure herself that he wouldn't take it again.

Nick let his hand drop to his side. "Anyway, they're all over the place wrapping and packing the pieces that can be moved out. I've got our workroom set up in the back, but I'm afraid we'll have to share it with them for a few days . . . just until they're finished moving everything."

"Shouldn't they have done that before?" Brooke asked. "I mean, it seems a little late after the work has already started."

Nick smirked. "Poor organization."

Brooke smiled. "I see. Mrs. Hemphill wouldn't be in that group, would she?"

"Of course," he said. "Mrs. Hemphill is in everything."

They stepped over a power saw someone had laid on the floor, then ducked under a ladder. A burly looking hulk blocked Brooke's way into the corridor, and he grinned down at her, not offering to move an inch.

"Hey, I know you," the man rumbled. "You were a couple grades ahead of me in school. Brooke something, right?"

Brooke looked up at him, but didn't recognize him at all. "Martin."

He laughed then, as if he'd stumbled on the "Sex Kitten of the Month." "Yeah, I remember reading about you in the paper. I was real sorry I never got to know you."

Brooke felt color climbing to the top of her cheekbones. "Excuse me," she said firmly. "I need to get to my work-room."

The hulk took a step to the side, just enough that she would brush him as she inched past. "You gonna be work-ing here every day, too?" he asked. "Hot damn. Nobody told me there were perks with this job. Maybe we'll get to know each other, after all."

Nick set his hand on the hulk's massive biceps. "Out of the way, pal," he said, his voice balancing on the edge of anger. "The only thing you're gonna get to know better is that power saw over there."

The hulk grinned and stepped back, and Brooke pushed past him. Taking a deep breath, she stumbled into Nick's office and told herself that the exchange was no big deal. Women had to deal with men like that all the time. So why was she on the verge of crying?

The image of that basketball player returned, and she wiped her clammy hands on her jeans. It wasn't the same thing, she told herself. This was innocent, harmless... someone who knew her... and her reputation....

"Ignorant jerk," Nick mumbled, coming up behind her. He turned Brooke around, and saw the turbulence on her face. "Are you all right?"

"Yes," she said too quickly. "It's just...I hate being treated like that."

"It won't happen again," Nick said. "One more word to you and I'll have that SOB fired."

She swallowed back the emotion in her throat, and this time when Nick nestled her hand in his she didn't pull away.

He led her out of the office, through the darkly lit hall, and into the large workroom where he had set up their tables. Several middle-aged women crouched over a box of artifacts, disagreeing about the proper way to wrap each piece.

Brooke recognized some of them. She had vague memories of the women who'd sat together at town picnics, picking away at gossip until the juiciest morsels were dried up. Roxy was right: she hadn't stayed around to listen to their gossip and their disapproval of her, but she had imagined. She let go of Nick's hand, and jammed hers back into her pocket.

"What do you think?" Nick asked her, drawing her attention from the women back to their work space. "Is this going to be okay?"

Brooke surveyed the large worktable, which was just tall enough to stand up at without putting strain on the back. To the left of it she saw a light table made of several pieces of frosted glass with fluorescent bulbs beneath to simulate sunlight through the stained glass. On the wall was a large pegboard with Nick's tools hanging neatly from it, and beneath it was a stack of storage bins of various sizes for glass. "It's perfect," Brooke said. "It's a lot like my studio in Tallahassee."

"A little cruder, maybe," Nick said. "But we really need to work on-site to keep from having to move the panels much. I think this'll do. After we've decided on our theme and the general direction of the project, I'll place the order for the glass and the lead came that we'll need."

The suddenly overwhelming reality of the project they faced hit Brooke, and she realized that until now she hadn't given the work itself that much thought. "There's so much to be done," she said. "It'll take weeks to do the cartoons of the glass, and then all the cutting and leading . . . I don't see how we can do this alone."

"Oh, we won't be doing it alone," Nick said, pulling out a drawer on the worktable and removing a stack of sketches. "We'll have to hire some more people experienced in cutting glass. I was going to ask you if you knew of anyone from Tallahassee who might be interested in helping us out."

Brooke sat on a tall stool and thought for a moment. "I have several people who've taken classes at my studio, who might come. But do we have enough in our budget to pay them?"

Nick shrugged and began to spread his sketches out across the table. "I don't know for sure what our budget's going to be yet. Abby Hemphill was right. It hasn't completely been approved. But, yeah, they'll have to put it in the budget. If we did this ourselves, it would take over a year."

"Maybe we could hire some high school kids to help with some of the other things," she said. "Like tracing the patterns, coloring them, cutting them out . . ."

"My nephew has agreed to help," Nick said. "And I'll call the high school and see if we could get some help from the art department."

Brooke sensed the sudden silence among the women behind them. It was so abrupt that she knew at once what they were thinking. "Do you think they'd really let some of their students work here with you—us?" she asked, barely above a whisper.

Nick glanced back at the women, noting the distasteful looks on their faces, the blatant disgust. He released a heavy sigh. "Well, maybe not," he mumbled. "Maybe we'll have to find assistants another way."

The women behind them began to whisper again, and Brooke's eyes connected with his, sharing the common bond of regret.

"These are some of my preliminary sketches," Nick said finally. "I had some ideas, so I thought I'd jot them down."

"Yes," she said, trying not to let the women distract her. "I have some sketches, too."

Brooke opened her portfolio. She glanced over her shoulder and saw that the ladies had gone back to their wrapping, though she was certain they mentally recorded every word she and Nick exchanged. "Well...I..." She cleared her throat, suddenly uncomfortable that her ideas would be open to the scrutiny of the Historical Society. "I thought we could do it in ethnic sections. We have a lot of different cultures living in Hayden. Hispanics, Jews, Italians, Indians, Blacks, Whites...I thought we could give them each several panels that represent their individual cultures."

She felt the women's eyes on her again and realized that she could have proposed Michelangelo's murals in the Sistine Chapel and they still wouldn't have been satisfied.

"That's good," Nick said, regarding the sketches she had penciled out. While the words indicated a compliment, she heard an unspoken *but* hanging on the end. "It's just that it's...pretty predictable."

"Predictable?" she asked. "Biblical stories are predictable. In stained glass, just about anything else is new."

"I like this one a lot," he said, reaching across her for one of her sketches. His shoulder brushed hers, and she caught the faint scent of his after-shave. Nick smelled of pine trees and ocean wind, and she remembered that it was the same fragrance he'd worn when he taught. It had distracted her then, too.

He held the sketch up and traced the lines with his finger. "An Indian woman nursing her child. This is sort of what I had in mind. Not the cultural aspect, but the personal. You know what I mean?"

She looked up at him, aware that he was a little too close for comfort. But in the chill of the room, his warmth was almost welcome. "No, not really."

Nick reached onto his stack of sketches, crude puzzle-pieced drawings that translated well to glass. "Like this one," he said.

It was the picture of an old, gnarled man, holding a child on his bony lap.

"That's beautiful," she whispered. "But what's your theme? Age? Family? Love?"

The sound of activity behind them ceased, and she knew that the women were listening intently, though they couldn't see the drawings. "All of them, sort of. I was thinking of portraying the most personal aspects of life. The most intimate emotions. Something that everyone can look at and say, 'I've felt that way.'"

"It sounds wonderful," Brooke said, "but it isn't that easy to translate emotions to stained glass. We need something more specific. Something like emotional events. Things happening that bring back associations. Like that picture of the mother nursing her child . . . that's an event that brings to mind an emotion."

"Right," Nick said, nodding slowly. His eyes were aglow with that special brainstorming spark Brooke had found so fresh and exciting years ago. "Events like birth and death and . . ."

"And a baby's first steps," she threw in. "And a christening."

"And a first kiss, and a wedding . . ."

Brooke's eyes absorbed the glow of his, and she caught her breath. "Stages of life," she said, forgetting that anyone else was present, and that anything she said would be spread around the town so that it wouldn't even be recognizable by the time it was repeated back to her. "Everyone could relate to the stages-of-life theme. Not just specific cultures or ages. Even little children who came to the museum would be able to relate to it."

Nick's face was tense with excitement. "I love it. It's perfect. The town wanted this to be a place that drew families, something a little more interesting than some dusty old artifacts that no one could be less interested in. I think this is just the feel they're looking for."

Brooke bit her lip and began pulling her charcoal out of her portfolio. "All right, then. The first thing to do is to decide exactly how to divide the panels, what stage of life each one will represent and start talking about the exact scenes we want there. Then we can get right into drawing the cartoons."

"Excuse me."

The words were delivered in a harsh, nasal voice, and Brooke and Nick turned to see that the women had come to their feet and were glaring at them as if they had just blasphemed. "Yes, Mrs. Inglish?" Nick asked the woman who had spoken.

"We couldn't help overhearing," the wiry woman said, stretching her chin high. "And we want you to know that the 'dusty old artifacts' that you referred to are precisely the mainstay of this museum. If you can't understand that, perhaps you don't belong here doing whatever it is you and that woman are trying to do."

Nick bit the inside of his lip. He crossed his arms and regarded the floor, schooling his features to remain calm. When he brought his eyes back to Mrs. Inglish's, he had managed to force a smile. "Of course we understand the importance of the artifacts, ladies. The problem, however, is that no one wants to come and look at them. We're trying to redefine the museum so that it'll appeal to more people."

"Forgive me if I don't believe that drawing cartoons on the windows of a museum will add to its appeal. You can do that in the elementary school. This is a solemn institution..."

Brooke set her hand on Nick's arm and stood up beside him. "Mrs. Inglish, we weren't talking about real cartoons. That's simply the term we use for the preliminary sketches of the windows. We swear there won't be any Bugs Bunnies on these windows."

Nick's grin broke through his frown, and he lowered his face to hide it.

"This may come as a surprise to you," Mrs. Inglish went on, more irate than before. "But we're taking this renovation very seriously. We all know what the two of you are up to in here."

Brooke's expression grew a degree more strained. "And what is that?"

"No good," the woman said, then nodded at her friends as if she'd just checkmated the champion.

Nick shook his head and turned back to the table, gathering all of the sketches and stuffing them into Brooke's portfolio. His breath was heavier, more restricted, as he grabbed Brooke's arm and started walking toward the door.

"Where are you going?" Mrs. Inglish asked.

"Someplace where we can work without interruptions," he said. "Because, you see, we take this renovation very seriously, too."

Mrs. Inglish mumbled something to the other women as Nick and Brooke left, something neither of them cared to imagine. The room erupted into a low roar of cackles and chirps.

"Where *are* we going?" Brooke asked when they were out of earshot.

"Well, there sure as hell isn't any place around here," he said. "I guess we'll go to my house."

Brooke stopped in her tracks. "No."

Nick turned and saw the determination in her expression. "What's the big deal, Brooke? We had some good brainstorming going. I don't want to let those biddies in there ruin it."

"It's bad enough that their gossip will be all over town before lunch," she said, "but if we go to your house today, while they're looking for something to say about us, we're only feeding it. I won't do that, Nick."

Nick leaned back against a wall, and his shoulders fell as he expelled a long breath. "It isn't that, really, is it, Brooke? You're afraid to go to my house with me for other reasons, aren't you?"

"Of course not."

His eyes were impatient, penetrating, as they locked her in their scrutiny. "Yes you are. You're afraid that we'll get there, all alone, and that something will happen between us. Aren't you?"

Brooke's mouth tightened into a thin line, and he saw the anger flaring in her eyes. "I can see now that maybe I was hasty," she said.

"What do you mean?"

"In telling Mrs. Hemphill I was staying!" she whispered. "I'm not up to rationalizing every decision I make with you, Nick. I'm not up to explaining myself constantly. Maybe this isn't such a good idea, after all."

Nick took her hand and pulled her into his office, closing the door behind them. She leaned back against the wall,

weary of all the battles she'd fought that morning. Nick
lifted his hands in apology. "I'm sorry," he said. "No more
pressures. Let's just try to work, okay? Don't quit on me
just when we've gotten started. I need you, Brooke. I can't
do this without you."

She looked up into his eyes and wished from her soul that
he hadn't said just those words in just that way. It made her
so much more aware of the chemistry between them, the
chemistry she was even less able to fight now that they were
adults than she had when she was in high school. She could
no more walk away from him now, she realized, than she
could end the gossip with a wave of a magic wand. Against
all her better judgment she nodded. "All right. Let's
work."

Relief drained Nick's face, making him appear as vulnerable as she felt. He turned to the cluttered desk and
cleared off a space for her. "We'll each take one side of the
desk, and maybe by the afternoon the Women's Hysterical
Society will have gone home."

Brooke couldn't help smiling at his deliberate mis-
nomer, and his naughty smile tugged at her heart.

"We're going to get through this, you know," he said.

Brooke's smile settled comfortably over her face, despite the sigh unraveling from her lungs. "I know," she
agreed.

BY THE END OF THE DAY Brooke and Nick had divided the
circular windows into eighty panels and had assigned a
different stage of life with minithemes to each group. They
stayed in the tiny office with the door closed until lunchtime. When they came out, they noticed the members of the
"Hysterical Society" nudging each other, and heard the
contractors' sneers. They went to a fast-food restaurant and
choked down a hamburger in Brooke's car, where they were

immune from the stares and gossip they might have encountered inside. Then, feeling refreshed, they braved curious eyes once again and locked themselves back in the office.

By the time they called it a day, the construction crews had left, and all of the women of the Historical Society were safely at home, no doubt lighting half the telephone lines in Hayden. Still, Brooke felt a major sense of accomplishment, a tingling pride that they were on the verge of creating something wonderful.

But when she drove home, that sense of pride sank as she realized that she had yet to face her family. She was certain they'd heard—from someone, if not Roxy—how she had told off Mrs. Hemphill and defied all the town gossips by staying and working with Nick on the windows.

And she was right. When she walked in, she saw them all sitting soberly in the living room, as still as statues, staring at her as if their silence eloquently demanded explanation. Her mother faced her with a hurt, how-could-you-do-this-to-me look; her father wore his stoic that's-gratitude-for-you visage; and Roxy regarded her with a martyred why-don't-you-just-shoot-me-and-put-me-out-of-my-misery expression.

Brooke excised the pain from her heart and told herself to make her explanation cut and dried, so that there wouldn't be tears and yelling and scars that never quite healed. She remembered the time her grandmother had died, and her parents had gathered her and Roxy into the living room to break the solemn news. Did her family view this moment as seriously as a death in the family?

"I thought of going straight to a hotel, since I had my suitcase with me," Brooke said, her voice raspy with emotion. "But I decided that I should at least come by and let you hear from my mouth that I *am* staying and I *am* going to be working with Nick on the windows. My work here shouldn't affect any of you at all. I'll find my own apartment tomorrow, and you won't even have to know I'm here."

She swallowed and saw that none of them, not her mother, her father, nor Roxy, was about to speak. Their expressions remained unchanged. Heartsick, she started slowly toward the door. Just before opening it, she turned back to them. Tears blurred her vision, and her mouth quivered. The words wobbled with emotion. "I'm truly sorry that my being here embarrasses all of you. But this town has taken enough from me. It owes me this chance to make my mark. And I'm going to do it."

She opened the door and started to walk out.

"Are you going to move in with that man?" Her mother's question stopped her before she'd crossed the threshold.

Brooke turned back to her mother, hardly believing what she'd heard. "No, I am not moving in with Nick. I told you, there is nothing going on between us."

"Then why would you sacrifice all of your dignity, all of the integrity you've worked so hard to rebuild in the last ten years, if he doesn't mean anything to you?"

"Because I'm an artist!" Brooke cried. "A good one. I've never had the opportunity to create anything of this magnitude!"

"Oh, you created something of this magnitude," her mother said. "About ten years ago."

Frustrated beyond control Brooke pressed her forehead against the edge of the open door and wiped the tears roughly from her face. After a moment she looked at Roxy, but found that her sister wasn't glaring at her any longer. Instead she stared despondently at the floor, as if Brooke's very presence drained her.

"Look, there's really no point in this," Brooke said as new tears rolled down her face. "I'm not ever going to make you believe me. You didn't believe me that nothing happened the first time, so why should you believe me now?"

"Because you're both single and attractive," her father blurted. "And you have a history."

"So what?" she asked. "We're two adults who have made a business decision. It isn't hurting anyone, it isn't betraying anyone..."

Her voice broke off, and she felt like a kid again, begging her daddy to let her stay out past ten o'clock. It was ludicrous, and she wasn't going to play the game any longer.

"I'll be at the Bluejay Inn," she said. And then she closed the door and left without looking back.

IT WAS ALMOST EIGHT when Brooke checked in at the Bluejay Inn. The room was hot and had a musty odor from age and traffic. She realized vaguely that she hadn't eaten, so she picked up the room-service menu and scanned it absently. Finally she dropped it onto the tightly made bed and admitted that she really wasn't hungry.

She lay down on the bed and stared at the ceiling, letting the quiet accompany her like just another hostile acquaintance. *It wasn't fair,* she thought. None of what had happened concerning Nick was fair. She was tired of being alone, tired of not trusting any of the men interested in her for fear that they'd heard about her reputation and expected to get lucky. She was tired of expecting the worst of people and being right. She was tired of not having a soul to confide in who wouldn't spread her deepest thoughts all over the state.

She closed her eyes as the tears seeped out and tried to find some sense to it all. What difference would it make, after all, if she and Nick did get involved? Weren't they both adults, unattached to anyone else, with a world of things in common? Wasn't that what had attracted them in the first place?

But it wasn't that simple, for in the town's eyes, he had been a statutory rapist, and she a child whore.

The most intense loneliness she had ever experienced coiled up in her heart, and she longed for a friend. But Nick was the only friend she had in town.

She sat up on the bed, wiped her eyes and reached for the telephone book. She found his number and stared at it. She just need to talk, she told herself. Needed to reaffirm that she had made the right decision to stay.

With a trembling hand, she picked up the phone and punched out his number, though she had no idea what she would say when he answered.

NICK HEARD THE PHONE from the shower and shut off the water. Grabbing the towel he had thrown over the bar, he stepped out, slung the towel around his waist and walked into his bedroom. He picked up the phone midring.

"Hello?"

"Nick?" Brooke's voice sounded hollow.

Nick changed ears and propped one wet foot on the edge of his bed. "Brooke? Are you all right?"

"Yeah, I'm fine," she said, her tone a little too bright. "I just...thought you should know, in case you had to reach me, that I've checked into the Bluejay Inn for the night. I'll find an apartment tomorrow, but—"

Her voice trailed off, and Nick planted his elbow on his knee and leaned forward, ignoring the rivulets of water dripping from his hair. "Why? I thought you were staying with your parents. Did—?'' He took a deep breath and raked his hand through his wet curls. "Aw, no. Did you have a fight with them about me?''

He heard her sniff and knew without a doubt that she'd been crying. The knowledge wound around his heart in skeins of regret.

"I just . . . felt it was better for all of us if I didn't stay at home.''

He dropped his forehead into his palm and asked himself what he was doing to her and when the torture for both of them would end. "Brooke, you need your family. It's a cruel town out there. Don't alienate them now.''

"They don't need me,'' she said. She caught the words on a sob, then muffled the sound.

Helpless, Nick stood straight and dropped his towel, reached for his jeans hanging over a chair. "What room are you in?'' he asked suddenly. "I'm coming over.''

"No, you can't do that!''

He held the phone with his shoulder and stepped into his pants. "The hell I can't. If it's just you and me in this, then we'll fight it together. I'm not going to let you suffer this alone. You *have* got a friend.''

"I know that,'' she said, her voice as soft and sad as it had been that night ten years ago, the last time he'd spoken to her before she left. "But I recognized the front-desk clerk, and she recognized me. She's one of those little ladies who's in all the civic clubs. If you came here, it'd be all over town by morning.''

"To hell with her,'' Nick said, though his voice lacked the bite to match such words. "Besides, she'd never even know I was there. So let me come over.'' His mouth pressed close to the phone. "I'll find something to make you laugh, or take you to a movie, or just let you cry. I'm a good listener, you know.''

He could sense the pain in her ragged breath, and he braced a hand on his windowsill and gazed out at the moonlight glittering on the canal. Instead, he saw her face, twisted in pain and distress, her soft cheeks shining with tears.

"Remember that time when you were in school, and you got a C on your English paper?" he asked. "Remember how upset you were when you came to my class...the overachiever who hadn't achieved? I was a good listener then, wasn't I?"

Brooke was quiet, but he knew that she remembered the way he had sat her down in the art room that day he'd caught her crying, pushed her hair back from her damp cheek, and insisted that she tell him what was bothering her. "Yes, you were," she whispered. "And you fixed everything. You talked to Mrs. Deere and got me another chance to do the paper."

"Yeah," he said softly. "I'm big on second chances."

The moment he said the words, Nick wished he hadn't, but when she spoke, he could tell that his words had stopped her tears. "I've always wondered what you said to her," Brooke said.

Nick dropped back to his bed and leaned back, wishing he could reach out and dry the tears he knew were glistening on her face.

"Oh, not much," he said. "Just that you were an overachiever who saw anything less than an A as absolute failure and that I had really been working you hard in art because of your unique talent. I told her it was all my fault and that I'd let up a little."

She laughed softly then. "Let up? You never let up on me. You demanded perfection."

"And I got it," he whispered.

Her silence sent a warm feeling rushing up inside him, untangling the confusion in his heart.

"What room are you in?" he asked again, a forbidden ache growing.

She didn't answer, and he felt his muscles stiffening like granite, waiting for the words that could break his shell.

"Trust me, Brooke," he said.

At once he realized that he had uttered that phrase before—those three little words packed with all the significance in the world. And just as she had denied them ten years earlier, she rejected them again.

"I don't want you to come, Nick," she said. "I just need a good night's sleep. I'll see you tomorrow, okay?"

His heart sank like lead, but in the fog of disappointment, he found his voice. "Brooke, you're not going to skip town on me again are you?"

"No," she said, her voice weary and innocently seductive. "I'll be there."

The line went dead, and Nick held the phone clutched in his hand, staring at it and knowing that, deep within, he didn't really trust her, either. What would it take to send her running this time? And who would be waiting for her when she did?

He dismissed the thought and hung up the phone and told himself that it wasn't love that had him reeling tonight. It was the frustration of unfinished business. It was that damnable loneliness that the very sight of her had created in his soul.

That, and the miserable sound of tears in her voice.

BROOKE LEANED OVER the hotel's bathroom sink and washed her face, looked in the mirror and saw a pale rendition of who she thought she was. Her eyes were red and swollen, and her hair fell around her face in silky tangles. She really should do something with it, she thought.

She heard a knock on the door and went to the window to peer out. Her mother stood at the door in the blue-white overhead light, and she saw her father waiting a few steps behind her. Her heart tripped, and she felt that misery that Nick had so successfully tamed rising back to threaten her again. Swallowing, she opened the door.

Her mother looked almost as battle-fatigued as Brooke herself when she stepped inside. "We didn't want you to stay in a hotel tonight," Alice Martin whispered, her lips trembling at the corners. "We love you, honey, and we want you to come home."

Brooke sighed and stepped back from the door, letting her parents into the room. They came in, looked around awkwardly and continued to stand as she lowered herself to the bed. "It's all right, Mom. I'm comfortable here."

"You can be comfortable at home," her father said, his gruff voice softened by his intention to make peace.

"No, not really," she said, shaking her head. "There's no comfort in all that fighting. I'm not used to it. I've lived alone for a long time. I just think it's best—"

"We won't nag you anymore," her mother interrupted. "Will we, George?"

"No, we won't," her father agreed, setting his arm around his wife's narrow shoulders. "We just want you with us. If we promise to keep our mouths shut, will you come home?"

Brooke looked critically at the floor, as if studying the worn-out carpet that clashed with the bedspread. She wondered if they could really share a home together again, without judging or condemning each other. After all this time, she doubted it. "I don't know..."

Her mother dropped into a chair, leaning toward her with her plea. "Do it for Roxy," her mother said, and Brooke looked up. "She needs you, Brooke. I'm worried about her. She's not happy, and I'm afraid we're losing her, too. Maybe having you there will help her some."

Brooke stood up and went to the window, peered out over the dark parking lot lit only with two blaring lights. From her window she could see the neon sign of a truck stop flashing its tacky glory. It hadn't been there ten years ago, she thought, but tonight the parking lot was full of eighteen wheelers and pickup trucks. Life had gone on in Hayden without her, just as Roxy's life had. "I don't see how I could help," she said, turning back to her parents. "She can barely tolerate me."

"It isn't just you," her mother said. "She's quiet like that with everybody. She just needs to get to know you again. We all do."

Brooke tried to see them without reproach, without the pain that fogged the vision of her heart. Too much time had passed to really go home and pick up where she'd left off, she told herself. But as Nick had reminded her tonight, it wasn't too late for a second chance.

"All right," she whispered wearily. "I'll come home."

Her parents offered faint smiles, but there wasn't a great deal of victory in their expressions. Too much had been lost between them. "I'll have supper waiting," her mother said. "I know you haven't eaten."

Brooke nodded. "I'll be there in about twenty minutes," she said. "I just have to get my things together and check out."

"Okay," her mother said awkwardly. She attempted a smile, and took a deep, uneven breath. "We'll see you at home, then."

"Yeah."

Brooke watched her parents walk toward the door, stiff with the emotion they both held trapped inside. "Mom? Dad?" she said just before they stepped outside.

They turned back to her, and she saw the naked love in both their faces. Suddenly she forgave them for all the mistrust, and all the pain. "I'll make you proud of me one of these days. I swear I will."

Her parents only smiled sadly and left her alone.

CHAPTER FIVE

SHADOWS SLID LIKE DANCING VISIONS of what might have been, along the moonlit wall of Nick's bedroom. It was almost midnight, but he felt about as sleepy as a hungry leopard. Wearily he slung his feet to the ivory carpet and rubbed his eyes, then let his fingers slide down his face. His gaze drifted to the window, where an oleander blew and danced in the breeze with the same cadence as the shadows on the opposite wall. Such were the origins of visions, he thought. Poisonous trees casting fantasies in a hopeful mind.

He got up and walked in darkness through the living room into the kitchen and opened the refrigerator, letting its light spill out to illuminate the room. He propped his elbow on the door and peered inside, at the half-full bottle of wine, the leftover pasta, and a lone apple.

Damn, he thought, staring vacantly at the food. She'd been crying tonight. Indirectly he always seemed to be responsible for Brooke's tears.

He thought of the sound of despair in her voice and wondered if she was, indeed, all right. Of course she wasn't, he decided, shutting the refrigerator and letting the darkness swallow him again. Because of him, there was a rift again, between Brooke and her parents. He must have been crazy asking her to come back here.

He went to the telephone on the kitchen wall, braced his elbows on the counter and closed his hand around the cool receiver. If he called her just to see how she was and woke her, would it be such a crime?

Deciding that there were worse things he could do, like get dressed and show up at her door—which didn't seem like such a bad idea—he looked up the number for the Bluejay Inn and dialed it.

It rang four times before the desk clerk—a man, rather than the woman Brooke had mentioned—answered.

"Would you please connect me to Brooke Martin's room?" he asked.

"Miss Martin checked out over two hours ago," the man said.

"She did? Why? Didn't she just check in?"

"All I know is what's on my books," the man said impatiently.

"Yes, thank you." Nick hung up the phone, raking a hand through his hair. His heartbeat accelerated to a threatening speed as thoughts spun wildly in his mind, all leading to the same result. *She's gone,* he thought. *She's left me again.*

Before he'd consciously decided to do so, Nick snatched up the phone again and dialed the number in Tallahassee he'd wanted to call a hundred times...the number he knew from memory, but had never dialed.

"Hello."

She answered on the first ring, and he caught his breath, though his heart fell miles to his feet. "Brooke, why did you—"

"This is Brooke Martin," her voice continued. "I'm not home right now, but if you'll leave your name and number I'll get back to you."

A recording! Nick realized, with some relief. He heard the beep and hesitated a moment. "Uh...it's Nick," he said. "I called the hotel and you'd checked out. I hope you haven't gone home, Brooke. It's too important to give up on that easily...the windows, I mean. Don't give up, Brooke. It's worth whatever it takes to see it through. I really hope you haven't gone home."

Then, unable to think of anything else to say, he dropped the phone back in its cradle and rested his forehead on his palm.

Damn, he thought. He'd said too much. And he hadn't said enough.

Well, there was no way to know for sure if she'd gone home until tomorrow, when he'd see whether or not she would show up for work. The trick, he thought, would be getting through the night.

THE QUESTION ANSWERED ITSELF the next morning when Nick looked up to see Brooke standing in his office doorway, shining like a ray of sunlight on a stormy day.

"Thank God," he said, wilting back in his chair in relief. "You're here."

Brooke smiled. "Well, that's some greeting."

He came to his feet and leaned haggardly over his desk. Dark circles were etched beneath his eyes, and he knew that his anxieties were written in every gesture he made. "Where were you?" he asked, schooling his voice to sound calm. "I called you last night. They said you'd checked out...."

Brooke dropped her portfolio onto a chair and looked at him with summer eyes that warmed the chill in his heart. "My parents came by after I talked to you," she said. "We sort of made peace, so I decided to go back."

He stared at her for a moment longer, but as the simple truth registered, a slow grin spread from his eyes right straight down to his heart. "I thought you went to Tallahassee," he whispered, knowing he shouldn't. "I thought you'd given up again."

A poignant expression softened Brooke's smooth features, and she shook her head. "I wouldn't abandon my partner without telling him."

Nick issued a deep breath in a half laugh. "Good."

They stood looking at each other for a moment, each contemplating the other. She thought how vulnerable he looked with red eyes and day-old stubble. He thought how sexy she looked with her hair pulled back in a ponytail, tiny wisps escaping to frame her face.

"So..." They spoke simultaneously, then smiled and hesitated.

"We'd better get to work before the Hysterical Society gets here," he said finally.

Brooke's smile died a little. "Too late. A few of them were driving up when I got here."

"Terrific," he said, coming around the desk. His white T-shirt looked wrinkled, as if he'd had other things on his mind when he'd dressed that morning. She thought of the sound of his voice on the phone last night, his plea to come over and comfort her. If anyone could have, it would have been him, she thought. Now, seeing him all ruffled and anxious, only one urge swept through her...the urge to comfort *him*, hold him in her arms, make him relax and beckon the sleep that had so obviously eluded him last night.

He glanced out the door, shrugging. "Well, at least it can't go on forever. They're bound to run out of artifacts soon."

A few of the women walked by and tried to look as if they weren't intentionally looking into the office as they passed.

"Morning ladies," Nick called in a pseudo-cheerful voice.

The women mumbled various greetings that their tones negated and walked on, looking for work to be done.

Brooke sank to her chair, aware that the electricity crackling between them was fast giving way to her own anxieties, her own fears. Through that door, she was the sordid topic of conversation that kept the women's day interesting, and that fact never left her mind as she worked.

For the next hour both Nick and Brooke tried to concentrate, but even with the door closed they could hear the incessant humming of power saws and electric sanders, of banging and crashing, of cursing and yelling over the noise. The office was becoming cramped and hot as they tried to spread out, and with each new panel they sketched, it became more cluttered.

After they'd been at it for more than two hours, Brooke threw down her charcoal. "This is never going to do," she said. "We need our workroom. That's what it's there for."

"They should be finished today," Nick said. "Things will be more normal tomorrow."

"In the meantime, we aren't really getting anything done. It's a mess in here. I don't know what I've done and what I haven't."

Nick leaned forward on his desk and propped his chin in his hand. His grin reached out and grabbed her heart. "Look, why don't we just use the time to go to Tampa to place our orders for the glass and lead came?"

Brooke looked at the stacks of papers that depicted some, but not all, of the panels. Even the ones they had roughed out didn't have details or exact colors—just the basic themes and ideas. "How can you order glass and lead when you don't know exactly how much you need yet?"

"I can't, really," he said. "But I can give them a ballpark figure and get some bids going on it, and when we're ready, we can give them exact amounts. Today's as good a day as any." He grinned. "Come on. Let me take you away from all this."

Nick's offer was sorely tempting, but something inside held Brooke back. Idly she fingered the chains at her throat. "We can't afford to waste the time, you know," she said. "I could take some of this home and work on it there while you go to Tampa."

He held out his hands, palms up, and shrugged innocently. "Hey, you're the expert. I need you with me."

A smile tugged at one side of her lips. "Don't give me that. If it weren't for your class, I wouldn't have ever gotten interested in stained glass. *You* taught *me*, remember?"

"Yeah, but you're the one who's been doing it for a living. You're way ahead of me."

Brooke shook her head. "Never. In my mind, you'll always be the teacher."

Nick's flip expression faded, and he looked down at his hands for a moment, then flicked a speck of dust off of his sketch. "I wish you could stop thinking of me that way."

Brooke averted her eyes when he looked at her. "I wish I could, too." She came to her feet, dusted off her pants as if she could shake away the growing sense of intimacy. "But maybe it's best that I do. It keeps the boundaries properly drawn."

Nick's eyes were penetrating, waiting for her to look at him without defense. "Do you really need those boundaries, Brooke?"

Brooke tossed a wisp of hair back from her face. "We all need boundaries, Nick. They're like the lead work on the windows. They help support us. They keep us from buckling and cracking with the weight of whatever we carry around."

"And they're nice and safe," he said quietly, not taking his eyes from her face.

"Yeah," she said, meeting his gaze directly. "They're nice and safe. And they don't hurt anybody."

Nick nodded and looked down at his hands again, as if some script he needed to get through the day was hidden there, in the lines of his palms. Finally he got to his feet, too suddenly, too brightly, and clapped his hands together. "Well, all right, then. Let's just take those boundaries and go to Tampa."

Aware that those boundaries were blurring with each hour, Brooke followed a few steps behind him as he lead her past the workers and out into the sunlight.

ABBY HEMPHILL STEPPED OVER a dusty power tool that someone had neglectfully left lying at the entrance to the museum and looked around for a sign of the culprit. *Who did these men think they were?* she wondered vaguely. From the way they slouched around, chomping on sandwiches and guzzling canned soda, you would think they owned the place.

It was a terrible day, she thought, when one had to face the fact that the town's museum had been turned into a loafing place for every idiot with a saw, as well as a love nest for Nick Marcello and that girl. It was a downright mockery to the solemnity of such a cultural institution.

Across the large room and through the corridor, Abby saw some of the ladies from the Historical Society, engaged in *constructive* work. *At least someone was doing what they were supposed to,* she thought.

Straightening her hair and pristinely dodging the cords and machinery in her way, Abby made her way to the room where the ladies had congregated. "Well," she huffed when she reached them, "it certainly is refreshing to see that not everyone is wasting the taxpayers' money."

The women looked up at her, all smiles and cordial greetings, which made her feel as if they, at least, gave her the respect she deserved, even if she did know very few of them beyond their names. It was difficult to hold positions of power, she told herself, and still maintain close friendships.

"It's lunch hour for the construction crews," Martha Inglish told her. "We were just thinking of going out to get a bite, ourselves. But we couldn't decide whether we could spare the time or not. Our two *artistes*—" she pronounced the word with great sarcasm "—are getting a little annoyed that they have to share a work space with us. We thought if we hurried we could finish this today."

"The Historical Society's duties should come first," Abby proclaimed. "Don't let them bully you."

"Oh, they aren't bullying us," Mrs. Inglish said. "In fact, we've hardly seen them in the last two days, since they've taken to locking themselves in his office. And we wouldn't *dream* of interrupting them."

The women snickered, but Mrs. Hemphill didn't find it at all amusing. "Locked in his office? Are you serious?"

"Well, not now. They left in that car of his about two hours ago."

"Left!" Mrs. Hemphill cried. "Those people are getting paid by the hour until the budget is approved! How dare they just leave?" She turned to the other women, surveying their faces for the answers she sought. "Have you actually *seen* them working? Cutting glass, painting it, whatever it is they do?"

The women all agreed that none of them had seen any such thing. "They just talked and whispered a lot when we could hear them," Mrs. Inglish said. "Who knows what's been going on in that office?"

"That does it!" Abby spun around and started out the door. "I'm going to put a stop to this today!" Determined to get the handling of the Hayden museum back under control, she marched out like a woman with a divine mission.

THE DUESENBERG'S ENGINE idled conspicuously at the red light in downtown Tampa, drawing admiring stares from the drivers around them. Nick had pulled the top down before they'd left Hayden, and the wind and sun had mingled to inject more energy and liveliness into his tired face.

The driver next to them, a businessman in a gold Mercedes, rolled down his window and leaned over to the passenger side. "Nice car!" he called.

Nick grinned. "Thanks."

The man dug into his pocket for a business card and stretched to hand it to Nick. "If you ever want to sell it, give me a call."

Nick took the card and noted that the light was still red. "Sorry. This baby's not for sale."

The light turned green, and the man shook his head regretfully. He gave the car a last look and drove off with a wave.

Brooke laughed and squinted over at Nick as the sun and wind hit her face. "You didn't even ask how much he was willing to pay," she said. "Aren't you even curious?"

Nick tossed the card to the floor. "Nope. Whatever it is, it's not enough. Some things just don't have a price."

Brooke set her elbow on the back of her leather seat and twisted around to see Nick more clearly as he drove. The act of driving made him seem more relaxed, more at home than she'd ever seen him. It was as if the Duesenberg held his power, his worth, his confidence. "Was the grandfather who left you this car a rich man?" she asked.

Nick made a sharp turn, swinging her toward him, and he laughed. "No, not by any stretch of the imagination. My grandfather was a cobbler."

"Then how could he afford a Duesenberg?"

Nick pulled onto a street with bottlenecked traffic and idled for a moment. "He didn't buy it," he said. "One of his best customers for twenty years owned this car, though. Grandpa made everything that man put on his feet, and the man had a deep appreciation for the quality in his work. When he died, he left the car to my grandpa. He wrote in his will that my grandfather was the only man he knew who understood the true meaning of the word *quality*. This car came to represent everything Grandpa believed in. It was his most prized possession."

A poignant smile touched Brooke's lips. "And he left it to you," she said.

"And he left it to me," Nick confirmed. "He told me that it wasn't meant to be parked in a museum, that he wanted me to drive it and depend on it like an old friend. So that's what I've done." He smiled as the memory played a sweet melody in his eyes. In a heavy Italian accent and with elaborate hand gestures, he said, "He told me, 'You putta care anda love into everything you do, Nicky, and that'sa quality. It don't matter about money. You love what you do, you'll be a rich man. That'sa what this car stands for.'"

Brooke sat back and set her hand on the door, looking at the car from a new perspective, experiencing the love and respect that every inch of it represented. "What was your grandfather like?" she asked.

Nick's soft sigh was a whisper, and his eyes twinkled. "Grandpa was the only one in my family who saw my talent as a gift instead of a curse. He gave me my first box of paints when I was six years old. He was ... special.''

Brooke's heart swelled at the look of love in his face. She told herself that if he ever looked at her with such sweet, unconditional love, she would abandon all her ''rules'' and ''reasons'' and devote herself to him completely. She wouldn't have a choice. ''You miss him, don't you?'' she asked.

''Yeah,'' he whispered. ''I miss him. But I have this car to remind me of him and all my zany memories of him. He's not gone, really.'' He smiled and glanced sideways at her as the traffic began moving again. ''He would have liked you.''

''I would have liked him,'' Brooke said, suddenly feeling as though she already knew the man who'd had such a profound impact on his grandson's life.

She looked around as the car pulled into a parking lot of an art gallery.

''What are we doing here?'' she asked.

''We've got enough bids on the glass.'' Brooke looked relaxed and sensuous to Nick as he reached over and brushed a wisp of hair away from her wet lip. He cut off his engine, letting quiet surround them. ''My grandfather always used to say that I could be whatever I aspired to be, and that others would see me as I saw myself. Well, I think maybe it's time I showed you how I see myself, so that you'll stop seeing me as a teacher. You know, I haven't taught in ten years, and I *have* had to make a living since then.''

''I know you have,'' Brooke said, feeling defensive.

''Do you?'' he asked, grinning with genuine amusement. ''What exactly do you think I've been doing?''

"Well, you've...I guess you've been—" She caught her breath and felt the sting of embarrassment. "You're an artist, of course."

"Well, at least you do realize that," he said. "But you obviously don't know if I'm a good one, or what that means in terms of who I am. To you, I'm still good ol' Mr. Marcello."

Brooke laughed. "Nick, you were never 'good ol' Mr. Marcello.'"

"Whatever," he said, opening the door and getting out. He came around the car and opened her door. "I brought you here to show you who I really am."

Atingle with anticipation, Brooke got out of the car—carefully, lest he ban her from riding in it again—and followed him into the small gallery that had a shining reputation among art lovers in Florida. It was one she had once secretly hoped would feature her own work someday, before she had decided to specialize in stained glass.

The gallery was quiet, though alive with the feel of exquisite art. Pieces hung from the slate-gray walls and graced lighted pedestals, which had been placed carefully throughout the rooms. Two patrons spoke in quiet tones to the gallery owner, a tall, wiry woman in billowy silk pants and an oversized silk blouse. Nick offered her a wave when they were inside.

"Nick!" she called, shattering the stillness. "It's been weeks! Darling, come over here right now and meet some of your admirers. We were just talking about you."

Brooke glanced up at Nick and noted his unfettered smile as he ushered her toward the people. In the midst of the gallery, surrounded by bits of artists' souls and reflections of his own, Nick looked more alive and at home than she had ever seen him.

"My admirers?" he asked as he approached the couple. "Helena loves to exaggerate."

"No exaggeration this time," the man said, shaking Nick's hand. "We were just asking how to reach you for a specially commissioned project."

"Mr. and Mrs. Winston, this is Nick Marcello," Helena said.

Nick set his hand possessively on Brooke's back. "I'd like you to meet Brooke Martin," he said. "She's my partner on my most recent project. I'm afraid I'm pretty tied up with it for a while."

The couple, from the "money is no object" strata of society, didn't settle for his polite rejection. Instead they went on to ply him with promises and offers, until Brooke decided to explore the museum and allow them to talk privately.

Feeling emotionally stimulated by the caliber of art she saw, Brooke strayed by the walls of paintings and sculptures until she found a collection hanging like visual poetry on one side of the gallery. Without looking for the signature in the bottom corner, Brooke knew instinctively that the collection was Nick's. The dark colors reached out with a contemplation of life that was distinctly Latin in passion and fervor and conviction.

"He's wonderful, isn't he?" Helena said in a deep, smoky voice as she walked up behind her.

Brooke glanced at her over her shoulder. "Yes," she said, her voice laced with a reverence she hadn't intended. "I didn't know he had anything on exhibit."

"Nick?" Helena asked, surprised. "You've got to be kidding, darling. Without him, I might as well close this gallery down. He's been one of my staple artists for years now."

"Really?" Brooke turned back to the paintings, study-ing one that looked like a girl engulfed in shadows—a girl with pale hair and green eyes . . . strangely familiar, yet ab-stracted, an incomplete puzzle.

"That's the one that couple likes most," Helena whis-pered, stepping closer to Brooke. "His work has such a rich, romantic feel. Sort of a longing, bewildered quality, you know?" She grinned and cast a sidelong look at Brooke, her brow quirking up with her obvious appraisal. "So, tell me. Are you the lady in his life? He's so private it's hard to tell if there is one."

Brooke knew her cheeks were turning a flaming pink. "No, not at all," she said quietly. "I'm a stained-glass art-ist. We're working together, that's all."

Helena sighed with dramatic disappointment and crossed her arms, her long, manicured fingernails tapping on her sleeve as she leaned back thoughtfully against the wall. Her tone was quiet when she spoke. "I've heard through the grapevine that there was some sort of scandal in his life a few years back. Sort of explains the mystery in his paint-ings, and the deep, underlying sexual fantasy there. And even a little of the sadness."

Brooke stepped down the wall, carefully absorbing the mood of each of the paintings, seeing . . . *feeling* vividly the sadness Helena spoke of, but moreover, the sexual under-tones, the raging desire, the secrets couched on every can-vas. She wondered if his sadness . . . and his desire . . . had the same origins as her own.

"How well do you know Nick?" Helena asked her, breaking into her reverie.

Brooke tore her eyes from the paintings and faced the tall woman. The gallery owner's expression was neither con-demning nor competitive . . . only curious. "I knew him for a while a few years ago," she said evasively. "But we were commissioned to do the stained glass . . ."

Helena's grin revealed that she wasn't buying the story. "No, darling. I asked 'How *well* do you know him?' not how long."

Brooke tried to match the woman's smile, but the strain almost prevented her from doing it. *Not well enough,* she started to say. But the words that came out were much more practical . . . much more benign. "Not well at all."

"Damn," Helena said, stepping away from the wall to look at Nick's paintings again. "I was hoping there was a romance brewing here. Something smoldering he'd want to paint about. You have such style . . . I figured if Nick had a type, you'd probably be it."

Brooke dipped her face and suddenly wished she had something to do with her hands. Nervously she crossed her arms. "I . . . I don't know about that," she said.

"Don't get me wrong," Helena went on. "It isn't that I've never seen him with anyone. He's brought an occasional date to the parties I've thrown . . . just no one he seemed terribly captivated by. I guess he saves up all his fascination for later," she said with a conspiratorial grin.

Brooke's heart plummeted to her stomach, and she turned back to the paintings, stricken, wondering about the "occasional dates," and whether her fantasies were dragging her down the wrong track.

"You two aren't over here exchanging criticism about my work, are you?" Nick asked from behind them. Brooke turned and saw him leaning against the wall, regarding her with a poignantly fragile look on his face. She couldn't help smiling, knowing without a doubt that her eyes revealed the tenderness she felt in her own heart. "Of course not."

"We were discussing the romantic fantasies that inspire you, darling," Helena said, and Brooke's eyes darted back to the paintings as she struggled to look preoccupied. But she could feel Nick's eyes on her, gently appraising her.

"My romantic fantasies, huh?" he asked, his voice dropping to a soft, sensuous tone as he focused completely on Brooke.

Helena didn't miss the subtle look, and she wasn't willing to let it go. "Brooke tells me you two hardly know each other."

Brooke met Nick's eyes and felt his gaze penetrating too deeply, searching her with an artist's eyes that filled in all the colorless places she had kept hidden away. "I was her art teacher a few years ago," he admitted. "She was my best student."

Helena's eyebrows lifted in sudden understanding, and she turned back to Brooke, studying her with a new, more critical eye. "I see."

Brooke lifted her chin, trying not to look so self-conscious. Desperate for a crutch to help her through this, she changed the subject. "Nick, your work is wonderful. I had no idea...."

"Thanks," he said, his modesty coming as naturally as his smile, though she could sense his pride in his eyes. "A guy's got to make a living."

"Give me a break," Brooke said. "This isn't just making a living."

He sighed and regarded the paintings with a subjective twinkle in his eyes. "No, this is more than that. It's just ... what I do."

"It's making *me* a living," Helena threw in, her raspy laugh rattling the room. "And frankly, darling, I can't imagine what I'm going to do if you don't plan to produce anything until that dreadful museum is finished."

"There are other artists, Helena," he said.

"Not like you, darling. Not like you."

THEY HAD BEEN on the road for thirty minutes before Nick threw out the question that he'd been holding since they'd entered the art gallery. "So, are you able to see past the teacher in me now? Am I a little more human?"

Brooke inclined her head pensively to one side and watched him as he drove. "Maybe a little less," she admitted. "Those paintings were fabulous, Nick. I mean it." She let her gaze travel to the other cars whizzing by. "I just wish you hadn't told Helena you were my teacher. She had just mentioned that there was some kind of scandal in your past. I think she knew I was the one the minute you told her that."

"So what?" Nick asked. "It isn't like it's some secret. Everybody in Hayden knows. Besides, Helena loves that sort of thing."

"I know." Brooke tried to smile, but found it difficult. "She also told me about the other women in your life. She's done quite a bit of speculating about your love life."

"Hasn't everybody?" Nick asked. "Most people around here do more than speculate, though. If they don't know something about me, they usually just make it up."

Brooke watched the wind flutter through his hair and squelched the urge to ask about those other women she hadn't even considered until today. Instead, she asked the second most pressing question on her mind.

"How do you do it? Really, Nick," she said. "How have you been able to stand living in Hayden all these years, when you could have gone to Tampa and had respect and admiration, and where no one would have known or cared what happened between us when you were teaching?"

He laughed lightly, as though he'd asked himself the same question a thousand times. "You know what they say about an artist needing to suffer. Besides, I'm too stubborn to let them run me out of town. I grew up here. I've never been one for running away from my problems.''

Brooke recognized the indictment of her actions, and she combed her fingers through her bangs. "Like me?" she asked.

Nick kept his eyes on the road as he answered. "You did what you had to do," he said in a flat voice. "I can't fault you for that."

She turned to face him in her seat, trying to make him understand. "Nick, those people are vicious. Maybe I'm not as strong as you. But the hostility...it's everywhere, in everybody in town. Like I killed each of their firstborn children, and they're determined to get me back for it."

"Then you're seeing the wrong people," Nick said. "Because, believe me, everybody in Hayden isn't like Abby Hemphill. There are good people there."

"Good people who love a good juicy piece of gossip," she whispered. "Good people who don't care who they hurt."

"Good people are good people," Nick said. "I hope you'll stay around this time long enough to see that."

The rest of the ride to Hayden was quiet as Brooke contemplated the goodness in the townspeople's hearts. It was difficult to imagine it, when even her parents were unable to see her for who she was and believed everything they'd ever been told about her. And she couldn't help feeling disturbed at the certainty Nick harbored that she would leave town again at the first provocation. When would he begin to trust her? What would it take?

It was mid-afternoon when the Duesenberg pulled back into the parking lot of the Hayden museum. Though the construction crews' trucks still filled the parking lot, the Lincolns and Oldsmobiles driven by the women of the Historical Society were gone.

"Alone at last," Nick said as he cut off his engine.

"The workroom is all ours," Brooke said, a smile finding its place on her face again. "Now we can get some real work done."

But as they climbed out of the car, Abby Hemphill pulled in beside them, dampening their hopes.

"Abby." Nick's greeting was strained as she got out of her car. "The ladies have gone home. I think you're finished here."

"Not quite," Abby bit out. "I just came by to inform you and your...your *mistress*...that I intend to block your budget approval tonight at the town council meeting. In fact I'm going to do my best to have your commission for this job revoked. I have witnesses that you've been behaving inappropriately on the taxpayers' money...locking yourselves all day behind closed doors, disappearing for hours at a time...together. Checking into hotel rooms..."

"What!"

"Wait a minute!"

Brooke and Nick's outraged responses were simultaneous, but Mrs. Hemphill forged ahead full speed.

"The meetings are open to the public, so if you care to fight for your jobs, I can't deny you the right to be there."

"You're damn straight we'll be there," Nick shouted.

Brooke's heart rampaged in her chest, and something close to panic threatened to choke her. "Mrs. Hemphill, I hope you have proof to back up these lies," she cried. "Otherwise, you're setting yourself up for a whopping case of slander!"

"Oh, I have all the proof I need, young lady," Abby Hemphill said.

And then, leaving them both stunned, she got into her car, slammed the door and screeched out of the parking lot.

CHAPTER SIX

THE EVIDENCE THAT Mrs. Hemphill presented at the meeting was flimsy at best, but in the minds of those present it seemed highly indicting.

Things began badly when Mrs. Inglish spoke to the council "on behalf of the Women's Historical Society," and explained how Nick and Brooke had exhibited a lack of respect for the museum when they referred to the exhibits as "dusty old artifacts." She went on to relate how they had abandoned their workroom and locked themselves in Nick's tiny office "for hours on end," adding that she wouldn't venture to guess what they were doing in there since she was "too much of a lady to imagine such things." And referring to her notes as though it had been her task to log their goings and comings, Mrs. Inglish outlined the number of times they had left the museum and disappeared "without a trace."

Brooke sat in her seat, her mouth clamped shut in anger as the accusations were fired at her. Nick bit his lip and continuously shook his head, but he remained silent, as well. But when Mrs. Hemphill pulled out her heavy artillery, Brooke felt as if the bottom of the world had dropped out.

"Mr. Chairman," Abby Hemphill said in a tone as authoritative as a courtroom attorney's. "I would like to submit a copy of a hotel bill that shows that Brooke Martin checked into the Bluejay Inn last night, then checked out two hours later.''

The council members buzzed with disapproval, and Brooke's mouth fell open in mute fury. Her spine shot ramrod straight, and her breath seemed to come in labored, heaving gasps. She sensed Nick looking at her, and she feared he would try to touch her to calm her, an act that would make her snap completely. He didn't.

Before Brooke's rage erupted, Horace Anderson, the chairman of the renovation committee on the town council—and ironically the museum curator—a sixty-year-old man who appeared as worn out as the twenty-year-old shoes he wore, looked at his watch and rubbed his face impatiently. "Abby, I'm sure this is going somewhere, but I can't imagine what all this has to do with Miss Martin and Mr. Marcello designing stained-glass windows."

"*Exactly,*" Abby Hemphill said. "It has nothing to do with stained-glass windows. But it has everything to do with wasting the taxpayers' money."

"Did the taxpayers pay the bill for that hotel room?" Horace asked, feigning confusion.

A contagious chuckle dominoed across the room. "No, of course not," Abby cried. "But if you'll—"

"Then I don't see how it pertains to this matter at all," Horace said. "And before we go on creating any more rumors, I think we should give our victims a chance to defend themselves. Miss Martin, Mr. Marcello, would either of you like to address these charges?"

"Hell, yes." Nick came to his feet before Brooke could. He braced his hands on the chair in front of him, leaning in Mrs. Hemphill's direction. She lifted her nose and crossed her arms, regarding him with try-to-weasel-out-of-this smugness. His voice was as spuriously gentle as the wind in the eye of a hurricane. "You've succeeded in smearing Brooke Martin's reputation and running her out of town once before, Abby. I'd like to think we're all a little older and a little wiser now, but I see some things never really change." He sighed and stood up straight, folded his arms and shook his head. "I hate to destroy the fantasies these kinky minds have devised, Horace, but Brooke and I were closed up in my office because the workroom that we would have preferred to work in was full of ladies of the Historical Society, who eavesdropped and interrupted us at every turn. Neither of us can work with someone looking critically over our shoulders. We're artists. Now, if you'd like evidence of the hours of work we've put in so far, you're welcome to come by the museum tomorrow and waste some more of our time."

Nick left the chair and began pacing around the room, looking each of his accusers in the eye, defying them to look away. "As for our leaving today, we went to Tampa to check out our suppliers and to get some bids on the museum. Those are some of the things that go along with designing stained-glass windows of this magnitude. However, I don't plan to account to you people every time I get in my car or close my door."

"My point," Abby interrupted, "is that these two people have a scandalous history that I don't think anyone here needs to be reminded of. My fear is that they're using this project as a means of finishing what they started. He hasn't addressed the issue of the Bluejay Inn, yet, has he?"

"I can't address it, Abby!" Nick shouted. "I wasn't there! And as far as Brooke is concerned, I think she'll agree that it is none of your malicious, back-biting business!"

"No, wait a minute!" Brooke stood up, drawing all eyes to her. She felt like an eighteen-year-old girl again, even though she'd pulled her hair back in a chignon and worn a pair of black slacks with a white blouse. Her appearance was far from the blousy, unusual style she usually embraced. She'd left her jewelry at home, except for a pair of white studs in her earlobes. The effect was severe, she hoped. Not at all vulnerable. Not at all seductive. Her voice waivered with restrained wrath when she spoke. "I would like to address the hotel issue, if it's all right."

Abby set her chin in her palm. "Go right ahead, dear," she said. "I can't wait."

Brooke offered the woman a sad, pitying smile. "I'm sure you can't. But I'm afraid I'm going to disappoint you, Mrs. Hemphill. The truth is that I had a disagreement with my family and decided that it would be best if I didn't stay at their house last night. I checked in, stayed awhile, and when they came and asked me to come home, I did. It's that simple."

"Then your parents were the only ones who visited you in the hotel room?" Abby asked skeptically.

"Absolutely," Brooke said. She turned to the other council members, her brows oppressively drawn together. "Why is it that I feel like I'm on trial here? Why am I having to defend everything I've done since I came into this town? Hayden is my home, too, and I'm tired of being made to feel I don't belong here. I came into this project against my better judgment, because I wanted a chance to work on something that could bring national attention to my career and to Nick's and to the museum in general. As for the money, I'm not even charging half what I ordinarily charge for a stained-glass commission, and I'm sure that there are much more lucrative things that Nick could be doing, as well." She turned to Horace, who listened with a deep, ponderous frown. "You asked *me* to come here, Horace. I didn't ask for the job. If we're wasting our time on this, tell us now. I'll just get right back to Tallahassee and pick up with my life.''

''Now, wait a minute,'' Horace blurted, halting her with an outstretched hand. ''That isn't what we want. I suppose a few of our members still need to be convinced, before we allocate the entire amount of your budget. I, personally, want you to do what you were hired to do, and I don't give a dog's damn where you sleep at night or what you do behind closed doors.'' He rubbed his weary eyes and looked around at his colleagues. ''Look, if they provided sketches of the windows and made some kind of presentation to show us what they're planning, would that put your minds at ease?''

Some of the audience agreed that it would, so Horace turned back to Nick and Brooke, who now stood side by side, allies against the world. ''All right then. This time next week, bring us those sketches, and I'm sure we won't have any trouble voting to approve your budget.''

Nick and Brooke looked at each other, astounded, then turned back to the council. ''All of our sketches?'' Nick asked. ''We're talking about eighty panels. We can't sketch all of those in enough detail to convince you people in one week!''

''We start with crude drawings,'' Brooke tried to explain. ''They look like puzzles. Unless you're used to looking at such things, you won't—''

''Do the best you can,'' Horace said, holding his hands palm up in apology. ''We'll have to go by whatever you can show us.''

Nick sighed and gazed at Brooke with troubled eyes, silently asking her if she was ready for the round-the-clock work it would take to prepare such a presentation. The look of unwavering determination on her face told him she was.

''All right,'' he said. ''We'll do the best we can.''

THE HALLWAY WAS DARK when Nick and Brooke exited the conference room, leaving the council to conduct other business. Light spilled out from a room being cleaned a few doors down, filtering just enough light for Nick to see Brooke. It reminded him of the evening ten years ago, when they'd negotiated the dark hallway of the high school on graduation night. Only, that night they weren't condemned until afterward.

Brooke leaned back against the wall and closed her eyes. She'd held together much better than he'd expected, but now Nick could see that she was very close to crying. He stepped toward her, reaching out to touch her arm, but Brooke recoiled. He dropped his hand helplessly and stood mutely watching her.

She looked up at him, and he saw the slivers of light playing on the incipient tears in her eyes. "They think we went to a hotel together," she said. "As long as we live, Nick, whatever we do, whatever choices we make, right or wrong, they'll see us that way."

He struggled to find the words to make the night's events seem less monumental, but he came up empty. "I know it's hard for you, Brooke. But not everyone believes it. Horace didn't."

"Yes, he did. He just didn't care." Her tears began to flow and she covered her mouth with her hand turning away from Nick, facing the wall. "It isn't fair."

"No, it isn't." Nick touched the back of her shoulder, and this time she didn't shrug him away. "We can't let it cripple us," he whispered. "That's what Abby Hemphill wants."

"Why?" Brooke turned back around, wiped at the tears in her eyes. "What have we *ever* done to that woman?" She swallowed her emotion, discarded the question as rhetorical, and tried to speak again. "Nick, we can't do all this in one week. It's physically impossible. Eighty panels?"

"We'll do what we can," he said. "I'm not willing to give up easily. We'll start working tonight. At my place."

"No!" she said again. "How many times do I have to tell you? We can't be caught alone at your house or anywhere except the museum. And then we'll *still* be gossiped about."

He threw up his hands in frustrated surrender. "Sorry. I just thought since I had coffee there, and food . . . We're going to be at this around the clock, you know. There's no avoiding it."

"Still," she said, putting him off with a trembling hand. "I just . . . I can't. Maybe tonight we should just work independently. I'll work at my parents', and you work at home."

Nick's discontent with the proposed arrangement was apparent but he didn't argue further. He took Brooke's hand in his, a gesture so natural that it didn't frighten her away, and they began walking down the corridor, past the lighted room where the janitor was cleaning. Holding his hand, Brooke could sense the weariness in Nick's muscles, the heaviness in his stride. Idly she recalled the ragged condition he'd been in that morning, as if he hadn't slept in days. She doubted tonight would provide him with much relaxation, either.

They rounded the corner where Mrs. Hemphill's office was and came to the door marked Records, where Roxy worked every afternoon. The lights were all off, creating an eerie, lonely atmosphere. The sound of their shoes against the floor was soft and rhythmic, but another sound, the sound of muffled voices inside the Records office, caught her attention.

Brooke's feet slowed. "Wait a minute," she whispered.

Nick stopped and looked down at her, still holding her hand. "What?"

"I heard voices in my sister's office."

Nick wasn't concerned. "It was probably the cleaning woman."

Brooke listened for another moment, staring into the darkness, concentrating. The hall had fallen quiet. "I guess it was," she said, and started to walk.

Before they reached the glass doors that opened into the parking lot, Brooke could see the light from the street lamps surrounding it. Only a few cars were still there, most belonging to the council members. But one, set apart from the cluster of others, caught her eye.

Roxy's car.

"That's my sister's car." Brooke turned back toward Roxy's office, trying to decide whether to barge in. "What if she's in trouble in there? She wouldn't be in some dark office this late at night if something weren't wrong." She dropped Nick's hand and started back up the hall. "I'm going to check on her."

Nick followed her back to the Records room, and again they heard two distinct but muffled voices: a man's and a woman's.

Brooke knocked on the closed door, though there was no light shining beneath it. "Roxy?" she called loudly.

The voices instantly stilled, but no one answered. "Roxy? It's Brooke," she said again. When there was still no answer, Brooke shoved open the door and snapped on the light.

The couple moved apart: Roxy and a young man with silky blond hair who looked vaguely familiar to Brooke. She noted that Roxy's hair was tousled and her neck and face were chafed from skin to stubble contact. Her sister's expression was one of panic, and she stumbled back, frantically trying to button her blouse.

"Roxy?" Brooke asked, torn between embarrassment that she had intruded and concern that her sister was too young to be headed in the direction she was obviously taking. As if the confrontation was too much for her to deal with, Roxy snatched up her purse and started for the door.

"Roxy!" Brooke said again.

Roxy reached the door where Brooke was standing and lashed at her with the biting emotion in her bronze eyes. "Leave me alone, Brooke," she said. "Just leave me the hell alone."

Before Brooke could speak, Roxy was halfway down the hall, with the man fast on her heels.

Brooke stood numbly in the doorway, reeling from the hatred she had seen in her sister's eyes. Nick's face mirrored her pain. "What was that all about?" he asked. "From all I could tell, they were just kissing. It isn't like we caught them at something catastrophic."

Brooke's tears tumbled down her face faster than she could wipe them away. "She hates me," she said. "That's what it's all about. I've lost her for good, and for the life of me, I don't know how to change that."

Nick pulled her against him, his warm body cocooning her in security and caring. It was foreign to Brooke, but something she sorely needed. Tonight she wasn't strong enough to deny it. "You can talk to her tomorrow, babe," he whispered. "But not tonight, when she's in this mood. Tonight, we're going to my house. No arguments, okay?"

The emotional warfare of the day had drained all the energy from Brooke's spirit, making her too weak to fight. She released a deep sob-ridden breath, and nodded. "No arguments," she said. "What have I got to lose, after all?"

THE RIDE TO NICK'S house was too quiet, and Nick had the uneasy feeling that Brooke was slipping away from him again. How could he blame her if she *did* want to disappear? First him, then the gossip, then her family, then the threat of losing the job, then more gossip?

He gave her a sidelong glance as he drove the Duesenberg through town and saw the melancholy expression in her eyes as she gazed out the window, the lights of the streets illuminating her face now and again. "What are you thinking?" he asked softly.

She shook her head dolefully. "Nothing, really. Just that I've never seen where you live. Until this morning, I'd never even been in your car." She looked over at him, and he would have given anything he owned to erase the sadness from her eyes. "Back in high school, the rumor was that *no one* rode in this car but you."

Nick grinned. "That was no rumor. I choose my passengers very carefully."

"I suppose I should feel honored."

"Don't you?"

She shrugged. "I'm not in high school anymore...." She looked longingly, thoughtfully, out the window, then brought her glistening eyes back to his shadowed face again. "Back then, riding in Mr. Marcello's Duesenberg would have been about equivalent to flying on the space shuttle. Now it only seems like one more complication."

Nick's heart fell, and his gentle smile faded from his face as he locked his eyes on the road. He was irritated, not at her, but at the Fates who had played such cruel games with their lives. Her conscience, molded by the disapproval of a ruthless town, would not allow her to act naturally. "I'm not going to complicate things any more for you, Brooke," he said, trying to make the promise as devoid of emotion as he could. "It's very simple. We're two artists working together for a few months. That's all."

"I know that, and you know that," she whispered.

Lack of sleep and an abundance of emotional blows combined to color his tone. "To hell with what anybody else knows, Brooke. When are you going to stop letting them get to you?"

"When are you going to *start?*" she returned. "It all seems to roll off your back."

"Would you rather I let it *break* my back? Jut lie down and let Abby Hemphill and anybody else tap dance across it? I had to scrape and claw for every ounce of self-respect I have, and I'm not giving it up for a bunch of shallow old biddies that no one ever listens to, anyway."

Brooke's eyes sharpened as she glared at him in the darkness. "How can you be so smug?"

Nick laughed mirthlessly. "Smug? You think it's smug not to cower in a corner just because some idiots out there in glass houses have nothing better to do with their time than to throw stones at me?"

"Are you saying that's what I've been doing? Cowering?"

Headlights from a passing car illuminated his face, then quickly disappeared. "I'm saying that there are a lot of excuses in life to keep from doing the hard things. I don't need excuses, Brooke. Maybe you do."

Nick pulled into his driveway, but Brooke didn't seem to notice. Instead she glowered at him in the darkness, silently denying his accusations. He let the car idle for a moment but when she didn't say anything, he got out to open the garage.

Brooke stewed as she watched him walk to the garage door and pull it open with a jerk. His words still stung, but deep in the back of her mind, she realized that she couldn't find a comeback because she feared he might be right. Maybe she did need excuses. Maybe she was afraid.

She exhaled deeply as he got back in the car and pulled into the shelter of the garage. When he had killed the engine, they sat quietly for a moment, neither of them making an attempt to get out.

"Look, maybe I was out of line," he said, the lack of enthusiasm in his tone making the apology seem less sincere.

"It's okay," she whispered, not sure she meant her words, either. "It's time I stopped hiding behind Mrs. Hemphill and all the others. It's time I really did grow up."

He looked at her in the thick darkness and offered a weak smile. "You look pretty grown up to me."

In the darkness Nick wondered if he'd made her skin turn that sunset shade of pink that had delighted him so when she was younger. Brooke cast her eyes down, unable to respond. The silence bound them like a warm blanket on a winter day, a blanket they had to share. The feeling was awkward, and finally, Nick opened his car door. "We'd better go in," he said.

They stepped into the kitchen from the garage, the residual emotions from their exchange still clinging to them like dampness after a storm. Brooke glanced around at the cluttered room that looked like a stop-off place for quick on-the-run meals. It was clean, though here and there lay a wadded napkin, an empty milk carton, a watered-down drink.

The faint, familiar smell of oil paints drew her deeper into the kitchen as Nick closed the door quietly and laid his things on the kitchen table. She peered through a door on the other side of the kitchen, where the strongest of the scents seemed to originate. "Is that your studio?" she asked.

"That's it," he said. "Go on in, if you want."

She turned on the light and tentatively stepped inside. The room was larger than the kitchen, and much more cluttered. Paintings in progress lined the oak floor of the room, but one back wall was made entirely of glass, overlooking a small canal lit with lanterns on either side. An easel dominated the middle of the floor with a stool and a small table next to it, where dozens of colors of paints waited in tubes to be used. Paintbrushes soaked nearby in mineral spirits.

"I think this is exactly what I pictured," Brooke said with a self-conscious smile. "The room even smells creative."

She turned back to the kitchen and saw Nick making coffee. His expression was still sober, but he seemed to try as hard as she to cast off the melancholy.

"Canvas seems to be your favorite medium," she said. "Why did you get interested in stained glass?"

He shrugged and plugged the coffeepot in. "I had ideas for some things that I thought would turn out better in glass, and I like the freedom to be versatile." He got two coffee mugs out of the cupboard, and set them on the counter. "What makes you specialize in glass? I would have thought you were leaning toward sculpture."

Brooke leaned against the doorway, suddenly feeling at home surrounded by an artist's tools, an artist's work, and an artist's understanding. It had been a long time since she had experienced such a sense of comfort in anyone else's home. "It's just such a beautiful art," she said. "The only one that sunlight plays a direct part in. I worked with it a lot in college, and I guess I got hooked. I was never that good at sculpture, really, anyway."

Nick stopped what he was doing and turned back to her, his eyes dark with disbelief. "Not good? You're kidding, right?"

"Well, maybe good enough to win a scholarship, but I don't think I could have ever produced anything good enough to sell."

Nick closed the cupboard door and turned to face her squarely. An astounded smile sparkled in his eyes, removing all traces of his earlier ire. "Brooke, has your memory really faded that much?"

Innocence softened her features, making him realize that she had, indeed, forgotten the power of her talent. "What do you mean?"

Nick abandoned the coffeepot, took her hand and closed it tightly in his. "Come here," he said.

Brooke let him lead her into his living room, a breathtaking showcase for some of the finest works of art she'd ever seen. The white carpet added contrast to the colors of the pieces hanging on the walls, and even the furniture served to accent the sculptures surrounding it.

Brooke's wondering eyes swept over each piece in turn, absorbing the richness of the beauty accumulated there. But Nick dropped her hand and touched her shoulders and gently turned her around, where a taller pedestal provided the centerpiece for the room.

It was *Infinity*, the sculpture of their two hands, embraced in gentle passion, their touch so poignant that even now she could feel the emotions that had driven her as she'd worked on it. She inclined her head in a moment of awe. "You kept it," she whispered.

"Of course I kept it," he said, his voice a warm vibration against her hair. "What did you think I did with it?"

Brooke laughed softly and brought her hands to her face. "I don't know. I guess I thought it was lying in your attic or something. Or that you'd thrown it away."

He led her to the sculpture, picked it up and set it in her hands. Immediately she felt the poignant familiarity of every line, the cool warmth of every vein chiseled there. She slid her hand over his clay one, then smoothed her other one across the smaller hand it embraced. Her heart ached with the sudden heartrending memory, the sudden shattering loss.

"Does that look like something that could be thrown away?" he asked quietly. "Brooke, you have no idea how powerful this piece is."

She had some idea as her heart hammered against her chest, but she wasn't sure it was exactly the kind of power Nick referred to. *Infinity* held the key to her past, the lock on her future. It was both the beginning and the end. But it was her beginning, her ending, and as bittersweet as it was, she cherished it in a way that—she was certain—no one else ever could. "I don't know what you mean," she whispered.

"I've had offers for it," he said. "People see it, and they want it. It strikes so much emotion within them. That's what art does, Brooke. That's why I've always known you were a born artist."

She frowned down at the hands, trying to see the work more objectively. "You had offers?" she repeated. "What kind of offers?"

"Helena at the gallery saw it a few months ago and offered me $25,000 for it," he said, watching her face carefully for her reaction.

There was none. It was almost as if she didn't hear.

"Did you hear me?" he asked.

"I heard you." She locked her eyes on the sculpture again, then quickly set it back on the pedestal and backed away, staring at it as if she weren't familiar with it, had *never* had intimate knowledge of it. Assigning it that kind of price tag cast it into the realm of something live and mysterious. It suddenly seemed like nothing an eighteen-year-old girl could have created.

"Why... why didn't you sell it?" she asked, still staring at the sculpture.

"Because it wasn't mine," he said.

She tore her eyes from the hands and looked up at him, stricken. "Yes, it was. I gave it to you."

"You gave it to me before everything fell apart," he said. "I always planned to give it back when I saw you."

He lifted the sculpture carefully and handed it to her. Tentatively she embraced it, not taking it from him, but holding it just as he did. "I want you to take it back," he whispered. "When you gave it to me, it was a poignant gesture to show me how you felt. But a lot's happened since then." He swallowed and looked down at the sculpture, unable to meet her eyes as he finished. "Neither of us feels that way anymore."

"But I don't want it," she said. "Really, I couldn't have—"

"Take it, Brooke," he whispered. "And when you start doubting your talent, you can remember just how powerful an artist you really are."

Brooke accepted the sculpture, but something in her heart sank when she did. It meant that the last spiritual connection between them was severed. The last physical evidence of the relationship that she had convinced herself was imagined, was being returned to her. There were no more feelings. No more desires.

At least, not on his part.

She was quiet as they worked for the rest of the evening, disheartened, though she knew that what he had done was exactly what she had intellectually wanted. She didn't want any more remnants of those feelings. It was best that they laid them to rest . . . early, while they still had choices.

But her heart remained miserably unconvinced, and more than once she was reminded of their phone call last night, and his haggard but relieved condition this morning. Besides, he'd kept the sculpture all these years, as if she'd entrusted her heart to him and knew he wouldn't let harm come to it.

But those were all translucent facts lacking in substance. For he'd admitted the truth himself. *"Neither of us feels that way anymore."* And as the night wore on, she tried with all her heart to hold on to that cold truth, and convince herself that she believed it.

IT WAS MIDNIGHT when Brooke slipped into her house and saw that Roxy was still up, sitting in the living room staring at some Korean Kung Fu movie on television.

"Hi," Brooke said.

Roxy didn't look away from the screen. "Hi."

Brooke wilted and dropped her case down on the couch, but she kept the wrapped sculpture in her hands. She was bone tired, and her spirit was full of holes, shot from every direction that day. She wanted nothing more than to collapse in bed and sleep unhindered, but Brooke knew that this talk with Roxy about the scene she'd interrupted earlier couldn't wait. At some point she had to start laying some kind of foundation for a new relationship.

"Look, about tonight—" Brooke started, but Roxy immediately cut in.

"I don't want to talk about it."

Brooke sat down next to her, looked at the screen and realized that her sister couldn't possibly have been interested in the badly dubbed film. Roxy had stayed up, Brooke surmised, exactly because she *did* want to talk about it.

"I want you to know that I only walked in on you because I heard your voice and the light was out, and I was afraid you were in trouble. I'm sorry, okay?"

Roxy didn't respond.

"Besides," Brooke went on. "You were just kissing. It's not a federal offense to kiss your boyfriend."

Roxy kept her blank stare on the television, her eyes so devoid of feeling that Brooke began to wonder if her sister was, indeed, preoccupied by the movie.

"Who was he, anyway?" Brooke asked.

Roxy pulled her feet up to the couch and wrapped her arms around her knees. "No one you know."

"I might surprise you," Brooke said. "The town's pretty small. I got to know a lot of the kids your age going to school functions when you were little. What's his name?"

"He's not my age," Roxy said belligerently. "He's older." The tension on Roxy's face grew more pronounced, and her lips quivered. "It doesn't matter anyway."

"Are you trying to hide him or something?" Brooke asked, hoping to make light of the situation in order to reach Roxy.

Roxy picked up the remote control and flipped the station, not bothering to answer.

"All right," Brooke said, crestfallen that her strategy hadn't worked. "It's none of my business. I can respect that."

She sat motionless for a moment, struggling for some common subject she could broach, something that wouldn't sound as if she was being nosy or judgmental. Her hands closed more tightly around the sculpture in her lap. Slowly she began unwrapping it.

"Do you remember this, Roxy?" she asked.

Roxy looked down at the sculpture and a grudging spark of interest ignited in her eyes. "That's the piece you did in high school. The one that won you the art scholarship."

Brooke nodded, turning the hands over, tracing the smooth lines with her fingertips. It fascinated her, for holding *Infinity* was like holding a part of herself she hadn't glimpsed in a decade. "Nick kept it all these years."

Roxy's gaze climbed to Brooke's face, amazement and wonder coloring out the jaded grays that had reigned there before. "You worked so hard on it. I always thought you had it, or that you'd sold it or . . . something."

Brooke moved her head from side to side. "I gave it to him. I couldn't have finished it without his help." She looked up and met Roxy's eyes. "Nick was a good teacher, Roxy."

The shutters over her sister's eyes drew shut again, and Roxy looked back at the television. "Why did he give it back?" she asked, her tone deliberately uninterested.

Brooke's eyes glazed over as she looked at the sculpture, but saw his real-life hand, protectively embracing hers tonight. "He said he always intended to. Just never had the chance until tonight." She laughed softly for a moment as the conversation played back over in her mind, sensual softness mingled with a sweet sadness. "He told me that a gallery owner in Tampa once offered him $25,000 for it. Can you believe that? And he turned it down."

Roxy's eyes left the screen and focused nakedly on her sister, her antagonism blatant. "Sentimental value," she muttered. "I guess passion does crazy things to a person."

Brooke's openness vanished. "It had nothing to do with passion," she said tightly. "He just felt that it was mine, and that he didn't have the right to sell it."

"So are *you* going to sell it?" Roxy asked.

Brooke looked at the sculpture and realized just how much it meant to her, now that she held it again. So much of her had gone into it. All her days, all her nights. All her thoughts, all her dreams...

Maybe it did have something to do with passion, after all. "No, I couldn't ever sell it. It means too much..." Quickly she looked up at Roxy, as if she'd caught herself in her own trap. "Nothing happened between us, Roxy, but I did care for him. It's over now. Our relationship is strictly business."

Roxy didn't seem content to let things go at that. Brooke saw the subtle challenge in her eyes. "If he doesn't mean anything to you, it seems like you could let it go. Especially since you haven't had it all this time, anyway."

"No," Brooke said, suddenly feeling as if the walls of free choice were closing in on her. She stood up and turned her back to her sister. "He could have sold it, but he didn't. I can't do it, either."

"Twenty-five thousand is a lot of money," Roxy said.

"They could offer me a hundred twenty-five and I wouldn't change my mind," she said. Then, looking down at the sculpture carefully cradled in her hands, she started out of the room. "Good night, Roxy. I'm going to bed."

IT WAS LATER that night, as Roxy lay awake in her bed, that she thought again of Brooke's attachment to the sculpture. *Twenty-five thousand dollars*. Just the thought of that amount of money made her palpitate. Twenty-five thousand dollars could take her so far away from this oppressive little town...

She turned over on her side, and thought of the sentiment Nick Marcello had shown in keeping the sculpture instead of selling it. She had to admit, it was a little out of character for the sex-hungry cradle-robber she'd always imagined him to be. But then the same old question that she supposed plagued everyone in Hayden cropped up again. What would a handsome, gifted art teacher see in an eighteen-year-old girl?

Brooke was different. The intuitive knowledge, the awe-struck memory, invaded her thoughts, making her admit that her sister had never been ordinary. There had always been something extradimensional about her. So much style. So much substance. So much emotion. Roxy remembered that no one in her life had ever made her feel quite as special as her big sister had when she was little.

Maybe she was still angry at Brooke for driving away that day and leaving her on the doorstep, she admitted in the solitude of darkness. Maybe that was the big sin she couldn't forgive her for. That and all the others that followed.

Time to grow up, Roxy told herself, staring at the ceiling. *Life won't let you stay innocent forever.* She knew that more than most people her age. She'd been fighting the inevitable for years. But the fight was coming to an end. If Brooke hadn't barged into her office tonight, her innocence would have been surrendered like the adoration she'd once had for her sister.

An angry tear rolled down her temple and over her ear, and she closed her hand over her mouth to muffle her sob.

When did choices get less consequential? When was it supposed to get easier to make it through each day? And when could she stop caring about the hopeless, heartless whispers behind her back, the people waiting for her to mess up so that she could wear Brooke's scarlet letter for a change?

It was inescapable, really, she thought, burying her face in her pillow. It was just a matter of time. Until the bomb dropped, she would go on making choices based on the fickle, fathomless whims of other people's traitorous hearts, and stave off the chaos within until she could run away like Brooke had.

But unlike Brooke, Roxy knew she would never look back.

CHAPTER SEVEN

PASSION DOES crazy things to a person.

Roxy's words played over and over in Brooke's mind constantly for the next few days, making her wonder if that passion—for her work, for her goals, and yes, even for Nick—was apparent in every scene she drew for the windows. She found herself completely absorbed in the life-altering events she depicted. Without even being aware of what the scenes represented, she drew a girl and boy reaching out, shyly, awkwardly, to touch each other's hands.

In response to that panel, Nick captured the nervous, gentle, and yet smoldering feelings of a first kiss.

Not knowing she followed that with her heart rather than her hands, Brooke drew a couple in wedding garb, kneeling before the priest who bound them for eternity, with the tiny mosaic of a church's stained-glass window behind him.

And then Nick drew a startlingly emotional black silhouette of that same man and woman, facing each other in gentle apprehension, before the backdrop of a sun-brightened curtain.

"That's...so beautiful."

Nick looked up from his sketch and saw tears forming in Brooke's eyes as she leaned across the table, watching his hand move across the page. Her eyes were shining with a prismatic luster that he could never have captured on paper. "You think so?" he asked.

She inhaled deeply and tried to steady her voice. "It's so emotional. It just tugs at something so deep..."

He watched her poignant struggle for words for a moment, then looked back at the silhouette on the paper, trying to view it from her perspective. Would anyone know, he wondered, that the faces cloaked in shadow were distinct and vivid in his mind? Did *she* know?

"Do you think it goes too far?" he asked quietly.

Brooke wet her lips, running a finger along the edge of the page. "I don't know," she whispered, as though the question was too important to address in a normal tone. "Maybe. I mean, the wedding night is definitely an important stage of life, but it's so personal..."

She knew, he thought, that the fantasy he had drawn was his own. She knew, and didn't want others to know, as well.

A sly grin nudged at his mouth. "Well, you started it, you know."

Brooke's answering smile was self-indicting. "What did I do?"

Nick flipped back through the drawings and pulled out the first of the falling-in-love sketches. "This one," he said, referring to the one of the young man and woman touching hands. "If that isn't personal, I don't know what is..."

"They're just touching hands," she protested.

"Just touching hands," Nick repeated, looking down at their own hands, lying so close to each other on the worktable. "But that one little gesture can open such a Pandora's box of emotions."

He could see from her downcast gaze that Brooke remembered, as well, a teacher and a young girl alone in a classroom, hands embraced, fingertips stroking, hearts pounding...

Brooke swallowed and pulled her feet into her seat, hugging her knees tightly. "Mrs. Hemphill will have a field day with this. Maybe we should throw out this whole series."

Nick knew that wasn't what she wanted to do. He leaned forward, his eyes soft and yet penetrating. "But we plan to spend at least seven panels on infancy, Brooke. And we must have outlined fifteen panels just on childhood. Why can't we spend equal time on something that affects everybody at one time or another?"

"Falling in love," she whispered with a note of surrender, looking back at the panels. "We can't really have the whole span of life without that, can we?"

"No," he said.

She was quiet for a moment as not-so-quiet thoughts passed over her face like movie credits on a screen. Finally she brought her clover-green eyes back to his. "All right," she said. "I know you're right."

Nick set his chin on two knuckles, gazing at the series in mute concentration. "But there's something missing," he said after a moment. "Something important that we left out."

Brooke looked down at the sketches, mentally checking for an oversight. "What?" she asked. "We have the first moment of awareness, the first kiss, the wedding, the wedding night . . ."

"The broken heart," Nick said. "We can't leave that out."

"The broken heart," she repeated in a whisper. Her eyes glossing over. "How could I forget?"

Nick sat back and found a blank sheet of paper, then began moving his hand across the page. She watched as he, once again, drew a silhouette. This time it could have been a man or a woman, surrounded by shadows with the backdrop of what would be color. The only break in the black of the silhouette was one white tear shimmering on the cheek. "How's that?" he whispered.

"Perfect," she answered. "Where should we put it? Before the kiss?"

"After the wedding," Nick mumbled as he continued to work on the sketch. "This is the broken heart of a third party. The one she didn't marry."

Brooke's gaze collided with his, and suddenly he knew he'd gone a step too far.

"That's funny," she said quietly. "I thought the heartbreak was hers."

Their eyes locked for a jagged shard of eternity, awareness burning like a chemical fire between them. Finally Nick looked back at the sketch. "Let's make this just between the two of them," he said, his voice a gentle rumble. "And put it between the kiss and the wedding. These two deserve a happy ending, don't you think?"

Brooke's smile was tentative. "What the heck," she whispered. "It doesn't have to be *that* close to real life."

"Neither of us feels that way anymore." He had uttered the words himself last night, but now the dismal thought left him as cold as the chill in the depth of her eyes. She cast her eyes downward and fingered the gold earring dangling against her jaw. He wondered how that earlobe would feel between his lips, how her hair would smell against his face.... He brought his pencil up to his lips, and chewed on the end.

Brooke's cheeks blushed with a subtle smear of pink, and Nick knew that she felt him watching her. Would it ease the ache in his soul, he wondered, if he reached out and swept her hair behind her ear? Or would it simply redefine the dull agony he'd grown accustomed to?

"Hey, Picasso." They both jumped at the alien voice intruding on the sizzling mood in the room, and turned to the door to see Sonny leaning against the casing, wearing tight jeans and a black leather jacket, with a helmet tucked under one elbow. His eyes swept around the room, as round as those of a toddler at Disney World.

"Sonny!" Nick's voice was a degree less than enthusiastic at the sight of his nephew, but he forced a smile. "Come on in." Nick turned to Brooke, touching her arm almost possessively. "Brooke Martin, I'd like you to meet my nephew, Sonny Castori."

Sonny stepped forward, regarding her with a sly grin, and extended a hand to Brooke. "If you don't mind my saying so," he said bluntly, "now I can see what all the fuss was about."

Knowing intuitively that he referred to the scandal, though he meant the remark as some kind of compliment, Brooke tried not to bristle. "It's nice to meet you, Sonny," she said.

"What brings you by here?" Nick asked. "I thought you were in school about this time."

Sonny glanced at his watch. "At five-thirty? Give me a break."

"Five-thirty?" Brooke pulled her watch out of her drawer and gaped at the time. "Nick, did we stop for lunch?"

Nick started to laugh. "No, I don't think so."

"Damn," Sonny said. "You mean you two have been in here working all day and didn't even know how much time had passed?"

Brooke flung a sweeping hand toward the drawings and flopped back in her chair. "We've gotten a lot done. But we still have a long way to go."

Sonny stepped over to the drawings, his expression one of awe-struck admiration. Carefully, he began to flip through the work. A long, slow whistle eased out on his breath. "Man, these are great. I mean ... these are *really* great."

Brooke's weary eyes brightened. "You think so?"

"Man." He turned back to Nick, not completely abandoning the drawings. "Listen, I just came by to see if I could take you up on your offer to use your studio tonight. But if I could help here ... man, I'd love to be a part of this. I could trace the drawings for you, or color them in, or whatever you need."

Nick looked at Brooke. "What do you think?"

"I think he'd be a godsend. I didn't think we'd have time to do color presentations, but with help we could."

Sonny took off his leather jacket, tossed it onto a chair and rubbed his hands together anxiously. "Just mark each piece in the color you want and I'll take it from there," he said.

Brooke's amused expression told Nick that she liked his nephew, which, he was sure, made the feeling mutual. Why that was important to him, he had no idea.

"I'll order a pizza," Nick said, heading for the phone. "Brooke can get you started."

Before he'd started to dial, Sonny and Brooke were head to head, and he knew she had hours more creativity in her before she would call it a day.

IT WAS AFTER ONE in the morning when Nick realized that Brooke was fast approaching the zombie dimension, and he had to admit that seventeen hours of work was about his own limit, as well.

When Nick had seen Brooke to her car and made sure that her doors were securely locked, he and Sonny ambled toward the Harley parked near the Duesenberg. "Your ma's gonna kill me for keeping you out so late."

"No problem," Sonny said. "I told her I was helping a friend wire a new room in his house. She thinks of it as career advancement."

Nick grinned as he remembered making up similar stories when he was younger. But quickly he wiped that grin away and told himself that he shouldn't encourage his nephew to deceive his parents. "I should have made you go home hours ago," he said more seriously. "You have school tomorrow."

Sonny shrugged and threw a leg over the Harley. "I've been staying up this late every night, anyway, working on my painting. It's the only time I can work without being interrupted." He pulled his helmet over his head and looked up at his uncle. "Hey, Picasso, I really appreciate your letting me help out on this. Can I come back tomorrow night?"

"You can come as often as you can," Nick assured him. "But don't thank us. Brooke and I needed help badly. We'll pay you as soon as we get a budget."

Sonny set his wrist on the handlebar, letting the keys dangle from his fingers. "She's a nice lady," he said. "Like I said earlier, I can see what all the fuss was about."

Nick issued a heavy sigh and looked in the direction she had driven. "Do me a favor and don't bring 'all the fuss' up in front of her anymore, huh? It's kind of a sore spot."

Sonny chuckled. "Yeah, sure. But really, man. I can't blame you for anything that happened with her. She's not like most women. Something about her...she's different."

Moonlight found a forum in Nick's eyes, lending him a vulnerable air as he smiled softly. "Yeah. She's definitely that."

Sonny kick-started his motor, revved it for a second before he pulled it off the stand. "Well, I'll see you tomorrow, then," he said.

Nick watched his nephew pull out of sight, one lone light disappearing with a grating shift of gears. For a moment he stood alone in the dark parking lot, feeling suddenly cold and empty...wondering if Brooke was home yet, if she had him on her mind, if she dwelled on the moment that had passed between them before Sonny had arrived today. He had never spent so much time in one day with anyone in his life, and yet he had felt strangely deprived when she had to leave. *Give it up, Marcello,* he told himself. *You're just tired.*

Maybe so, he thought, but tired or not it was going to be a futile task getting Brooke Martin out of his mind tonight.

THE ONLY LIGHT still glowing in the house when Brooke came in was the reading lamp in Roxy's room. She passed by the room quietly and saw that the door was ajar, casting a bright triangle of light on the comparative darkness in the hallway.

Brooke pushed the door open enough to see that Roxy lay asleep on top of her bedspread, still fully dressed right down to her shoes. A stack of travel brochures cluttered the bed beside her sister, like propaganda fairy tales of Canada, Washington, Colorado, Jamaica, Illinois—places with nothing in common, except that they were all far away. Frowning, Brooke lowered herself to the bed, careful not to disturb the girl and reached out to stroke the soft tangle of hair back from her face. Roxy looked so young tonight...so innocent. So unhampered by the bevy of secrets she hid behind her eyes. Tonight she looked almost happy. Tears tightened Brooke's throat, and regret filled her weary heart. Why had she let herself miss these last few years with Roxy and lose touch with the crises that had altered her spirit? Was her pride really worth it? she wondered.

At Brooke's touch, Roxy stirred, lifted her head up and squinted, disoriented.

Brooke withdrew her hand. "Sorry I woke you," she whispered. "I saw your light on..."

Roxy sat up, looked around her. "Musta dozed off," she muttered. "What time is it?"

"One-thirty," Brooke said.

Roxy pushed her hair out of her face and settled her groggy eyes on her sister. "And you just got in?"

"With all the work I have to get done in the next few days, I don't have time to sleep at all," Brooke whispered. "Unfortunately my body demands it."

Brooke knew the wheels in Roxy's sleepy brain were turning, adding up the late hour and her work with Nick and coming up with the same conclusion that everyone else in town would have. Unwilling to argue about it now, Brooke glanced down at the travel brochures, picking one up. "You going somewhere, Roxy?"

Roxy pulled her shoes off with her toes, watching them drop to the floor. "As soon as I graduate and save up enough money."

Brooke tried to keep her expression neutral as she watched her sister slide off the bed and peel back the bed covers. "Where?"

Roxy slipped between the covers, still fully clothed. "As far from this town as I can get," she said.

The words hit Brooke like an icy tide, but she didn't speak. What was there to say, after all? That Roxy shouldn't run away from her problems? That the grass really wasn't greener on the other side? Her own credibility left something to be desired, so instead of digging deeper into Roxy's psyche, Brooke sat silently beside her for a few minutes as Roxy fell back to sleep, and wondered if she had imagined the misery in her sister's voice. Were the travel brochures just bits of a dream, she wondered, or crucial parts of an escape plan? And what, exactly, did Roxy feel she had to escape *from*?

The feeling that she had failed her sister by not being around enough assailed Brooke, exhausting her even more than she already was. Quietly she turned off Roxy's light and went to her own room, where *Infinity* sat on the bedside table, profoundly reminding her that she hadn't always failed. She just hadn't allowed herself to succeed, at least not at relationships. What would have been different, she wondered, if she had stayed in town ten years ago and faced the gossip? Would she and Roxy be friends? Would she and Nick be lovers? Would it have ever led to anything more than inevitable heartbreak? Or was it simply the forbidden aspect that had drawn them together before?

For the life of her, she didn't know the answers. But as she fell asleep, one image preyed on her mind, blossoming from a still picture into a moving fantasy. Two shadows embracing on the verge of consummation...of a marriage, of a love affair, of a future. And in her mind, there was no doubt whose faces Nick had drawn in the panels today. Brooke saw them vividly, as well.

IT WAS TEN O'CLOCK on the night before the presentation when Sonny finally left Brooke and Nick alone, where they sat solemnly in Nick's house scrutinizing the work they had accomplished in the previous week. The drawings fell far short of what they had hoped for, for only half the drawings were finished, and none were done in any great detail.

Thanks to Sonny, they did have color, but even so, the outcome of the upcoming meeting looked pretty grim.

Nick reached for the half-full bottle of wine chilling in a bucket on his coffee table and slipped down to the carpet to sit across from Brooke, who sat cross-legged, leaning back against the legs of a chair, studying the panels she would have loved to have a second shot at. He poured more wine into her glass, the sloshing sound punctuating the rythym of an old Billy Joel song.

"We gave it our best shot," he said quietly. "And we can take care of some last-minute details tomorrow."

"Yeah," she whispered. She leaned her head back against the cushions of the chair and sipped her wine. She was tired, so tired—mentally, emotionally, spiritually—and her frayed emotions seemed ready to unravel with just the right stress. "They're going to hate it, you know. Not one person on that town council has enough imagination to see what we see here."

Nick propped his wrists on his knees, letting his glass hang from his hand. "Oh, I don't know. Don't forget that it was their imaginations that drove you out of town to begin with."

"You're right," she said, conceding the point. "It's just that their imaginations lean in the wrong directions."

"We'll do what we can to generate their enthusiasm," Nick said, his voice little more than a whisper. "That's all we can do."

Brooke lifted her glass to her lips. He was too close, facing her on the carpet, and she could smell the wine scent on his breath, and that maddening after-shave. "If we were two ordinary artists making a presentation, maybe that would work," she said quietly. "But we won't just be dragging these sketches in there tomorrow night. We'll be dragging in our history together and our alleged affair and everything that's ever been said about us . . ."

"To hell with what's said about us," he whispered. "We both know the truth."

She stretched out her legs before her, indolently allowing one to brush Nick's hip. A warm feeling syruped through her with the potency of melted honey, making the tragedy of their plight seem that much more pronounced. "Why are we always the losers?" she asked. "Why can't we win, just once in a while?"

Nick took a long sip from his glass, reached for the bottle and poured himself some more. "Because we're more honorable than they are and we don't play dirty."

Brooke looked into her almost-empty glass, considering it for a moment. "Where does that get us?" she asked. "Unemployed, alone, frustrated . . ."

"Are you frustrated?" The question was a breathy whisper, and Brooke met Nick's eyes, dark as midnight and smoldering like the smoky remains of a dormant fire. His gaze dropped to her lips, and she wet them unconsciously.

"Aren't you?" she asked, knowing she was walking a line that was far too narrow.

Nick's tongue slipped across his lips, and she watched it with too much interest. "Frustration is just one of those emotions I always associate with you," he said. "But I figure you're worth it."

"Am I?" Not taking her eyes from his, she brought the glass to her lips and finished her wine. Her eyes sparkled with emerald mist, but there was no smile hidden there. Only solemnity, as if the subject they broached now held a sacredness that neither of them dared to taint. She picked up the bottle and filled her glass again. Closing her eyes, she took a long drink, knowing that Nick's gaze remained warmly on her, as physical as a gentle touch. "Maybe the windows just weren't meant to be," she whispered. "And maybe that's my fault. I'm so sorry, Nick."

Nick lifted her hand, held it in both his own, lighting her nerve endings with fingertip sparks that found a home in her heart. She opened her eyes, saw him gazing down at her fingers as he fondled them. "No, it's never been your fault," he said. "I'm the one who's sorry."

"For what?" she asked.

"For asking you to put your business on hold and come here for something that wasn't even a sure thing. For disrupting your life . . . again."

Brooke's fingers laced with his as their palms came together, and she leaned closer to him, inclining her head. "It's okay, Nick. It was time for me to come home."

His face was only inches from hers, and she could see the desire in his eyes and sense the apprehension in his heart. His hand released hers and moved slowly up her arm, cradling her elbow as if it were some piece of fragile sculpture. "But you've lost so much," he said.

"You're the one who's lost everything," she whispered as his eyes swept from her tousled hair to her mouth, down her chin and back up to her eyes, memorizing her expression longingly in detail. "And I don't know how I will ever forgive myself," she went on, "if I make you lose the second most significant job of your career."

His eyebrows drew together in troubled surprise, his face moved closer, and she sensed, more than felt, his hand moving up her neck and into the roots of her hair, molding to the back of her head. Her eyelids grew heavy as she felt his gaze probing into her deepest, darkest chambers, where secret, forbidden emotions lay buried like sealed treasures. "I wouldn't have minded either loss," he whispered, "if I'd come out of them with you."

The startling admission was like a warm salve on Brooke's aching heart. His eyes were eloquent with honesty and emotion, but cloaked with a sadness that went much deeper than the losses he had faced. It almost hinted at the losses still to come....

With all her spirit, Brooke wished she could hold that sadness at bay, and somehow bribe the Fates that kept detouring them from an instinctive path.

His fingers massaged the nape of her neck, pulling her infinitesimally closer, until their lips were a breath's distance apart. He paused a moment, looking down at her moist lips, offering her the chance, she knew, to back away. One last chance to cling to her defense that the gossip was unfounded, that there was nothing going on. One last chance to end the fantasy plaguing them both for years.

She let that chance pass her by and waited breathlessly for the replay of the most heightened moment of her life, the moment that had been so quickly, so cruelly ended ten years before.

Finally his lips descended on hers, wet and warm, his tongue making a slow, agonizingly sweet entrance. She felt his jaw beneath her hand, rough and rugged, strong, moving as the kiss deepened. His arms closed around her back, pulling her tighter against him, cradling her as her head dipped back. In her mind's eye was a slow-motion replay of a heart pounding madly, breath thinning, and palms tingling in desperate need of the feel of bare skin.

He abandoned her lips with a low moan, leaving them red and hungry, and trailed to her neck, up to the delicate shell of her ear, then back down to her throat, as if he wanted to taste and feel and breathe her, everywhere at once, before cruel fate took her away from him again. He sucked in a long breath, fanning it out across her skin. "You smell...just like I remember..."

Before the words had completely been uttered, Brooke captured his mouth with her own again. Her fingers made a sensuous journey across his stubbled jaw, learning the angles and texture, so that she might sculpt it later, in her mind. The kiss grew more urgent, and she felt his breath heaving in his chest, his heart hammering against her breast, and a low moan of hungry relief forming in his throat.

But just as the tide of desire swept them both into its arc, the subtle nag of intellect intruded. Without a second of warning, Nick grabbed her arms and broke the kiss and set her back from him.

She looked up at him, her shamrock-green eyes clouded with desire and confusion, misty with the sting of emotions that couldn't be cut off. But behind those eyes, he could see the subtle hint of relief.

"One frustration after another," he whispered on a ragged, tremulous breath. "But I know the ground rules."

Brooke sat motionless—stricken with profound disappointment, self-censure and maybe the slightest peppering of relief—as Nick pulled himself off the floor, then extended his hand for her to take. He pulled her to her feet, and she stood looking up at him, the look in her eyes telling him without question that it wouldn't take much persuasion to make her dispense with those rules. But Nick didn't persuade.

She swallowed, trying to steady her breath. "Guess I should go," she whispered.

He nodded and slid his shaky hands into his pockets. "Yeah, I guess."

She sucked in a deep, cleansing breath, but found that it did nothing to banish the cluttered, clashing emotions within her. She started to stack some of the sketches, but he reached out and stopped her hand.

"But I was just—"

"I'll get them later," he said. "I'll bring them to the museum tomorrow."

"Okay." She looked up at him with hurt, bewildered eyes, wondering what she had done wrong to make him so anxious for her to leave. "I'll see you then."

She felt him watching her as she gathered her purse and her case, and started toward the door.

"Eight o'clock?" he asked.

"Sure," she said.

He took a few steps to follow her to the door, but when Brooke glanced back, he stopped, as if moving too close would make him abandon those rules. "Try and get some sleep. Tomorrow's going to be rough."

She lifted her brows and offered a self-conscious smile that told him sleeping would be the last thing she'd do tonight. "I'll try."

He followed a few steps behind her to her car, watching her get in and dig nervously through her purse for her keys. When she found them, she gazed down at them for a moment, as if struggling with a question she couldn't make herself ask.

"Hey, Brooke?"

She looked up at Nick, saw him standing back in the darkness, hands jammed in his pockets, and his eyes as vulnerable and gentle as she had ever seen them in her life. "Uh-huh?"

"If we'd had the chance to see it through, this is the same way it would have wound up that night ten years ago," he said. "Not because of what anyone would say, but because we're both too smart to move that fast. I thought it was important that you knew that."

She felt her eyes filling with mist, and she smiled up at him as relief and gratitude played symphonies in her heart.

He wasn't turning her away, she thought. He was just proving to her what they felt went deeper than lust. It was rooted in affection, in respect and maybe in something more. "Thank you, Nick," she whispered. "I did need to know that."

As she pulled out of the driveway and started down the street, she saw him standing alone in his yard, watching over her like a gentle spirit. In a way she knew that was exactly what he was. For he had found a home in her heart, without her even inviting him in.

CHAPTER EIGHT

THE TOWN COUNCIL MEETING the following night was open
to the public, and as Nick sat next to Brooke at the front of
the room watching the people filing in, he wondered why
the telephone lines in Hayden hadn't overloaded during the
past week. The people who came couldn't be less interested in hearing the presentation of the stained-glass windows, he thought, as he watched their eyes sweep over the
room and settle anxiously on himself and Brooke. What
they really wanted was to be firsthand witnesses to any
smutty little allegations he and Brooke faced, so that they
could light up the telephone lines again.

He recognized some of the students he'd taught in
school, Brooke's classmates, all gawking at her as if she
were some legend they were finally getting a glimpse of after all these years. Others were his own ex-classmates, or
active grapevine contributors who wouldn't have missed
tonight if they'd been stricken with disease. Some, like
Brooke's family and his own were conspicuously absent.
Nick leaned toward Brooke, who sat next to him, rigid and
expressionless. "Do you believe this?"

"Of course," she said. "This could be the best enter-
tainment the town's seen all year."

"All decade," he muttered.

She shook her head and looked down at her hands, and
he saw the threat of tears in her eyes. "Only this time they

get to see exhibits one and two firsthand. Last time they only enjoyed the dirt in print.''

Nick wanted to reach for her hand and reassure her somehow, but he couldn't escape the feeling that if he did, cameras would begin flashing around the room and they'd be the headline story in tomorrow's news. The mayor, Ed Brimley, got to his feet at the center of the table and banged his gavel on a wooden block. ''Could we have some order here?'' he said loudly. ''We have a lot of business to take care of tonight, and I'd like to get started.''

It took a good ten minutes for the crowd to quiet, but when it did, the mayor turned the meeting over to Horace Anderson, who stood looking wearily across the crowd with strict admonishment in his expression.

''I'd like to remind you people,'' he said in a gruff, no-nonsense tone, ''that our intention here tonight is to listen to the presentation Mr. Marcello and Miss Martin have prepared concerning the stained-glass windows in the museum, and then to vote to approve or reject their commission, at which time we can approve or reject their budget.'' He slipped his thumbs through the suspenders tucked under his coat and turned meaningfully to Abby Hemphill. ''This is not about personal accusations or gossip. So don't anybody waste our time with that stuff tonight.''

A murmur of disappointment undulated through the crowd, and Nick glanced toward Brooke, noting that the corners of her mouth trembled slightly.

''Now, Nick, Brooke, the floor is yours,'' Horace said.

Nick and Brooke stood up, and Sonny, from across the room, stepped forward, as well, to assist them in setting up the first group of the panel sketches they intended to explain. A round of whispers and mumbles were heard as they spread the drawings across the five easels they had set side by side in the room. When he finished, Nick ventured a glance at Brooke.

Her cheeks were flushed in sunburn pink, and he knew she struggled with all her courage to keep from letting the stares and whispers daunt her. He should have done this alone, he told himself with self-reproach. He should have insisted that she stay home and let him make the presentation without her.

She finished arranging the panels on her end and looked up at him. Their eyes met, and he thought how beautiful she looked in the oversized emerald sweater that matched the green of her eyes. She looked fragile and vulnerable. The apprehension on her face, the strain, made him want to turn back to the crowd and crucify each of them in turn, the way they had crucified her. Instead he began the speech he had prepared for this night, hoping the town would defer its judgment and give them just a little more time....

BROOKE'S NERVOUS TERROR calmed a bit as Nick explained the stages of life theme to the council members and spectators, and she found herself getting lost, yet again, in the passion in his voice as he explained the concept of each group of panels. She glanced over the faces in the crowd. They were no longer gaping at her, for their interest had shifted completely to the poignant drawings, incomplete though they were.

He's magic, she thought, her gaze, drifting to Nick again. With just the excitement in his voice and the zest in his eyes and the gestures of his hands he had captured their imaginations and shown them the beauty that went beyond what they had done on paper. He explained the process of creating the stained glass and the dimensions that couldn't be seen here. And with a few simple words, he had made them imagine the colors as they might be, with the sun filtering through.

When Nick's presentation came to an end, a hush fell over the room, undisturbed for a moment as the audience absorbed what he'd said. "We'd be happy to answer any questions anyone might have," he said finally, breaking the silence.

Hands went up throughout the audience, and Horace recognized one person by name. "How many people will you have to hire to help you with this?" the questioner asked.

"Quite a few if we're to stay on schedule and have the windows finished on time," he said. "We plan to hire experienced people to help cut the glass and some inexperienced help, part-time workers like teenagers, to help with some of the less intricate things. And then, of course, we'll have to have someone to install the panels, which should be included in the cost of the construction, rather than our budget."

"How can we justify putting all this money into the windows," someone else asked, before Horace could identify him, "when we won't get any of it back? The museum is nonprofit. There's no hope of ever getting a return on this investment."

"Excuse me," Brooke piped in, desperately wanting to add her input to the argument. "I'd like to address that question." All eyes went to her, and she stood up, determined not to wilt beneath their judicious scrutiny. "*None* of the pieces exhibited in the museum is actually going to produce a profit for the town," she said. "The whole purpose of a museum is to enrich the community and draw people from other communities to share in it. The return is nonmonetary. But the rewards from something like this are educational, cultural, spiritual ones. We stand to draw a lot of the tourists from Orlando on the eastern side of the state, and from the Gulf towns on the west, if we just have something intriguing enough to offer.''

Abby Hemphill slapped her hands theatrically on the table and bolted out of her seat. ''I've sat here and listened to this nonsense long enough!'' she blurted out. ''We cannot spend our taxpayers' hard-earned money to paint topless women on the windows of our museum!''

Nick spun around. ''Topless women?'' he returned, astounded. ''Mrs. Hemphill, if you see a topless woman in any of these panels, would you kindly point her out to me right now?''

''That one!'' Mrs. Hemphill said, coming around the table and waving a finger at one of the panels still displayed.

''That's a woman breastfeeding her baby!'' Nick shouted. ''Some people consider that a viable stage of life that brings to mind a very gentle emotion.''

''What about that smutty little scene over there?'' Abby asked, flinging her pointed finger to one panel from the ''falling in love'' series Brooke had been most concerned about.

''That's a boy and a girl's first kiss,'' Nick said, his voice dropping in pitch. ''Despite the misconceptions of some of the gutter minds in this town, there is nothing smutty about a simple kiss!''

Brooke felt tears burning in her eyes, and she touched Nick's arm, hoping to stop him from flinging any more accusations at the townsfolk, who would, no doubt, make them pay for his words later. ''Mrs. Hemphill,'' she said in a voice surprisingly steady, ''Nick and I were very careful to choose life events that everyone could relate to. Emotions people all over the world share.''

Mrs. Hemphill went to the series in question and jerked one of the pictures off of the easel, waving it as if the audience hadn't seen it closely enough before. Fury constricted Brooke's throat, stopping her breath, as she saw that it was the poignant silhouettes Nick had done of the man and woman on their wedding night. "Do you people really want *this* on windows where *children* can see them?" Abby asked.

"While I admit that this portrays a man and woman's wedding night," Nick said in a voice quivering with rage, "it's apparent that they are only *looking* at each other, Abby. They are done in opaque silhouette, and they are not even *touching!* It comes *after* the wedding panel, and that's the *only* way you would ever know that it represents the consummation of a marriage. You do remember that event in life, don't you, Abby? Or is that something that you and your husband skipped altogether?"

Brooke closed her eyes and wilted back against a table as Mrs. Hemphill stiffened in livid fury. "I . . . beg . . . your . . . pardon!" she shouted. "I will not stand here and tolerate this!"

"Then sit the hell down," Horace Anderson called out. "You're both out of order. And this is not one woman's decision. We have a whole town that can decide if this is a project worth pursuing. Personally I'm pretty damn impressed, and I recommend that we go ahead with it. It's about time Hayden had something besides an overactive grapevine to get excited about."

Nick flopped back into his seat, his lips compressed and nostrils flaring with each heavy breath. Brooke sat down beside him, feeling the anger, the tension in every inch of his body, and she knew intuitively that his anger was directed more at himself than at Mrs. Hemphill. He leaned forward, propped his elbows on his thighs, crossed his hands in front of his face and stared vacantly at the council members, who were preparing to vote.

"Any more discussion?" Horace asked. Then, without allowing much time for response, he banged his gavel. "All right, then, let's vote."

As the council members voiced their votes one by one, it became apparent that the decision was pretty evenly divided. By the time it was all over, however, there were a few more votes in favor of the windows than there were against them.

"Then let the record show that we voted—again—" Horace emphasized the word with vexation, "to commission Nick Marcello and Brooke Martin to design and create the stained-glass windows for the museum. I'll expect a budget approval from the finance committee by the end of the week."

With a final bang of his gavel, the meeting was adjourned. An eruption of voices suddenly filled the room, and Nick dropped his face in his hands.

Brooke set her hand on his shoulder and leaned toward him. "Nick, it's okay. We won."

"No thanks to me," he muttered.

"You handled it a lot better than I would have," she said. "That woman brings out the worst in people."

He looked up at her, self-deprecation evident in every line of his ruddy face. "I can't believe I let her get to me like that. I can't believe I reacted that way."

Sonny zigzagged through the crowd and leaned over to slap his uncle on the back. "Hey, Picasso, you really skewered her good."

Nick shot him an unappreciative look, and Brooke shook her head, warning Sonny to stop the teasing.

Sonny's grin faded. "Hey, you're not upset about that, are you? I mean, you won. It's a go."

"Yeah, yeah," Nick said. He stood up and started to gather the drawings. "Let's just get our stuff and get the hell out of here."

Across the room he saw Mrs. Hemphill in a corner, surrounded by her cronies, babbling with nonstop fury. She was cooking something up already, he knew. She wasn't going to let this go easily.

"Congratulations," Horace Anderson said from behind him.

Nick turned around and shook Horace's hand. "Thanks for your help," he said quietly.

"Don't thank me yet," Horace said, his gruff voice taking the edge off the victory. "Just between you and me, I'm concerned that the budget won't come through. You didn't do much to smooth out Abby's ruffled feathers tonight, you know. She can be pretty vindictive when she wants to be."

"Tell me about it," Nick said, his eyes straying to the angry woman again.

"Horace," Brooke asked, keeping her voice too quiet for anyone to hear, "do you really think she can block the budget approval? I mean, can't she be outvoted?"

"Of course," Horace said, "and that's exactly what I hope will happen. But you never know about these things. It depends on which way the wind blows, and how loud that woman yells."

He left them alone to speak to some of the other council members, and Brooke and Nick only stood staring at each other. "This is a nightmare," she whispered. "I thought it would be over tonight one way or another, but here we are, no better off."

Sonny shrugged, not entirely clear what the dismal mood was about. "Sure, you're better off. At least we can go

Here are your BIG WIN Game Tickets, worth from $5.00 to $1,000,000.00 each. Scratch off the PINK METALLIC STRIP on each of your sweepstakes tickets to see what you could win and mail your entry right away. (See official rules in back of book for details!)

This could be your lucky day - GOOD LUCK!

THE BIG WIN

TICKET 1
Scratch PINK METALLIC STRIP to reveal potential value of this ticket if it is a winning ticket. Return all game tickets intact.

LUCKY NUMBER

5F053984

THE BIG WIN

TICKET 2
Scratch PINK METALLIC STRIP to reveal potential value of this ticket if it is a winning ticket. Return all game tickets intact.

LUCKY NUMBER

1L051569

THE BIG WIN

TICKET 3
Scratch PINK METALLIC STRIP to reveal potential value of this ticket if it is a winning ticket. Return all game tickets intact.

LUCKY NUMBER

2F051220

THE BIG WIN

TICKET 4
Scratch PINK METALLIC STRIP to reveal potential value of this ticket if it is a winning ticket. Return all game tickets intact.

LUCKY NUMBER

4F054512

FREE BOOKS

TICKET 5
We're giving away brand new books to selected individuals. Scratch PINK METALLIC STRIP for number of free books you will receive.

AUTHORIZATION CODE

130107-742

FREE GIFT

TICKET 6
We have an outstanding added gift for you if you are accepting our free books. Scratch PINK METALLIC STRIP to reveal gift.

AUTHORIZATION CODE

130107-742

YES! Enter my Lucky Numbers in The BIG WIN Sweepstakes and tell me if I've won any cash prize. If PINK METALLIC STRIP is scratched off on ticket #5, I will also receive one or more FREE Harlequin Supperromance® novels along with the FREE GIFT on ticket #6, as explained on the opposite page. U-H-SR-11/89 134 CIH KA77

NAME _____

ADDRESS _____ APT. _____

CITY _____ STATE _____ ZIP _____

FOLD AND DETACH ALONG THIS DOTTED LINE—RETURN ALL GAME TICKETS INTACT.

Carefully
detach card
along dotted
lines and
mail today!

*Play
all your
BIG WIN
tickets
and get
everything
you're
entitled to—
including
FREE BOOKS
and a
FREE GIFT!*

ahead with our work...finish the cartoons... At least some
of the townspeople agree that this project is worthwhile."

Brooke scanned the faces in the crowd, saw that some of
the audience lingered with interest near the panels displayed on the easels. They did like them, she mused. She
scanned more of the faces, seeing those people engaged in
angry conversation as well as those snickering with gossip
and comments and throwing amused glances her way.

Her gaze rested on a face at the back of the room, a
man's face. He was leaning indolently in the doorway and
looking at her as if waiting to catch her eye.

"Skip," she whispered.

Nick heard her and turned in the direction where she was
looking, and saw Brooke's ex-husband. She heard Nick's
slow intake of breath, saw his posture stiffen. "Was he here
the whole time?" he asked.

She shrugged, but didn't take her eyes from Skip. "I
guess so."

She stepped forward, offering Skip a tentative smile, and
thought how grown up he looked, as if the years since she'd
last seen him had refined him. He wore a blue sports coat
and dark slacks and even a tie, which he'd rarely worn in
the old days except when the team was ordered to dress for
the press. He looked at her with that same old look he used
to get before they were married, the look that said he felt
something special for her, even though neither of them
knew exactly what it was.

As she started toward him, Skip came to meet her
halfway.

"It's good to see you, Skip," she said, a genuine smile on
her lips. "I didn't know you were here."

He gestured toward the last row of seats. "Yeah. I came
in late and sat at the back."

"Oh. Then I guess you heard all the fireworks."

He smiled, but it failed to reach his eyes. "There always seem to be fireworks where you and Marcello are concerned."

Recognizing the trace of bitterness in his words, Brooke looked back over her shoulder to Nick and saw the sober way he watched them as he gathered the cartoons.

"I was surprised when I heard you were back in town," Skip went on, drawing her gaze back to him, "I guess I came tonight to see it for myself."

Her smile faltered. "Yeah, I'm here."

Skip shuffled his feet on the floor, studied them for a moment, then met her eyes again. "You never would come home to Hayden even once when we were married." His voice was flat, but laced with a shadow of pain. "I guess it just took the right person asking you."

"Nick didn't ask me to come back," Brooke replied. "Horace Anderson did. Until I got here, I didn't even know Nick was involved." She averted her eyes, then took a long breath. "I came home because I've grown up, Skip. I just felt like it was time."

Skip's eyes strayed past her shoulder, to where Nick stood. She looked back again, saw that Nick had stopped his work completely and was watching them with tender dread in his eyes. Did he think she would grab Skip's hand and run away with him? she wondered. Did he think she even compared Skip to him?

"Time for what?" Skip asked quietly. "To pick up where you left off?"

"To make things right," she whispered.

Their eyes came together again, and she saw a gentle, accepting smile in the depths of his cobalt eyes. "Well, maybe those are one and the same," he admitted.

Brooke reached up to touch his face in silent thanks that he had matured enough to stop condemning her. He pressed his hand over hers, brought it down, and nestled it in both his own. The touch held a brotherly affection that made a tiny wave of nostalgic joy swim through her. Had he forgiven her for not loving him? Had he forgiven himself for marrying her?

"Well, you have work to do," he said quietly.

Brooke nodded and withdrew her hand, letting it fall to her side. She watched wistfully as Skip walked away, wishing with all her heart that they could be confidants again, friends who could count on each other. But the relationship was tainted now, she thought, for they had tried to become lovers. And that hadn't had any more chance to work than things with Nick had.

She turned back to Nick, who had resumed his work again, as if he didn't care that her ex-husband had drawn her away from him. She stepped toward him and began stacking the sketches herself.

"So, are you going to see him later?" he asked, his tone brittle with feigned disinterest.

"I don't know," she said. "I suppose I'll run into him a few more times while I'm here."

"Yeah," he mumbled. "Like you ran into him at Florida State?"

Brooke stopped her work and looked up at him. The room was emptying rapidly, and only a few people lingered behind. He'd uttered the comment just under his breath, but she could feel the anger swelling just beneath the surface. "Nick, I don't have any hostile feelings toward Skip. There's no reason why I wouldn't be cordial to him when I see him. He was my husband."

Visibly, anger rushed up to color Nick's face, and she saw him struggle with the same dark look that he'd worn when Mrs. Hemphill pushed him over the cliff of his control. His eyes were dark and glowing with anger as they fixed on her.

"I know who he was," he whispered through his teeth. "You don't ever have to remind me who he was."

"Nick, I was just—"

Nick threw his hands up and took a few steps back. "Look, I'm just tired. I need to crash..." He jammed the drawings into his case, and roughly dismantled the easels that Sonny hadn't gotten to yet. "Do you need a ride home or what?"

"No, I have my car," she said stiffly.

"Then I'll see you tomorrow," he told her.

"Yeah," she said. "Tomorrow."

Brooke watched as he gathered the last of their presentation tools and flung them into boxes. Every movement was staccato. She started to speak, but found that her heart was in her throat. He was angry with her, he was hurt...

He was jealous.

The thought barely had time to inscribe itself on her mind when the woman she'd recognized as the mayor's secretary stepped into the room. "Miss Martin? You have a telephone call. Your sister. She says it's important."

"All right." Reluctantly Brooke turned and started for the door. "I'll be right there."

Before she left the room, she looked back and saw Nick standing motionless, gazing at her with tired, regretful eyes. Feeling cold and miserably—unnaturally—alienated from him, Brooke rushed for the phone.

THE MAYOR'S OFFICE was only partially lighted, and the secretary, who had stopped in to leave her notes after the meeting and found the phone ringing, led her to the telephone. Quickly Brooke picked up the phone. "Roxy?"

"Thank heaven they caught you!" Roxy was barely audible over the line, but Brooke could still hear the quiver in her voice. "I was afraid no one would answer the phone, or that..."

"Roxy, what's wrong?"

Roxy dragged in a shaky breath, and Brooke could tell that she was crying. "I need your help," she said. "I'm sort of... stranded."

"Stranded? Where?"

Roxy cleared her throat, and Brooke heard the terror in her pitch. "You know that bar about a block from the Bluejay Inn? The After Hours?"

Brooke's brows burrowed together, and a sick feeling rose in her stomach. What was Roxy doing "stranded" alone at a rough place like that? It was the kind of place where hoods and hookers hung out, where people got shot or stabbed on Saturday nights, where young women who wandered in could lose their virtue. She glanced at the mayor's secretary, who tried to pretend she wasn't listening. "Yes, I know the place," she said.

"Well, could you come pick me up?"

Brooke pushed her questions to the back of her mind. "I'll be there in five minutes," she said.

"It'll take at least ten," Roxy told her.

"I'll be there in five," Brooke said again, and slammed down the phone.

TRUE TO HER WORD Brooke made it to the After Hours Bar within five minutes. She pulled into the parking lot and saw a cluster of bearded men in denim and leather turn around and ogle her as she put her car in park. Roxy was nowhere to be seen. She opened her car door and got halfway out, her lights still on and her motor still idling.

"Hey, darlin', you lookin' for me?" one of the men from the small crowd called out, and the others joined in with rounds of catcalls and vulgar remarks.

Trying to ignore them, Brooke looked around frantically for a sign of Roxy. Was she waiting inside for Brooke?
Did Roxy expect her to walk past those morons to find her?

She was just about to turn off her ignition and take her
chances going inside, when she saw Roxy slip out from the
shadows at the far corner of the building.

"Roxy!"

The men turned around, and their enthusiasm heightened. "There she is!"

"We thought you'd gone home, honey."

"You weren't hiding from us, were you?"

They started moving threateningly toward Roxy, and she
began to run toward the car. When she reached it, she
yanked open the door and almost fell inside.

Brooke was pulling out of the parking lot before Roxy
even had time to sit up, and more importantly before any
of the men had reached the car.

"They're like animals," Roxy cried, her sobs quaking her
shoulders. "Vicious, filthy animals."

Brooke caught her breath and became aware that she was
shaking, as well. "Did they hurt you?"

"No. I'm okay."

Brooke drove for several miles before she was certain her
voice was steady enough to ask the questions that had to be
asked. "Roxy, what in God's name were you doing there?"

Roxy swallowed a sob, wiped her face, and lifted her
chin. "Bill and I . . . we stopped in for a drink. . . ."

"A drink?" Brooke cut in. "Roxy, you're seventeen!
You aren't old enough to buy liquor. Didn't they check
your ID?"

"No!" Roxy flung back.

Brooke bit her lip, and decided to report the sleazy bar
at the first opportunity. "Where is this *Bill*?"

Roxy didn't answer for a moment, and finally she spoke, slowly choosing her words. "He . . . he had an emergency, and had to leave . . ."

"He took you to a sleazy bar and *left* you there alone?" Brooke shouted. "Is he crazy? Are *you* crazy?"

Roxy glared out the window, tears streaming down her pale cheeks. "I don't need this from you, Brooke."

Brooke tried to contain her fury as she negotiated the dark streets leading to their neighborhood. "I hope you don't intend to see him again," she said finally.

Roxy didn't say a word.

"Roxy? You don't, do you?" she demanded.

Roxy remained silent, staring out the window.

"Roxy, you don't have to put up with this. You can do better than some insensitive idiot who—"

"You don't know anything about it!" Roxy screamed. "So just get off my back!"

Despair stabbed Brooke's heart. "All right, Roxy," she whispered, pulling into their driveway. "I'll get off your back. But promise me that if anything like this happens again, you'll call me."

"That's what I did, isn't it?" Roxy asked, her tone softer than before.

"Yes," Brooke said. "That's what you did."

Roxy got out of the car and started toward the house. The lights were off, and Brooke knew her parents were sleeping soundly, completely unaware that Roxy was going through some sort of crisis that even Brooke didn't know how to handle. She locked the car and followed her sister to the porch.

Roxy stopped before she reached the front door. "Don't tell them, Brooke. Okay?"

Brooke regarded her sister for a moment, saw the vital plea in her face. "That's asking a lot, Roxy."

"I've never asked you for anything before," Roxy said. "Not until tonight. I need you to promise me that you won't tell them."

Brooke saw the red, swollen evidence of misery and heartache in Roxy's eyes. She had no idea what her sister was going through, but going to her parents would only alienate Roxy further. Instead she vowed privately she would find a way to take Roxy under her wing, win her trust and guide her in the right direction again.

Releasing a long, weary sigh that bled her of any energy remaining after the emotional evening, Brooke acquiesced. "All right," she whispered, though her better judgment warned her against it. "I promise."

CHAPTER NINE

NICK LOCKED HIS DUESENBERG in the garage and brought the sketches into his kitchen and set them down carefully, so as not to tear or bend them. Then, in direct contrast to that gentleness, he slammed his fist on the counter. Leaning over it, he clutched the edges of the countertop, his knuckles whitening with the force of his self-reproach.

Damn! What had come over him tonight?

Gritting his teeth, he kicked the cabinet at his knees, then headed into the living room, where he flung himself onto the couch, covering his face with both hands.

He couldn't believe he had insulted Abby Hemphill in front of two hundred people. But the worst sin he'd committed tonight was reacting to Brooke's speaking to Skip Nelson. *You don't ever have to remind me who he was.*

If that wasn't a red flag that he was as jealous as a schoolkid losing his first girl, he didn't know what was. *Damn!*

The doorbell rang, and he sat forward, looking in the direction of the door, wondering with dread if Brooke had come to try and appease him. What did she want from him? Hadn't he shown herculean control last night when he'd stopped the progression of their passion? Did he honestly think he could be that noble tonight, when his nerves were frayed and his arms fairly ached for the feel of her?

Swallowing his frustration, he stood up and went to the door. Pulling it open, he started at the sight of his mother,

Anna, and Vinnie, who had only visited him as a group once before that he could remember. And that was the first week he'd moved in.

"Ma, Anna, Vinnie. What's going on?" He ushered them in and closed the door. In their somber faces, he saw that he had reason to be alarmed.

"We came to talk to you." Vinnie's words were delivered with clipped gruffness.

"About what?" he asked.

"About what you're doing to Sonny," Anna said.

Nick frowned and shook his head, wondering if he'd missed something. "What do you mean, 'what I'm doing to Sonny'?"

"Encouraging him in this art business," his mother threw in.

"How could you?" Anna asked, glaring at him with disgust. "How could you undermine our authority as his parents? Are *you* anybody's father? Do you know what it's like to go through adolescence with a child?"

"Adolescence! The kid's nineteen!" Nick leaned wearily against his wall, telling himself that he was engaging in a losing argument, that he should stay calm. "Look, Anna, if I've upset you, I'm sorry. I didn't mean to—"

"Upset me!" she shouted. "I want to know how you could do this! When you know how we feel about him wasting his life!"

"Anna, you're overreacting," Nick said. "The kid has talent. I didn't do anything to cultivate that. He's done it himself."

"Yeah?" Vinnie asked, stepping across the room until his massive frame pressed threateningly close to Nick. "Then how come when we found that paint and stuff in his room tonight and told him to get rid of it, he told us that if we wouldn't let him paint at home, he'd come over *here* and do it?''

"What are you people afraid of?" Nick shouted. "It's not like the kid's on drugs or something. He has a hobby, for God's sake."

"You should know better than anybody," his mother said, shaking her long finger at him, "that hobbies can turn into occupations. Next thing you know he'll want to waste four years going to college to study something that'll make him a worthless pauper when he could be making good money working with his father."

Nick collapsed on the couch, wondering just how far his control was expected to stretch tonight. "Oh, man. I thought I'd finished fighting this battle fourteen years ago. I never in a million years thought I'd have to hash this out with you again, Ma."

Anna sat down next to her brother, her face as intent as he'd ever seen it. He looked at her, wondering if she'd forgotten all the fights that had taken place between him and his father all those years ago, when he had been about Sonny's age. Hadn't she learned *anything* about human determination from the way he had conducted his own life?

"I want the best for my son, Nick," she told him, her tone quieter as she made an earnest attempt to reason with him. "I want him to have good working values, and I want him to be able to earn a living."

Nick released a frustrated laugh and sprang off the couch, gesturing around him, at the home that proved—to him, at least—that he had worth. "Don't *I* support myself?" he asked. "Don't I do okay? The bank that holds my mortgage doesn't have any complaints."

"You don't even have a family!" Anna shouted, as though that meant the ultimate failure. "How is Sonny ever gonna support a family drawing pictures? If it could be done, wouldn't you have done it by now?''

Nick strode across the room, rubbing the back of his neck, desperate not to explode in front of these people who meant so much to him. Trying to contain his rising wrath, he went to the window, propped a foot on the sill and looked out over the small canal behind his house. "My not marrying has nothing to do with my art."

"It has everything to do with your art!" his mother belted out. "If it weren't for that art you wouldn't have been wasting your time teaching ten years ago, with so much time on your hands that you'd do something so foolish as to sleep with your student! And you wouldn't be involved with a married woman today!"

"What?" The question whiplashed across the room as he spun around to confront that accusation on his mother's face.

"That Brooke Martin woman. She ruined your good name once already. And don't think we haven't heard about the latest episodes."

Nick opened his mouth to respond, but caught himself, bit his lip and told himself that he'd burned enough bridges tonight. It wouldn't pay to throw his family out of his house. Regardless of their refusal to understand him, he needed them. "First of all," he said in a voice exceedingly calm despite the fire raging within him, "Brooke Martin is not a married woman. She happens to be divorced."

"In the eyes of God and the Church she's still married!" his mother shouted. "What is it with you, that you go so blind when it comes to her? Is it some perversion, that you would lust after her when she was a child and still do it today under the pretense of so-called work?"

Nick held his breath for a moment and coiled his hands into fists at his sides. He closed his eyes and reminded himself that he loved his mother. This was nothing new, after all. She'd been on him since the first day she'd discovered his intention to study art, as if it had proved he was less than a man.

Meeting his mother's eyes again, he tried to find words to make her understand. "Brooke Martin is the *only* woman I have ever met who understood my passion for my work," he said in a voice just above a whisper. "She is the *only* person I've ever cared for who didn't see it as a flaw in my character. She is the *only* human being on the face of this earth who can share that love of art with me, because it means as much to her as it does to me."

He reached out for his mother's arm, knowing she could feel that he was shaking. "Ma, I love you, but you have never understood the first thing about me. I learned to accept that a long time ago, and it doesn't even hurt me anymore. But don't you do that to Sonny. He's a great kid, and he deserves a chance to become what he wants. If that's an electrician, fine. But if it's not, you can't force him to give up what means something to him."

"You're not going to help us are you?" Vinnie asked, astounded.

Nick turned to his brother-in-law, stiff and rigid, like a tiger about to attack. "Vinnie, I'm not going to help Sonny defy you in any way. I won't condone rebellion or disrespect. But he's *not* an adolescent. He's nineteen years old, and if he wants to use my studio because he feels he has something in his soul that needs expressing, he's welcome to it. And your trying to stop him is only going to make his passion for it that much stronger. Believe me, I've been there."

"I can't believe this," Anna shouted, tears coming to her eyes. "You're going to put us through this all over again, aren't you? All the fighting you and pop did when we were kids, you're wishing it on us, now, aren't you?"

A fissure of pity cracked through his anger, making Nick realize that his sister would never understand that embracing a gift from God did not amount to weakness or a betrayal of loved ones.

"I'm not wishing anything on you, Sis," Nick said. "You're bringing it on yourself."

Anna blotted the tears spilling down her face. "Let's go, Vinnie," she said. "Ma."

Nick's mother only stood in the center of the floor, glaring up at him with furious incrimination in her eyes, with disgust, with every negative emotion a mother could feel for a son. It didn't hurt half as bad as it had when he was Sonny's age, he thought.

"Give the kid some room, Ma," he entreated. "A little paint never killed anybody."

His mother didn't say anything as she followed Anna and Vinnie out of the living room. Nick was left standing alone, feeling as if the entire western hemisphere had collapsed tonight, without the good grace of taking him along.

BROOKE'S ROOM SEEMED DARKER than usual, perhaps because the sky was overcast, alienating the moonlight, or perhaps because her heart was stormy with turbulent emotions she couldn't contain. Roxy, Skip, Mrs. Hemphill, Nick... Worries and fears and more worries raged in her mind, making it impossible for her to sleep.

She heard the phone ring in another part of the house and wondered who could be calling so late. Roxy's boyfriend, perhaps, wondering if she'd made it home or gotten molested and left for dead? The thought made Brooke seethe, and she sat up and wadded her pillow.

A knock sounded lightly on her door, and Roxy opened it and looked inside. "Telephone," she said.

Brooke looked at the glowing numbers on the clock, then hurried out of bed. "Who is it?" she asked, knowing the answer even as she asked.

"Didn't say," Roxy told her, "but I have a strong hunch."

Brooke got out of bed and went barefoot out into the hall, and clearly saw the look in her sister's eye. The look that said, *If there's nothing between you, why is he calling at nearly midnight?* But there was more to that look, Brooke thought as she went to the kitchen telephone. Maybe a little more understanding and a little less judgment.

Brooke sat down on the stool next to the telephone and dipped her head as she picked it up. "Nick?" she asked.

"Yeah, it's me." Nick's voice was deep, gravelly, thick with pain. "Look, I know it's late..."

Brooke heard a click and knew that Roxy had hung up the extension. Nick paused for a moment.

"It's okay," she said. "I wasn't asleep."

She heard him sigh, sensed his struggle for the right words. "Look, I... I was just trying to sleep, but after the crummy day I've had, it's not easy. And I couldn't stop thinking that I owe you an apology. I didn't mean to snap at you, after everything else we went through tonight. You didn't need that."

"It's okay," she said again. "I understand."

"Do you?" he asked.

She was quiet a moment, wondering if she did understand, after all. Hadn't he jumped on her about something that had nothing to do with him? Hadn't he read more into her conversation with Skip than there was?

Nick's voice was raspy and heavy when he spoke again. "When I found out that you had married him—" his words trailed off, and he cleared his throat, found his voice again "—I think I went a little crazy. Tonight, seeing you with him again . . . it just brought back all the old anger . . ."

A warm fever rushed through her, making her heart forget the stings of all the accusing arrows that had come at her tonight. "Oh, Nick. I haven't seen him in years. We were just saying hello."

"I know," Nick assured her. "And it isn't like we're . . . an item or anything. You can talk to anyone you like. That's why I wanted to apologize."

"It isn't like we're an item . . ." The words weighed her spirits down, making Brooke wish from the deepest chamber of her heart that things were just a little different, that the people of Hayden cared just a little less, that their consciences and honor and nobility weren't so important. "Look, it's been a tough day for all of us. You don't have to apologize. I didn't mean to run out so fast, but my sister was in trouble."

"Is everything all right with her?" he asked.

Brooke wilted against the counter, thankful there was someone she could confide in, if not her parents. "Oh, Nick. She was stranded at some sleazy bar. Her date left her there, and she had to call me to go get her. I drove up there, and all these hoods were standing outside boozing it up. She had been hiding behind the building waiting for me."

"Who the hell is this guy she's dating?" Nick asked, as irritated as if he was talking about his own sister.

"Some guy named Bill. That's all I can get out of her. I can't understand. One minute she's acting like I'm overreacting, the next she's hiding behind a building in absolute terror. I've got to keep an eye on her from now on. She's headed for trouble. I can see it."

Nick was quiet for a moment, and she could sense his concern. "Why don't you ask her to help us out at the museum? Maybe you two could get to know each other again if you worked together."

Brooke was skeptical. "I don't know. There's a real sore spot there when it comes to my having anything to do with you, Nick. I don't know if she could handle it. Besides, she already works at city hall and goes to school."

"Well," Nick said, "it was just a thought. School's out next week for spring break, and she could help at night and during regular school hours. We need all the help we can get." He released a deep breath, and she could hear the self-deprecation in his tone. "Of course, after my diplomacy at the meeting tonight, we might not have jobs ourselves by the end of the week."

Brooke's expression softened, though he wasn't there to see it. She wished she could be with him to convince him that he hadn't done anything wrong. "Don't be so hard on yourself, Nick. You said what needed to be said. Mrs. Hemphill was going to jump on us, anyway. If the chuckles I heard were any indication, I'd say a few of the people there wanted to give you a trophy."

"How come you always know how to make me feel better? My own mother can't even do that."

"Oh, but that's not a mother's job," Brooke teased. "Her job is to make you feel guilty and paranoid...."

Nick was silent and she wondered if she'd hit closer to home than she knew.

"And what's your job?" he asked after a moment.

"To be your friend," she said without hesitation. She was quiet for a moment, weighing her words, wondering if she dared go on. The memory of the night before washed over her, when he'd held her and kissed her with passion so intense that she knew he felt more for her, as well. But then he had sent her away. She hadn't yet gotten over the disappointment, but the gesture had only made her feel more certain that what she felt for Nick was more than chemistry, more than ancient history. And for some reason the gossip of others didn't matter so much anymore. Yes, she thought! Maybe it was time they crossed over the boundaries of friendship.

"And maybe..." she whispered, frightened at the emotions leading her into naked honesty.

"Maybe what?" he asked.

"Maybe a little more," she whispered.

WHAT MORE? The question plagued Nick late into the night, long after he should have been asleep. What more did she want to be? His confidante? *His lover?*

More troubling, though, was the counter question, shooting at him from the back of his heart. What if she didn't want those things?

"If you can'ta have whata you want, Nicky, then want whata you have." His grandfather's old saw flew through his mind on the wings of a memory, and he pictured the old, thin-haired man with his back curved from slumping over the shoes on his work bench. He vividly remembered the first time he'd said the words to him, when Nick had been ten or eleven, mourning the fact that his parents wouldn't send him to the art camp in southern Florida he'd read about.

"But it isn't fair," he'd mumbled, kicking at a rock in his grandpa's front yard. "I've saved the money myself, and it's just for two weeks. What do they care?"

"They care!" his grandfather had shouted, slapping his hands together. "And they won't let you go and that'sa that." Nick remembered how surprised he'd been when his grandfather had thrust his sketchpad and watercolor set at him, defying the boy to complain. "So stop moping and make the best of what you have! It won't get any better unless you make it so."

He had picked up the pieces of his spirit, dusted them off and angrily lunged into a painting that had set the tone for those he had done for the rest of his career. Emotions had emerged in blacks, blues and browns, for he'd discovered early it was those dark shades that revealed the mysteries in his soul.

Only, now the color he saw foremost in his mind, the color he felt most inclined to mix on his palette, was the emerald-green color of Brooke Martin's eyes. If she never loved him, if she never wanted him, if she never needed him, he would always have her engraved on his soul like templates from which everything else he painted was inspired. Would his grandfather have been so earnest in that advice, to accept what he could not change, if he had even once seen Brooke's smile?

Wearily Nick gave up on the idea of sleep, got out of bed, pulled on a pair of gym shorts and went out to the garage, where he kept a can of the special car wax he had ordered for the Duesenberg. Mechanically, methodically, as if ministering to someone he loved, he began to apply the wax in small, gentle circles.

Nick's mind drifted back to the night before, when he had held Brooke in his arms and felt her response to his kiss. She had melted, just as she had ten years earlier. She had touched his face, measuring the angles and textures with the tips of her fingers. She had made him feel so...hungry.

Maybe he had been crazy to stop things when he had, he told himself now. But in his heart, he had known how important it was to keep himself from pulling her under before she was entirely ready. Now that she'd had time to think, did she still want to be pulled under? Or was his imagination just convincing him so?

Hope welled up in his heart as he stroked the wax off his car with the firm but gentle hand of a lover. Hope that, perhaps, they would finally have a chance. Hope that he wouldn't have to keep being the noble one. Hope that, in this case, his grandfather's advice didn't apply.

ROXY'S DOOR WAS OPEN when Brooke went back to her room, and she saw her sister sitting at her desk in a long, pink gown with her bare feet crossed on the floor, examining a paper under the dim light of her lamp.

"Studying?" Brooke asked quietly.

Roxy looked up. "No, I was just going over my savings account," she said. "I thought I'd have more money saved by now."

Brooke went into the room and sat down on the bed. "What are you saving for?"

"My escape," Roxy whispered. She closed her bankbook, and swiveled around on her chair to face her sister. There was no hostility in her voice or her expression . . . no belligerence in her manner. Only a gentle sadness that touched Brooke's heart.

"Escape from what, Roxy?" Brooke asked. "Me?"

"No," her sister said. She looked down at her gown, picking at a white dot on the fabric. "From this town. From the people here."

A faint note of alarm rang out in Brooke's head. "Are you planning to get married or something?" she asked.

Roxy laughed aloud, but there was no mirth in her eyes. "No, I don't plan to get married. I just want to leave town when I graduate. Like you did. I want a chance to be somebody . . . different."

Brooke pulled her feet up onto the bed and gazed at her sister, trying to view her as a grown woman, rather than as the little sister she wanted so desperately to protect. "I like who you are already," she said.

Roxy's smile was genuine as she met her sister's eyes. "But you don't know me that well, do you?"

Brooke stood up and ambled to the desk. She leaned a hip against it and faced Roxy. Roxy's face looked so mature for her age, Brooke thought, and she wondered what went on behind those beautiful, guarded amber eyes. "I'd like to fix that," she said.

Roxy looked away. Brooke's honesty made the moment more awkward.

"Listen, I don't know if you're interested at all, but Nick and I need to hire some people to help us at the museum. If you really want to make some more money, you could work there whenever you could spare the time."

Roxy looked up at her, trepidation darkening her eyes. "With you and Nick?" she asked skeptically. "I do need the money. But I don't know, Brooke. I'm not real good at hiding the way I feel."

Brooke reached for a curl of Roxy's soft hair and tugged lightly on it. "That's okay," she whispered. She laughed gently and shrugged. "We couldn't have paid you for a while, anyway. At least not until our budget is approved. It probably wasn't a good idea."

Roxy regarded the bankbook on her desk as an unreadable expression passed across her face. After a moment she glanced back up at Brooke. "What would I have to do?" she asked tentatively.

"Just simple things, like tracing the patterns, numbering them, cutting them... That way Nick and I can concentrate on the more technical work."

Roxy sat back in her chair and ran her hand through the roots of her hair. "You know, spring break is all next week. I have to work at City Hall for a few hours a day, but I could still put in a lot of time at the museum."

A smile began in Brooke's eyes and traveled to her lips. "Are you saying you want the job?"

"I guess," Roxy said. "When do I start?"

"We could use you tomorrow," Brooke said carefully, "if you don't mind working on Saturday."

Roxy nodded. "Just wake me up, and I'll go with you."

Brooke set her hand on Roxy's shoulder and wished she were close enough to her sister to lean over and kiss her. But it was too soon for that. She would take things one step at a time. "I'll get you up at seven. Wear something you won't mind getting dirty."

She started toward the door, then turned back. "And Roxy," she said. "About Nick...you'll like him if you give him a chance. Really, you will."

Roxy's gaze fell to the floor, so Brooke left her alone, telling herself she could only expect one miracle at a time.

NICK WAS AT THE MUSEUM at eight o'clock the next morning, fatigued from lack of sleep, but anxious to see Brooke and probe her for the "more" she had alluded to on the telephone last night. He had finished waxing his car, changed the oil and conditioned the leather upholstery before he'd finally gone inside and surrendered to sleep. But even in slumber he had felt the subtle anticipation of tomorrow. And now tomorrow was today. He couldn't wait to get her alone.

He heard the door open and close and the sound of rubber-soled sneakers across the museum's dusty, cluttered floor. But it wasn't Brooke who appeared at the work-room door.

"Hey, Picasso."

Nick tried not to look disappointed at the sight of his nephew leaning in his doorway, his tall frame slightly slumped in dejection. That smile that he had grown accustomed to seeing was conspicuously absent, and Sonny looked as if he'd gotten about as much sleep as Nick had last night.

"Hey, Sonny. You okay?"

"Yeah," Sonny said, stepping into the room and sliding his hands into the pockets of his black jeans. "Look man, I'm really sorry about last night. Ma told me about them ambushing you."

Nick sat on a stool and leaned back against the worktable, regarding his nephew with grim eyes. "They're worried about you." He uttered a gentle, self-deprecating laugh. "They're afraid you'll turn out like me or something."

"There are worse things I could do," Sonny said. He looked down at the floor, and Nick noted the deep frown was beginning to cut permanent lines in the boy's forehead, making him appear much older than his years. "What's so wrong with it, Nick? What do they care?"

"It's the work ethic," Nick tried to explain. "They honestly can't respect anyone who doesn't break his back all day to make a living."

"But you work harder than anybody I know," Sonny said. "I've never been to your house that you weren't deep in the middle of some project. And here, on these windows, you've been at it day and night. What do they want? Blood?"

Nick grinned. "Maybe a little."

Sonny went to the worktable, picked up a mat knife, turned it over in his hands. "Well, I'm sick of them telling me what I'm gonna do with my life," he said. "I think I want to go to college and study art. I think I want to see if I can do anything with it.''

Nick rubbed his forehead, wishing his encouragement of Sonny didn't mean direct defiance of his family. How would his grandfather have handled this? he asked himself. He searched his memory for his grandfather's sympathetic words of support peppered with caution.

"What do I know?" he'd said once as he hammered on the heel of a shoe he was repairing. *"I'll tell you what I know. I know that life'sa too short to spend doing what other people say. God don't dole out talents he don't expecta you to use."*

He had held up the shoe he'd been working on, as if it keenly illustrated the point he was making. *"If I'd had a talent like yours, I wouldn't be in here pulling on leather, I'll tell you that."*

"What would you have done, Grandpa?" Nick had asked with amusement.

His grandpa's eyes had lit up like the candles at St. Theresa's. *"I'd have been a race car driver,"* he'd exclaimed.

Now, a grin tugged at Nick's lips as he looked at his nephew. "You know, if you go with your gut, there are going to be a lot of fights to come. Take it from me, the family may never understand. And that hurts, Sonny. Sometimes even I wonder if it's worth it."

"But that's just it," Sonny said, setting down the knife and balling one hand into a fist. "It's not like it's something I can just turn off. I want it bad."

Nick cocked a one-sided grin and turned his hands palm up. "What can I say?" he asked. "I've been there. I'm still there. You happen to come from a long line of dreamers."

"Dreamers?" Sonny asked, confused.

Nick smiled and rubbed the indention just above his lips with an idle finger. "I was just thinking of grandpa," he said.

"The one who kept getting arrested for reckless driving?" Sonny asked.

Nick chuckled in spite of himself. "Yep. He had a record as long as my arm." He looked up at Sonny's bewildered face, and decided that he owed his nephew exactly what his grandfather had offered him. Courage. Hope. And even permission if he needed it. "It's your life, Sonny," he said. "You're the only one who can live it."

"Then will you let me keep working here, helping you guys out? Will you teach me when you have time?"

Nick regarded Sonny, wondering if his grandfather had risked the wrath of his family to give him the wings he needed. His family would see helping Sonny as the ultimate betrayal, the corruption of an innocent mind. But he'd been accused of worse things, he supposed. "I don't know, Sonny. Anna's my sister."

"She's my mother!" Sonny said, his face red. "But she doesn't understand! No one does, except you. I'm counting on you, man. I'm nineteen years old. When do I get to decide what I want to do with my life?"

Nick turned back to the table, saw all the work that still needed to be done. He needed Sonny's talent and passion, and Sonny could learn a lot about precision and detail from working with him and Brooke.

"You're going to put us through this all over again, aren't you?"

His sister's words echoed in his mind, and he weighed the pain they evoked against the plea he saw in his nephew's eyes. "Are you sure you're ready for this?" he asked.

"I've never been more sure of anything," Sonny said. "You won't regret it, Nick."

Nick laughed dryly and admitted that if he did have regrets, they'd be at home in his heart. "All right, Sonny," he said with a sigh that seemed to pull some life out of him. "We'll do it your way."

The echo of the door sounded throughout the museum, and Nick knew that Brooke had arrived. His heart sank in disappointment, for he wouldn't get that chance to talk to her alone. Not right away, anyway.

For a moment, as his heart thudded in anticipation, he realized that those regrets about hiring Sonny were blossoming even sooner than he'd expected.

CHAPTER TEN

BROOKE RECOGNIZED Roxy's tension the moment she led her into the museum, over the electrical cords and around idle equipment used in the renovation. Because it was Saturday, the construction crews were off, and she breathed a sigh of relief that she would be able to break Roxy in with relative peace and quiet, and that they wouldn't have to endure catcalls every few steps.

"You've been working around all this?" Roxy asked.

Brooke looked over her shoulder. Her sister looked fifteen today, she thought, with her hair pulled back in a ponytail, wearing an old pair of jeans with a hole in one knee and a Hayden High School Tigers football jersey. "Yeah. You should see it on weekdays. The noise level is so high you can hardly hear yourself think, and you can't walk through here without fearing for your life. The construction workers act like prison inmates who haven't seen a woman in years." She tossed a half smile over her shoulder. "I'm starting to get used to it, though. Our workroom is back through there."

Roxy hesitated and started to hang back. She crossed her arms, drawing her shoulders up defensively. Was she nervous about meeting Nick? Brooke wondered. Or was it just her distaste for him that was already making her feel uncomfortable?

Slowly, because Roxy seemed to lag behind, she led her down the dark corridor to the workroom. Before she reached it, Brooke could see that the lights were on. She heard Nick's voice, then another's. Sonny? she wondered. Maybe that was good, she thought. Maybe his being there might help Roxy to feel more at ease.

She stepped into the doorway, waiting for Roxy to catch up, and saw Nick slumped in his chair with his feet propped on the table and Sonny, leaning back against the wall across the room.

"Hi."

Her eyes collided with Nick's, pensive and anticipating, and she felt a rush of heat through her veins. Had she really told him last night that she wanted them to be more than friends? Was that thought playing through his mind now, as it was through hers?

Suddenly Nick's eyes shifted to Roxy behind her, and she saw him drop his feet and sit upright. "Hi."

"Roxy has decided to work for us part-time," Brooke said. "She needed some extra money, and I told her how badly we needed help."

Nick came to his feet, offering her sister a smile that would have charmed her right down to her toes if she hadn't already erected such strong barriers. "Hi, Roxy," he said. "I'm Nick."

"I know." The words were clipped and delivered in a way that made it clear she wasn't interested in friendship.

Nick looked amused when he shot a glance at Brooke. He turned back to Roxy and gestured toward Sonny. "This is my nephew, Sonny Castori. He's going to be helping out here some, too."

Roxy cleared her throat and tried to smile cordially at the young man in the black T-shirt. "Hi."

The weary clouds passed out of Sonny's eyes, and he brightened at the sight of the small blond standing at the door. "Hey, I remember you," he said. "You went to Hayden High, didn't you?"

"Still do," Roxy said.

Sonny grinned and slid his hands into his back pockets, and took a cocky step toward her. "Yeah. I remember seeing you in Ole Lady Hannah's class a couple years ago. I was in the class across the courtyard. You sat by the window."

The awkward smile tugging on Roxy's lips was difficult to miss, but it was evident she struggled to look unaffected. "I don't remember you," she said.

Sonny shrugged and ruffled his dark mop of hair. "Yeah, so what else is new? I have one of those faces that's real easy to forget."

Roxy allowed her smile to spread, and as if to distract herself from her grudging interest in Sonny she stepped over to the worktable, perusing the tools and patterns lying there. Behind her, Nick gave Brooke a wink that said he knew it would work out with Roxy, if Sonny had anything to do with it.

Brooke wasn't convinced, however, and decided that Nick should be warned of Roxy's reluctance. She set down the case she was carrying on the table. "Before we get started," she said, looking pointedly at Nick, "I need some help getting some things out of my trunk."

Sonny started for the door, but Nick stopped him a little too obviously. "I'll go," he said. "Sonny, why don't you just show Roxy where everything is for now? We'll be right back."

Roxy turned and looked at Nick, then at Brooke. She dropped her gaze to the floor, as if she knew without a doubt that Nick had more on his mind than getting anything out of Brooke's car.

Oblivious to Roxy's disapproving glare, Nick took Brooke's arm and escorted her back out into the corridor. She looked so beautiful today, he thought, with only a plain white T-shirt that accented her tan, and a pair of baggy muslin trousers in army green. Her usual delicate gold chains hung around her neck and dipped down her chest, and her gold earrings hung long and loose like the unbound strings of her hair. "So you talked her into it, huh?" he asked quietly as they walked.

"Yes," Brooke whispered. "But she's a little skeptical about it working out. She isn't exactly crazy about you, you know. She believes everything she's ever heard about us."

Nick caught her hand as they reached his office, and without warning, pulled Brooke inside. He pushed her gently against the wall, trapping her with a hand over either side of her head. Brooke's breath grew short and shaky, and she swallowed hard and looked up into the smoky black eyes trapping her in their sweet prison. "What does she believe?" he whispered, his face teasingly close to hers. He smelled of mint and soap, and the misty warmth of his breath made her mouth go dry.

"That...that you and I are..."

"More than friends?" he whispered. His gaze dropped to her lips, and she slid her tongue across them.

"Nick..."

"You said that to me last night," Nick said, his voice husky, "and I couldn't sleep for the rest of the night. I wanted to be alone with you today. I wanted to talk to you..." He nuzzled his face into her hair, and she closed her eyes and breathed in a sweet, traitorous breath. "You smell so good..." he whispered.

She felt her breath expelling in a shaky susurration, and wished with all her heart that they could be alone...that she could hold him.... "Nick, things are still real touchy with her," she said weakly. "We have to be careful when she's here."

"When can we stop being careful?" he asked.

Her gaze fell to his lips, and she saw the light glistening in them. A secret burning welled from deep inside her... urgently telling her that the wait wouldn't be easy. "Later," she whispered. "We'll have time later."

"Oh, Brooke," he whispered. "Later is such a long time." As if he couldn't stand the wait, Nick's mouth descended slowly, until at last it made sweet contact with her bottom lip, full and wet and aching for his taste. She drew in a sharp breath as his tongue swept across it. His teeth closed gently over her mouth and he suckled with a soft pressure that made her close her eyes and rise up on her toes. His hands moved to her face, framing it like an exquisite painting, moving it slowly as his mouth moved to her top lip. Trembling, she reached out to grab the sides of his shirt and pulled him closer against her.

His hunger grew more voracious as she ambushed the soft, slippery wetness. His tongue flirted inside the warm recess of her mouth, teased, retreated, then courted hers until he robbed her of her very breath, but returned it to her sweetened with his own. With that kiss he altered her will and erased the shadows that stood between them.

But suddenly, like an alarm waking one from the stupor of a dream, Brooke heard Roxy's and Sonny's voices from the room at the end of the hall, reminding them that they weren't alone.

They broke apart as their frustrated sighs filled the air. "Later," he whispered in a shaky voice.

"Later," she agreed. Then, before either of them forgot the solid reasons to stay apart, he propelled her back toward the workroom.

THE FOUR OF THEM worked diligently for hours, Nick and Brooke enlarging sketches and numbering them to keep the pattern pieces from getting lost, and Sonny and Roxy tracing pictures through sheets of carbon so that there would be three precise copies of each: the cartoon, the paper pattern and the working drawing.

Although Roxy occasionally exchanged a quip with Sonny, she was quiet for the most part, hardly speaking to Nick at all. Her silence added another level of tension to the already charged atmosphere, and Nick saw the way she alienated not just him, but Brooke, as well. It was nearing lunchtime, when Brooke had left the room to retrieve something from Nick's office and Sonny had gone to run an errand, that Nick found himself alone with Roxy.

"You're doing great," he said, looking over her shoulder at the drawing she'd just finished tracing. "I'm glad you decided to help us out."

"Thanks."

Undaunted by her brevity, Nick pulled up a stool and sat down next to her. "Are you interested in art, too?" he asked.

Roxy's face pinkened, but she didn't look at him. "No. The art teachers at school now aren't nearly as interesting as they were when Brooke was there."

Nick accepted the verbal dart with a lift of his brows. "Ouch."

Roxy didn't find his response amusing. Still not looking at him, she continued to work.

Nick sighed and glanced toward the door, wishing he could break through the defenses of this complicated young woman who meant so much to Brooke.

"Look, Roxy," he began, setting his hands on his thighs and leaning toward her. "I know you don't like me, and there's no law that says you have to. But I wish you'd give

Brooke a little slack. She's been pretty torn up over the way things have been going with you lately.''

Roxy's lips tightened as she began retracing the lines she'd already done. "I don't know what you're talking about."

"Your sister," Nick persisted, not fooled by her feigned concentration. "Roxy, if I had never been in the picture, you'd still see her as the sweet, sensitive, caring person you know she is. You'd really like her if you gave her a chance."

For the first time since she'd walked into the room, Roxy looked at him fully. "Funny. She told me the same thing about you."

They heard footsteps approaching the room, and Roxy turned back to her work station. Nick studied her for a moment, searching for a clue to unlock her bitter resentment. But she was too tightly barricaded, he decided.

Brooke came back into the room, carrying a stack of fresh paper. She hesitated when she saw Nick sitting beside her sister. "It's getting late," she said, putting the paper on the table and surveying both their faces for a hint as to what had transpired while she was gone. "I think I'll take Roxy to lunch. We don't want her to starve to death on her first day here."

Roxy pretended to be too engrossed in her work to eat. "It's okay," she mumbled.

"I want to," Brooke said, feigning brightness, despite the clouds hanging over the room. She turned back to Nick. "Can you do without us for an hour?"

"I'll manage," he said. "You go ahead."

Nick watched as Roxy reluctantly put up her tools and followed Brooke from the room. He wondered if he and Brooke had really made any progress after all. Somehow he felt as if he'd taken three steps back for every two he took forward.

"More than friends..."

How the hell could they be that, he asked himself with frustration, if they were hardly ever alone and had the shadows and whispers of a million other people surround them when they were? He leaned over the table and braced his chin with the heels of his hands. *Damn.* He was losing it. His mother was right. He *was* getting obsessed with her, just as he had when she'd been eighteen. He couldn't get her scent out of his mind. Couldn't get her taste off his lips. Couldn't get her memory out of his heart.

And they could be more than friends, if he could just get around her sister, his nephew, her parents, his family and the whole cursed town. If he could just have her alone for a little while.

The idea preyed on his mind until he lost the concentration he needed to reproduce the cartoons correctly. Finally he decided that if he couldn't fill one hunger, he'd fill another of a different kind.

He wondered if there was a long line at McDonalds this time of day.

"SONNY SEEMS TO LIKE YOU," Brooke told Roxy as they sat in the popular little café, Back Street Deli, which drew people from miles around for its savory cheeseburgers. "What do you think?"

Roxy moved the uneaten potato chips around her plate with an idle finger. "I hope you don't plan to try to push us together," she said. "The last thing I need right now is another man in my life."

The weary way she spoke, as if she were a thirty-five-year-old divorcée who'd traveled the fast lane, disturbed Brooke. Roxy was too young to be so bitter. "I don't plan to do anything like that," she said. "But you've got to admit he's cute."

"If you like his type," Roxy said, indifferently. She pushed her half-eaten burger away, and set down her wadded napkin.

Brooke cleared her throat and tried once again to find a subject they could share. "So, do you like the work?"

Roxy nodded. "It beats filing at city hall. All the hassles..."

"You could quit and work for us full-time," Brooke said. "You said you were leaving town after you graduated, anyway. It isn't like you'd be giving up anything long-term."

Roxy studied the wood grain on the table, feeling the texture of the lines with her fingertips. "I can't really count on your budget coming through, can I?" she asked. "What happens if I quit my job, and then Mrs. Hemphill pulls the rug out from under you? That's her favorite pastime, you know."

Brooke didn't have an argument for that. "Well, maybe you can think about it after the budget's approved."

Roxy nodded noncommittally.

Brooke broke a French fry in half, nibbling on it absently. "It hasn't been so hard today, has it?" she went on. "Working with Nick, I mean?"

Roxy scanned the room idly, as if bored by the conversation. "I guess it's just like he told me this morning. There's no law that says I have to like him."

Brooke set her French fry down and knitted her brows together. "He told you that?"

"Yeah," Roxy said, bringing her jaded gold eyes back to her sister. "He thought it was more important that I like you."

"Well," Brooke said. "I suppose that's true." She laced her hands together on the table, still trying to imagine the conversation. Had Roxy sniped at Nick when she'd left the room? Had Nick made Roxy angry? A heaviness settled over her at the idea that her two favorite people might have the capacity to hurt each other.

She watched her sister, desperate to find the words that could break the ice between them. Last night she had almost felt close to Roxy. They had met each other halfway, to bridge the gap between them, and when Roxy had accepted the job Brooke offered, Brooke had embraced a false hope that their relationship was healing. But now Roxy's exposure to Nick seemed to have made her close down yet again.

"Are you—?"

"Do you—?"

Their words came out simultaneously, and they each stopped, yielding to the other.

Feeling the renewed awkwardness between them, Brooke tried again. "Are you ready to go back?" she asked quietly.

Roxy came to her feet. "I was going to ask the same."

Brooke left a tip on the table and followed her sister to the cash register near the door. She was busy digging through her bag for her credit card when she heard, "Hi, Rox. How's it goin'?"

Brooke looked up to see the man she had seen with her sister in the dark office at City Hall last week, standing with his arm around a woman who looked to be at least five months pregnant.

Roxy's face turned a startling shade of crimson as she shot a guilty look Brooke's way. "Hi. I'm . . . I'm fine . . ."

Knowing that her thoughts flashed across her face like the messages of a neon sign, Brooke forcefully kept her jaw from going slack.

She glanced too conspicuously at the woman's left hand and saw a wedding ring sparkling there. On his hand was a matching band, confirming that the two were married to each other.

"Bill, the hostess is waiting at our table," the woman said quietly, tugging on his sleeve.

A wave of dizziness swept over Brooke, and she gaped at them as they moved past her and Roxy. Her eyes clashed with Roxy's in harsh reprobation. Incipient tears glistened in her sister's eyes, and Brooke wondered if they were tears of shame or grief.

Mechanically she paid the bill with her credit card, knowing that the cashier could have charged her three hundred dollars for a cheeseburger, and she would have signed for it without a thought. All that mattered at the moment was that her little sister was involved with a married man. All that mattered was that Roxy was straddling the edge of a scandal, one that would ruin her life just as Brooke's had been ruined.

Neither said a word as they got into the car. Quietly, but on the verge of tears, she pulled the car out of its parking space, waited for a break in the traffic, then headed for the museum a few miles away.

"It's not what you think." Roxy's voice was weak.

"Oh?" Brooke asked, her voice restrained. "What do I think?"

One tear spilled over Roxy's lashes and she lifted a shaky hand to wipe it away. "I don't know," she whispered.

"I'll tell you what I think," Brooke said, unable to stop herself. "I think you're having an affair with a married man. And despite how that infuriates and upsets me, it does explain a few things. Like why you have to meet in dark offices at night, and why he has sudden 'emergencies' come up that force him into leaving you stranded in sleazy bars." She slammed to a stop at a red light, and sat seething until it changed color.

Roxy sat like a cold, rigid statue in the seat next to her, holding in whatever feelings she had.

"His wife is *pregnant!*" Brooke railed on, growing angrier the longer Roxy sat quiet. "Don't you even care about that? Doesn't that bother you at all?"

"Don't you dare judge me," Roxy said through her teeth, the pitch of her voice rising with every word, "when you were sleeping with your art teacher at my age! Maybe it runs in the family, Brooke. Maybe those promiscuous genes just run in our family!"

Brooke screeched into the parking lot, killed the engine and sat smoldering for just a moment before she could make herself get out. "You can't blame this on me or your godforsaken genes," she said. "This is something that *you* are going to be accountable for, Roxy. No one else. I want you to think about that."

"Think about it?" Roxy cried. "Do you think I've thought about anything else in the past few weeks?"

Brooke dropped her face into her hands and tried to stop the tears beginning to roll down her cheeks. She smeared them away with a clammy hand and inhaled a shallow breath. "You're going to get hurt, Roxy," she said. "It isn't worth it."

Roxy shook her head and opened her car door. "I can't talk to you about this," she said. "There is no way you would ever understand."

And before Brooke could stop her, Roxy had bolted out of the car and disappeared into the museum.

NICK AND SONNY WERE in the workroom when Roxy came in alone, her eyes bloodshot and puffy.

Sonny was on the floor, tying one of his sneakers. "Hey, beautiful," he said fliply, then, seeing her fragile expression, he came to his feet. His face mirrored her stricken expression. "What's wrong?"

"Excuse me." Roxy pushed past him to the table. "I have work to do."

"Okay," Sonny said, shooting a "What's with her?" look to Nick. "Sure."

Nick went to the door and looked up the hallway for Brooke, then turned back to Roxy, a poignant frown marking his brows. "Where's Brooke?"

"Coming, I guess," Roxy said.

Nick stood still for a moment, evaluating Roxy's condition and finally coming to the conclusion that Brooke was probably upset as well. "I'll be right back," he said quietly and left the room.

Moments later he found Brooke still sitting in her car, slumped over her steering wheel, weeping into the square of her arms. His heart collapsed, and opening her door, he pulled her into his embrace. "Come on," he coaxed quietly. "It's hot out here. Let's go in. I want you to tell me what happened."

Brooke wilted in his arms, allowing his strength to wrap her in a cocoon of security, of warmth, but it didn't completely chase away the frosty places inside her. "I...can't."

"Yes, you can," he whispered. He drew her against him and urged her out of the car, holding her close as they walked inside. Quietly he pulled her into his office and shut the door behind them. He set her down in a chair and took the one opposite her. Leaning toward her, he stroked her hair back from her damp cheek and dried her tears beneath her eyes with the pad of his thumb. "Now, what happened?"

Brooke saw that the pain in his own eyes was as great as that in hers. "I met Roxy's boyfriend," she whispered. "Her married boyfriend...and his pregnant wife."

Nick moaned, sat back in his chair and closed his eyes.

Brooke stood up and walked to a bookshelf behind his desk, resting her fist on one shelf. "What is she trying to do? Create her own scandal? Ruin her life?"

Nick looked up at her, struggling for the answers she so sorely needed. "Maybe it's not what you think," he ventured. "Maybe there's not really anything going on. I've been watching her today, and she doesn't seem like the home-wrecker type. She's withdrawn, and...almost shy. Sonny keeps trying to flirt with her, and she honestly doesn't seem to know how to respond to it. Not like someone who's had all that much experience with men."

"Oh, Nick," Brooke cried, spinning around. "She practically admitted it. Said we both had promiscuity in our genes! She thinks she's following in my footsteps!"

"Ah, so that's it." Nick took her hand and pulled her closer. "So it's time to turn the tables and make you out to be the one who has to defend herself, huh? Sort of takes the focus off her, doesn't it?"

"That's not what she's doing!" Brooke said. "She really sees me that way!"

"Then she doesn't see you at all," he returned. Her sobs crested again, and he rose up and held her against him.

Brooke laid her forehead against his collarbone and flattened her hands over his chest. His arms tightened around her, but it felt too good. Too right. Too comfortable.

She broke away from him and stumbled back. "We've got to go back in there," she whispered, wiping her eyes on her sleeve. "They'll think we're—"

"Brooke, stop worrying what they think!"

"I can't!" she shouted. "Don't you see? If she thinks we're involved now, it'll confirm that we were having an affair before. Somehow that's how she justifies what she's doing now. You don't understand what it's like having the people you love the most think the worst possible things about you!''

"Don't I?" Nick asked, his dark face reddening with the futility of this constant fight. "Don't you think I've had my share of defending to do? Just last night, my own mother told me that you were still married under God's eyes, and accused me of having some sort of perverted obsession with you!''

Brooke shook her head, unable to deal with the tornado of emotions. She opened the door and started over the threshold. "I have work to do," she muttered. "I can't talk about this—''

Nick grabbed her arm, his grip rough and unyielding. "Brooke, when are you going to realize that no one blamed you!" he said, lowering his volume, though he couldn't tame the intensity in his words. "It was me. I was the villain. I was the one who committed the worst crime a teacher can commit.''

Brooke stopped and looked up at him, fathomless pain and sorrow coloring her eyes. "What crime?"

Nick dropped her arm, his own fatigue making his emotions shine like raw onyx in his eyes. "My crime was falling in love with my student," he said.

Assaulted by the charged, belated confession that could have changed so much so many years ago, Brooke reeled back into the hall. It was then that she saw Roxy from the corner of her eye, standing motionless only a few feet up the hall.

And she knew that her sister had heard the confession, as well.

CHAPTER ELEVEN

BROOKE TRIED TO KEEP her frayed emotions in check for the rest of the day, but they were too sharp and jagged, too fresh, too extreme. Pain and anger swirled through her head like a drug as she worked in a solitary corner of the room, but in its wake came the sweet, burning sting of love. Nick had loved her when she was in high school, and somehow that made everything look different. The scandal wasn't nearly so debilitating when she realized there was a genuine feeling behind their attraction. And now she wondered if he still cared....

Roxy didn't say a word the rest of the afternoon, but Brooke couldn't ignore the massive amount of work she produced, with precision and diligence. Even Sonny was a little too quiet, and when Nick finally suggested that they quit working at sundown rather than continuing into the night, Brooke was relieved.

The sisters drove home in silence, and as they pulled into the driveway of their parents' house, Brooke looked over at Roxy, pale and small and looking as though a strong wind could shatter her into a million pieces. She cut off her engine, but made no move to get out. "Look, Roxy, I know you heard what Nick said today." Her tone was quiet, hesitant. "I want you to know that it's the first I've heard of it, too. But it doesn't change anything. No matter how I felt about him or he felt about me, we didn't do anything wrong back then."

"And I haven't done anything wrong, either," Roxy whispered, staring dully out the window toward the house.

Brooke wet her lips, tried to keep her voice even, despite the anger reviving inside her. "You've gotten involved with a married man."

She saw Roxy's bottom lip quivering and knew she was about to cry again. "You don't know anything about it."

Brooke dropped her forehead on the steering wheel for a moment, counting out her breaths until she could speak without reproach. "Then tell me," Brooke pleaded. "Don't make me guess. Do you love him? Is that it?"

Roxy uttered a harsh, cold laugh that only made her seem more distraught. "Love has nothing to do with it."

Brooke focused her astonished eyes on her sister, desperate to view the world as Roxy did just long enough to understand. "Then what is it?"

"It's power," Roxy said, meeting Brooke's eyes directly, injecting all her energy into every word she uttered. "That's what it's all about. And if you can feel better about what happened to you in high school by believing that Nick Marcello was in love with you, fine. But the plain simple truth is that he had power over you, and he used it. That's what men do best."

Brooke gaped at her sister, fresh, futile tears in her eyes. "How did you get so bitter, and so stoic?" Brooke asked on an incredulous whisper. "Where did you get such a distorted view of things?"

"From watching my big sister," Roxy said simply. Then, leaving Brooke to deal with that pronouncement alone, Roxy got out of the car and went inside.

Paralyzed by despair, Brooke sat in the car for a moment, staring toward the house with eyes as lusterless as twilight. Her parents were inside, no doubt, brimming with a million questions about Roxy's first day at the museum, full of a million unspoken reservations about both of their daughters working with Nick. She couldn't face it tonight, she thought, not when Roxy's words had scraped deeper into already-bleeding wounds.

Brooke cranked her car and backed out of the driveway, not certain where she would go. After a while she found herself cutting back through the darkness, toward the museum, the only place she knew of where she could be alone.

Since the side door could only be unlocked with Nick's key, she parked on the street and went to the front door to use her own. The door opened and closed with an echoing thud, and she smelled the familiar scent of sawdust and paint, of dust and Spackle.

Leaving the large room dark, Brooke made her way to the middle of it and sat down on a drop cloth crumpled there, crossed her legs and peered up at the boarded places where her windows would go when they were finished. Would she and Nick really be able to capture the true stages of life? she asked herself. Would they really be able to show the misery, the deceit, the lies? Would they really be able to reveal the truth behind the faces they portrayed there?

But truth was such an abstract term, she thought miserably, rubbing her eyes and realizing that she had cried every trace of makeup off long ago. Roxy's truth was that there was no such thing as love—only power. But love was what gave one power. And that was Brooke's own truth.

She heard a noise through the darkness and gasped. Swinging around, she saw Nick standing in the doorway, enshrouded in shadows and watching her with the gentlest look she'd ever seen on his face.

"I thought you had gone home," she said, her voice echoing in the large room.

He shook his head. "No. I thought I'd stay awhile."

Brooke looked down at the drop cloth beneath her. "I had another round with Roxy," she said, "so I couldn't face going home tonight. I just needed to think."

Nick went to the wall and turned on one dim light near Brooke. It cast her in a soft yellow circle against the darkness beyond, and made her face look more pale and more racked with despair.

Brooke squinted at the sudden burst of light and looked toward him, struggling to see the poignant look on his face. Her heart tripped out of time as he slowly stepped toward her, the light drawing him into its circle and blending over his face and chest, lending him the odd aura of a spirit coming to life at her heart's request. Slowly he stooped down in front of her, touched her cheek with a warm, strong hand that reminded her he was so much more than spirit. His fingers fondled the long earring dangling against her jaw, then settled on her soft earlobe, as velvety warm as her expression.

Her face tipped up to him, naked emotion glimmering in her eyes. "What you said today..." Her words were more breath than voice.

"That I fell in love with you ten years ago," he said. "It was true, Brooke."

Her heart swelled and shifted as it had when he'd said it earlier. "And I was in love with you," she whispered tragically. "When do we stop paying for that?"

Nick leaned closer to face her, set his bent legs beside her and lifted her hand at the wrist. Tenderly he pressed it against his own open hand, his fingers spreading against her smaller, more delicate ones. "Why don't we stop paying right now?" he asked.

Their fingers laced together in mutual surrender, and Brooke felt the power, the strength, even the restraint in his hand, just as she had felt it when she was eighteen. Her eyes fluttered to his, and she felt her heart melting and warming her whole body, just as his black pupils seemed to melt and darken the irises focused on her. He brought her hand to his mouth, slipped his fingers from between hers and closed his lips over one delicate fingertip, laving it with his tongue. She held her breath and swallowed hard as he tasted each one in turn, tickling her and igniting deep craving. Gently he moved his mouth to her palm, stroked his tongue across the center, sending a shiver fluttering down her spine. His face was rough with stubble, warm with desire, taut with anticipation as her fingertips quietly adored it.

He moved her hand down to his pounding chest, and his fingertips feathered up her bare arm, bringing with them compound sensations that culminated in a sweet shudder when his hand reached her neck. She turned her face and kissed his wrist, soft and sinewy and sprinkled with soft black hair.

His heart stumbled into triple beats at the gentle kiss, and she felt his chest pumping laboriously as his breathing grew heavier.

Like the gentle nudge of a soft breeze, he urged her closer. Their mouths connected with the strength of ten years' dreams, ten years' nightmares. She felt relief and release and at the same time, a burning new imprisonment from which only he could set her free. His tongue thrust against hers with unleashed ardor as a low moan issued from some chamber deep within him. She felt the moan in their kiss, just as she felt the slow, savoring movement of his hands over her ribs. A fever flushed her skin as he slipped her blouse out of the waistband of her pants and eased his hand under the jersey to the bare skin just below her breasts. His breath came in shallow susurrations as their tongues swirled and mated, retreated and teased. He nipped at her bottom lip, outlining it with his tongue.

"Oh, Brooke." The word came as an admonition, a whisper of defeat, a moan of frustration...and yet, surrender. His hands moved upward, pulling her shirt with them, until he grazed the silky cup of her bra. She felt him trembling as he found the front clasp and released it, then closed warm, calloused hands over the ivory mounds peaking in the center of his palms.

"I knew...you'd feel like this," he whispered against her lips. "I felt it in my mind a thousand times..."

She tried to speak, but found her throat full of words that couldn't be uttered. Her only expression came within their kiss, where the mating dance had begun ten long years before. She slipped her hand through his hair and felt tears coming to her eyes because its texture felt just as it had so long ago.

His hands slipped to her hips, and he coaxed her up to her knees. He pulled his own feet beneath him and rolled his lips away from her mouth, trailing wet candent paths down her chin, over her throat, past the shirt wadded over his wrists.

With a hunger that gripped her as well, he caught one rosebud nipple in his mouth. She gasped at the jolt of desire that passed through her as his mouth played games with her, the stubble on his jaw chafing her skin, making her arch back trusting him to cradle her completely. Slowly he worked the shirt over her arms and pulled it over her head. Her bra fell with it to the floor, leaving her breasts naked, except for the gold chains dressing them in bare extravagance, full and as aroused as the hot cradle of her womanhood.

His mouth claimed hers again as his fingers molded over the swells of flesh, teasing the wildfire raging through her.

With hands too unsteady to be graceful, she found the buttons of his shirt and began to release them. Slowly she peeled the shirt off his shoulders, baring the hard, tanned chest that she had sketched a million times in her mind, exposing the strength that she had felt wrapped in, every time she'd ever been in his presence, revealing the passion that breathed through and around him as his chest rose and fell. Her hands slid over him, through the dark hair sprinkled there, over the brown nipples hardening with her touch. Their kiss ended and Nick released a fevered sigh. Brooke nuzzled against his neck.

"You smell...so good..." she whispered. "I could breathe nothing but you..."

He moved her against him, her breasts teasing his own male nipples dauntlessly. She felt his arousal at the juncture of her legs, igniting an urgency in her core. "You can breathe me anytime you want," he said.

"I want you now," she whispered.

He pressed his forehead to hers, moving his lips forward to barely brush hers, maddening her with the tentativeness of his kiss. "I've wanted you for eleven years," he breathed. "Since long before you graduated. Do you know how many fantasies that is?"

"Yes," she said. "I know."

His lips met hers again, and his hands moved down the smooth skin of her ribs, to the waistband of her slacks. She inhaled his breath in gasps as he slipped his hands inside, cupping the warm flesh as he crushed her harder against his own rigid need. Drugged and dazed in the haze of his kiss, she felt her pants sliding down her hips, felt him lowering her to the drop cloth, felt his hands gliding down her legs.

He discarded her pants, then stood up enough to shed his own jeans. And suddenly his weight was upon her, anchoring her, bare skin against fevered flesh, sending tremors coursing through them both.

His mouth devoured hers again, following the rhythm of their bodies as he teased her, not within her, frustrating her to distraction, robbing the breath from her lungs.

Her hands moved down his back, to his lean hips, urging him to stop the misery, the hunger, the ache. When she was near the crest of frenzy, he moved his hands beneath her, lifting her up to meet him.

She cried out the moment he joined her and felt a painful rush of emotion and adrenaline that threatened to overwhelm her completely. His depth and fullness flustered her to mindlessness, wrapping her in bright-colored darkness, whirling her into full nothingness, launching her into the deepest heights.

He moved within her until she thought she would burst with the exquisite feelings taking her over, and when her world exploded into fragments all resembling him, she felt him shudder against her.

But like the windows, each had the power to reassemble the pieces into masterpieces of passion. For of all the work they had created together, this was the greatest work of all.

They lay together on the drop cloth for a long while, entangled in each other's love. She rested her head on his chest, heard his heart hammering beneath her ear. Her fingers cherished the hair defining his chest, and now and again she moved her mouth down to feel the precious texture she had dreamed of so many times.

"I have to ask you something," he whispered when his breath had returned to normal. "Something that's bothered me all these years."

"Ask," she said.

"Did you . . . did you love him?"

He didn't have to say Skip's name, for she knew instinctively whom he meant. "I tried to," she said.

Pain colored his face, and he closed his eyes. "Why?"

"Because," she said, rising up on one elbow. "I had lost so much, and so had you. You lost your job, Nick. And your reputation. And I thought you could never forgive me for that."

"Forgive you?" he repeated, stricken, his eyes opening. "Brooke, there was nothing to forgive. Getting fired from that nice, safe teaching job was probably the best thing that could have happened to me, because it forced me to rely on my talents. If I were still teaching, I may have never taken that plunge."

Her eyes rounded with disbelief, with profound hope. "You must have blamed me a little," she whispered. "You must have."

"What I blamed you for," he whispered, "was forgetting me so soon."

"Forgetting you?" she asked. "I *never* forgot you. Not in all these years."

"You got married," he said, his voice taking on a bitter tone, although his hands still worked gentle magic in her hair.

She sat up, the soft light shimmering over her bare skin and dancing like tiny specks of firelight on her gold chains. "But Nick, you never came after me. I had this fantasy that you would ride after me on your white horse, and that we could just be lovers without anyone caring. But I finally realized it was just a fantasy, because I never heard from you again. After a while, I decided that you probably saw me as some silly little schoolgirl with an embarrassing crush on her teacher."

Nick hiked himself up on his elbow, his eyes full of disbelief. "Brooke, didn't you feel how I reacted to you that night? Couldn't you see what I felt for you? Wasn't it apparent?"

Brooke released a breath and shook her head. "I thought I was kidding myself," she said. "And then Skip was there when I felt so lonely and so alienated from everything I loved and knew. I guess I thought marriage to him was an escape from all the turmoil . . . all the memories. I was wrong. . . ."

Nick sat up completely and took her by the shoulders, making her see the truth in his eyes. "Brooke, I didn't come after you, because I wanted the scandal to die down before I found you again. But I felt like the sculpture was my bond with you. *Infinity* meant everything you and I should have been . . . everything that I believed we *would* be." He took a deep breath, swallowed and steadied his voice. "But I wanted to give you the chance to find peace."

Tears filled Brooke's eyes. "The only peace I've ever had in my whole life," she whispered, "is when I've been with you."

Nick pulled her into his arms, and salty tears seeped into their kiss. His hands slid down her arms, savoring her skin, making her shiver with renewed desire. His mouth left hers and roved over her face, kissing away the tears. "I love you, Brooke," he whispered. "I loved you then, and I love you now."

Heat spread like a liquid fire through her bloodstream, and she felt his body coming to sweet life once again. "I love you," she breathed as he began to move against her.

Their lovemaking was slower this time, more full of feelings that couldn't be expressed solely through words or smiles or touches. It was the union of two souls that had been waiting for each other for too long. It was a quiet feeling, a soft feeling, a peaceful feeling.

And afterward, when Nick held her, it was with no demands or expectations, no conditions or accusations, only burning, life-giving love, and Brooke fell asleep in his arms.

THE TELEPHONE at the Martin's house rang at nine-thirty, but Roxy, who had been alone in her room for most of the evening, didn't answer it. She was busy turning the pages of the scrapbook she'd kept as a little girl, searching the joyful faces in the cracked and faded photographs for a sign of the happiness she had known before Brooke had left home.

Her one-time hero worship of her protective big sister was a fantasy, she told herself, for Brooke could no more protect Roxy now than Roxy could have protected her ten years ago.

Her mother knocked on her door and stuck her head in, interrupting her reverie. "Telephone, Roxy. Someone named Sonny."

Roxy frowned and looked at the extension, which was lying on the table. "Sonny? What does he want?"

Her mother smiled. "I guess he wants to talk to you," she said.

Roxy's head moved slowly from side to side, and she cast a beseeching look at her mother. "No. Tell him I'm not here."

Her mother stepped into the room, still smiling, as if she had caught her shy, awkward daughter on the threshold of her first budding romance. "I've already told him you're home. You know, with that attitude it's no wonder that you're sitting at home on a Saturday night. Now, answer that phone."

Roxy watched her mother leave the room. Reluctantly she took a deep breath and picked up the phone. "Hello?"

"Yo, Roxy, it's me. Sonny."

Roxy sighed impatiently. "I know. What is it?"

"What is it?" Sonny asked. "It's . . . nothing. I was just sitting here thinking about . . . today . . . and I wondered how you were feeling."

"I'm fine," she said.

He hesitated a moment, and she realized that, just maybe, the conversation wasn't easy for him, either. Maybe he had sat looking at the telephone for a while, and only now had summoned the courage to call.

"Listen, I know it's late and everything, but...would you like to go out for a Coke or pizza? I could have you home by eleven."

Roxy caught her reflection in her dresser mirror, saw the dark circles from too much crying today, the pallid color of her complexion, the bedraggled state of her hair. What could Sonny possibly see in her, on a day when she was at her absolute worst? "Why?" she asked suspiciously.

"Why?" Sonny laughed, but it didn't disguise the tension in his voice. "Well, why not? I mean, I'm hungry, what can I say?" He laughed nervously again. "To tell you the truth, I didn't really expect to catch you at home tonight, but I figured I'd take a chance."

She sat quietly, unable to believe his invitation was that simple. There had to be more.

"I don't want you to think it's *normal* for me to be home on a Saturday night," Sonny qualified quickly. "Usually I have this long line of wild women lined up at my door, and they drag me dancing and partying until all hours. But it's so exhausting, you know, my busy social schedule...."

A grin made its slow journey across Roxy's lips, but she didn't speak.

"So, what do you say?" he asked. "You feel like going somewhere? I could be there in ten minutes."

Her smile faded, and she felt her mouth go dry. "No. I couldn't get ready. I look awful...."

"Hey, Roxy," Sonny cut in. "If you look anything like you looked today, you'll knock my socks off."

She frowned, wondering if he could really be serious. She had cried off her makeup around noon, and her eyes had been puffy and swollen. She wasn't one to keep up with the latest trends, but she was pretty certain that her look today wasn't "in." "No, really. I can't...."

"Oh, I get it," Sonny said. "You've got one of those mud packs on your face, right? And all that greasy conditioning gunk in your hair? And sponges between your toes while you paint them?"

She laughed in spite of herself. "No!"

"Then what could be so bad?" he asked, more seriously. "My standards are real low these days."

Roxy laughed again, becoming more uninhibited the more he carried on. "Thanks a lot."

"Hey, I'm trying to raise them some," he said. "What can I say? So will you wash the mud off of your face and come with me, or not?"

She smiled softly and brought her other hand up to the telephone. Something deep inside her urged her to say yes, but the part of her that had kept score over the past year and had filed away deductions concerning men, warned her to stay at home. "I really can't," she said.

Sonny gave a great, exaggerated sigh. "All right," he huffed. "Then I guess I'll have to resort to that line of wild women outside my door."

"I guess."

"But I'm not fooled," he went on, undaunted. "I can hear it in your voice that you really want to come. At least you aren't snapping at me anymore." He paused a moment, lowering his pitch. "Maybe I *won't* go out with those wild women. Maybe I'll just save myself for you."

A soul-deep smile welled up inside her chest and pushed out all the pain and misery she'd been dragging around with her. "I'll see you at the museum tomorrow," Roxy said, and for the first time, realized she actually looked forward to it.

"I'll count the minutes," Sonny teased. "Don't leave the mud on too long, now, okay?"

Roxy hung up the phone and kept her hand over the receiver for a moment, smiling down at it. Funny, she thought. Ten minutes earlier she hadn't believed there was a person in this world who could make her smile today.

Sonny had proved her wrong. She only wished she was wrong about other things, as well.

IT WAS ELEVEN O'CLOCK when Nick woke Brooke. She nuzzled against him, and with all his being he wished he could just lie there and hold her all night. He fondled the chains still draped across her chest, twisting the longest one on his finger. "Next time we'll have a bed," he whispered, "and I'll hold you until morning. But now we've got to get you home."

Brooke yawned and stretched with feline sensuality that stirred the smoldering embers of his desire. "Yeah. Don't want to give Roxy or my parents more ammunition," she said. She looked at Nick and saw how relaxed he appeared, as if their loving tonight had erased the past ten years. "You know, everything they think about us, we made it true tonight."

"Regrets?" he whispered.

Brooke thought about it and found that her doubts were overshadowed by the incredible fire he had kindled inside her. "No," she said finally. "No regrets."

She left him lying on the drop cloth, propped on one elbow, as she found her clothes and pulled them on.

Nick grabbed her hand and stopped her as she started to button her blouse. Slowly he stroked one perfect nipple with his fingertip and smiled up at her, his eyes sparkling.

"You sure you don't want to just go on back to my house?" he asked.

She sighed. "I can't."

He reached up to kiss her, gently, sweetly, then murmured, "I know."

He got dressed himself and walked her to her car, then stood and watched her drive off into the darkness. An aching emptiness gnawed inside him the moment she was out of sight, and he looked at his watch, counting the hours until he would see her again.

WRAPPED IN THE SPIRITUAL COCOON of Nick's love, Brooke went home that night. She said good-night to her parents, who were up late watching a movie on the VCR, then passed by Roxy's room and saw that the light was off.

She stepped into the doorway, watching Roxy sleeping soundly in her bed. Her sister's features were soft and youthful in repose, as innocent as they had been when she was a child. Quietly Brooke reached down and pulled a blanket up around her.

Her heart twisted again at what she had discovered about her sister that day. Little Roxy, who used to crawl in bed with her and look at the clouds, involved with a married man!

She sighed and went back to the door, leaned against the casing. The tragedy of it all, she thought, was that Roxy was missing the exclusive feeling of love that Brooke felt tonight. She wouldn't find that in sleazy bars and secret affairs. Yes, its intensity left Brooke without control, but if it was right, that madness provided a sweet new sense of command, a poignant power that was new to her.

Quietly she went to her room and got out of her clothes, trying to get Roxy's problems out of her mind so that she could bask in the memory of Nick's arms around her.

CHAPTER TWELVE

ABBY HEMPHILL HUNG UP the telephone and checked off one more name on the long list on her clipboard. Already she'd convinced over fifty townspeople to support her committee's decision not to grant the money necessary for the stained-glass windows. When Horace tried to supercede their verdict, they would all be there, backing her up. It hadn't been that difficult, she mused. All she'd had to do was point out the enormous amount of money in question, the more immediate needs of Hayden's schools and government offices and the proof she had that the "artists" in question were more concerned with each other than with the pretense of their windows.

She was a reasonable woman, after all, she thought, and the town was filled with reasonable people. They were engaged in making a reasonable decision, one that put control of this project back where it belonged in the first place.

She glanced down at the gold watch shackling her wrist, noting that it was after noon. By now Nick Marcello had probably been notified of the committee's decision. Already, no doubt, they were desperately rallying together what little support they had left in the town. Wouldn't they be surprised when they saw how outnumbered they were?

She went to the end table across the immaculately decorated living room—quite appropriate for a woman of her station—and flicked off a piece of dust that was illuminated between the shadowed bars cast by the vertical blinds on the windows.

It was so quiet. Too quiet.

The quiet made her feel cold, lonely, detached...and she chafed her arms with her hands and wandered into the study, to the small file cabinet where she kept her personal things. There was no need to lock it anymore, as she once had. The kids were all grown and gone, and Gerald...well, Gerald would never in a million years have cared about anything she held dear.

She pulled out an overstuffed scrapbook, blew off the dust and opened it. A soft smile played over her face as memories of her glory days assailed her. She had been in control then. No one had ever questioned it. And she had been a good role model for all those who looked up to her.

Maybe too good.

Her eyes fell on an old, fading snapshot of a young man, grinning at the camera as if he planned to pounce on the photographer as soon as the camera snapped. He had, too, she mused. He had chased her across the park, and when he'd caught her, he had tickled her until she'd collapsed with screams of glee....

She turned the page, seeing herself, young and pretty and full of spirit, brandishing the tiny engagement ring he had saved for a year to buy her.

"It's hardly more than a crumb," her father had pointed out distastefully. *"It'll probably turn your finger green."*

And then her mother had gotten all puffed up and told her she had to consider what people would think. It wasn't appropriate, her mother said, that a debutante would marry the son of a woman who cleaned houses for a living.

Little by little they had chipped away at him, until she began to blame him more and more for not being from the right side of the tracks, for not being someone her social circle respected, for not being the man her parents wanted her to marry.

Eventually she had chosen propriety over love, and Gerald Hemphill, a more *appropriate* choice from a wealthy family, had come along and proposed to her.

But there were those who wouldn't have understood her choice, who would have followed their instincts or their traitorous hearts, who would have dived headfirst into the wrong kind of relationship. People like Brooke Martin, or Nick Marcello. People who *knew* their actions were inappropriate and didn't care.

She flipped through the pages and saw other snapshots of the young man in various candid poses that brought back stirrings of unsettling memories. He had married since then, she'd heard through the grapevine. Had two children and a horse named Smitty and a wife who had no more money than he had. She wondered if he was happy, or if ever, in the dead of night when his family was sleeping and life stood quietly frozen, he thought of her. She wondered if his memories were pleasant, or if he still blamed her for the choice she had made. He had never understood her need to live her life right, no matter what sacrifices had to be made.

There had to be a consequence for choosing the easy way—as Brooke and Nick had done—even if she was the one to administer those consequences. Propriety, after all, was the most important thing.

"WHAT WE'RE SAYING," Horace Anderson said in a roundabout manner to keep from making the news sound as cruel as it was, "is that we realize the personal sacrifices both of you have made for the windows, and we appreciate it and intend to compensate you for your time. However—"

"However, we're fired, right?" Nick finished, making the job easier for him. He leaned forward, elbows on his knees, tapping his mouth with steepled fingers as he surveyed most of the members of the town council on one side of the table, and Mrs. Hemphill and her followers on the other. He and Brooke had guessed what had transpired the moment Horace called him that morning to ask them to attend the evening meeting. The somber tone of his voice had been an immediate clue.

"No, not fired," Horace said, his face pinched with distaste at the hateful task he'd been assigned. "Technically the job has been approved, and you've been approved to do it. We just..." He lowered his eyes in defeat, and slumped over the table. "We just can't pay you."

Brooke looked at Nick and saw that he was as confused as she. Nick stood up and regarded Abby Hemphill, who sat perched on the edge of her seat with her nose high and a satisfied smile adorning her lips, a victory grin he recognized. She had worn it the night he'd lost his teaching job. "Let me get this straight," he said quietly. "The budget wasn't adequate to cover the expenses of our salaries, or the expenses of the windows altogether?"

"The budget was more than inadequate," the mayor threw in. "It was nonexistent."

"But as I've said, we're not firing you," Horace repeated, as if that softened the blow.

Nick fixed his astonished eyes on Horace, impatient with his inability to be direct. "Why the hell not?" he asked. "Is that supposed to be some consolation?"

Horace rubbed his face, and Brooke could see that the ordeal was costing him a great deal. She reached up and touched Nick's arm to calm him. He peered down at her, saw the censure in her expression and turned back to Horace.

Horace cleared his throat and tried to explain. "Because I want people to know that you were capable of doing the job, and that this decision had nothing to do with you...." He looked down the table at Mrs. Hemphill. "I want them to know who's responsible for this."

"So, what you're saying," Brooke began, struggling to get the ruling clearer in her mind, "is that it's over? All the work we've done? All our plans...they're worth nothing? The windows were just figments of our imaginations?"

Horace sat back wearily in his chair and rubbed his stomach. "I guess that's about it," he said. "The renovation will continue, but there won't be any stained-glass windows."

The harsh reality of the decree assailed Brooke. No stained-glass windows...no redemption from Hayden... no excuse to stay....

Her heart plummeted and her misty eyes flitted to Nick's. Was history destined to repeat itself? Another job lost, another relationship broken, another defeat to overcome? Would she follow the script Abby Hemphill had written for her and leave town again? Would ten more barren years go by before either of them could sort out the regrets and mistakes they'd made...by trying one more time...by succumbing to their desires...by falling in love...?

The emotions evident on Nick's face told Brooke that the same questions plagued his mind, as well. He turned back to her, holding out his hand. Knowing how it looked, but for the first time in her life not giving a damn, Brooke accepted his hand and laced her fingers through his. Then, without saying another word that could be rebutted or repeated, the two left the meeting together.

By the time they reached the parking lot great sobs racked Brooke's shoulders and hindered her steps. Nick pulled her against him and held her quietly for a fragment of eternity. Combined with all the other fragments of time they'd shared, it still was too little. "Don't cry," he whispered after several moments had passed. "It's gonna be okay."

His futile promise broke her mood of despair, turning it into acid anger instead. "She's done it again," Brooke rasped. "How could she do this to us again?"

"I don't know," he whispered. "I don't know."

Nick held her beneath the light of a street lamp illuminating the parking lot, her tears soaking his shirt. Behind them the door to the building opened, and the somber council members spilled out one by one, along with Abby Hemphill's team of supporters who bubbled and buzzed with the elation of their "moral victory."

But what was it a victory over? Brooke asked herself miserably. Was it over the distaste of a misunderstood relationship? Over the happiness of two people who'd done no one harm? Over their future, their peace? Nick opened Brooke's car door and she got in, and he slipped in next to her, holding her hand. Together they watched those who had condemned them going to their cars and driving away without even a look back. Abby Hemphill, in all her glory, was one of the last to leave the building. They watched her march to her powder-blue Cadillac, get in and start the engine. When she pulled out of her space, she made a U-turn and drove up beside Brooke's car. Her automatic window drifted down, and within the solitary shadows of the car, they could see Abby's cold, smug smile. "I trust you'll have your things out of the museum as soon as possible," she said. "And leave your forwarding address, darling, so Horace can send you a check for the little bit you've done."

"What makes you think she's leaving?" Nick asked, his tone scathing.

"Well, maybe I was a little premature," she said, chuckling. "I assumed she had to make a living. One of you really should, you know." Then, rolling up her window and disappearing behind the tinted glass, Abby Hemphill drove away.

They sat silently for a moment, neither willing to broach the subject the woman had raised. What was there to say, when they both knew that Brooke's business was hours away and that Nick had opted long ago not to let the town run him away?

Finally Nick spoke. His voice was shaky...his tone tentative. "Well, I guess I'll go to the museum tonight and gather up our things."

"I can't believe this," Brooke whispered, her tears blurring her vision of the Hayden City Hall and the buildings of downtown beyond. Despite its hatred of her, there was something innocent about the town that Brooke still loved. "We were doing those windows for them. So that they would know...and see...that we really are decent people. Valued members of this town...."

Nick sighed heavily and pulled her against him again. "Maybe that wasn't a good enough reason," he whispered. "There are some people who would never be convinced."

Brooke wiped her tears and gazed off into the distance after Mrs. Hemphill. Her anger shot bursts of adrenaline through her, giving her an energy that demanded a confrontation. Maybe some people never could be convinced, she thought, but they could be confronted. They could be made to think. And they could be forced to see the truth in themselves, no matter how ugly it was.

"So, you want to come back to the museum with me?" Nick asked.

Slowly Brooke shook her head. "Not yet. There's something I need to take care of first."

Nick cupped her chin, turning her face back to his. His eyes were a misty black beneath the light in her car, and she saw him swallow. "Brooke, you aren't going to leave now, are you?" he asked. "Not yet?"

"No, Nick," she said. "I'll see you later tonight. I promise."

Slowly he got out of her car, dropped a kiss on her lips and locked her in. As she drove away, she looked in her rearview mirror, saw him standing there watching her with sad apprehension and dread in his eyes. The tragedy was that she didn't know how to banish that pain from his heart. All she did know was that, whether it helped matters or not, there were a few things she had to settle with Mrs. Hemphill tonight.

ABBY HEMPHILL'S HOUSE was located on the upper class side of town, nestled in a neighborhood of bankers, lawyers and doctors. Brooke pulled into the woman's driveway and peered through the darkness to the huge Tudor-style house. It was much too extravagant for a principal's salary, she thought, or a town council member's. But everyone in town knew that both Abby and Gerald Hemphill came from old money, and that they had brought equal portions of wealth into the marriage.

Abby Hemphill probably hadn't had to worry about money a day in her life, Brooke thought as she sat in her car, and yet she was so concerned about the money Brooke and Nick would have made. Idly Brooke wondered if the hateful woman had ever known the feeling of accomplishment, of creating something out of your own heart and with your own hands, of seeing a project through, of sharing it with another human being. Abby had probably never in her life known the unconditional kind of love that came from passionate involvement and struggle.

In a way Brooke almost felt sorry for her.

She got out of the car, not knowing what she planned to say to the woman, but trusting that the words would come when she called for them. Hands trembling with the emotions wreaking havoc in her soul, Brooke went up the wide steps to the door and rang the bell. A chorus of chimes rang out, filling the house with an aura of regal authority. She stood still, one hand in the pocket of her windbreaker, the other clutched around the strap of her purse as she waited for her self-appointed archenemy to answer.

In just a moment the door opened, and Mrs. Hemphill stood looking at her. Abby's expression became instantly guarded, as if she braced herself for a physical attack.

"I'd like to talk to you, Mrs. Hemphill," Brooke said, her tone dangerously calm. "You don't have to worry. No screaming, no yelling, nothing distasteful. Just one adult to another."

Abby Hemphill crossed her arms and stroked the column of her throat with her index finger. "I don't really believe you and I have anything to discuss. My mind certainly won't be changed."

"I'm not here to change your mind," Brooke said, stepping inside despite the fact that she hadn't been invited. "I just want to try to understand." She turned around inside the foyer, making it clear that Abby would have to contend with her. Stiffly, Abby closed the door, bolted it and turned back to Brooke. "I wanted to ask you to explain it to me," Brooke went on, "this vendetta you have against Nick and me."

Abby smiled condescendingly and she inclined her head. "It's no vendetta. It's business."

"Was it business ten years ago," Brooke asked, "when you told lies about what you saw Nick and me doing in the art room? Was it business when Hayden High School lost the best art teacher they've ever had? Was it business when you spread smut around town about what we were doing when we were working day and night on those windows, knowing that you would do everything in your power to pull the rug out from under us?"

Mrs. Hemphill's pale, pampered skin faded to a rose color. "Whether you can understand this or not, the town trusts me and my committee to oversee how their money is spent. I can't allow town funds to be spent to help with the pretense for your little affair."

Brooke told herself not to cry and tightened her lips to keep them from trembling. "If Nick and I were involved— on our own time—what difference would it make to you, anyway?" she asked. "Why do you care so much?"

"Because you brought scandal upon my husband's school ten years ago!" she shouted. "It took us months to recover from that, and I won't have it tainting our museum!"

"*You* brought scandal on me!" Brooke returned, the fraying thread of her control snapping her words. "I *still* haven't recovered from it, and it was all a bunch of lies! All it amounted to was two people *kissing*. And I've had to pay for that every day since!" She paced across the room, groping for the reins of her control. She spun around, knowing that her eyes glistened with tears, knowing that she was exposing all her wounds to Abby Hemphill. "Is your life so empty that you have to do cruel, bitter things like this to find reasons to get up in the mornings? Haven't you ever been devoted to something or someone just for the beauty of it? Haven't you ever loved?"

Myriad emotions passed like a color wheel over Abby's face, and Brooke saw the well of tears in her eyes. "Get out!" Abby said, reaching for the door. "You are not welcome in my house."

Knowing that she'd said even more than she had come to say, Brooke started toward the door. But behind her another door swung open.

"Mom? Is everything all right?"

Brooke turned around and saw her sister's lover—the infamous, mysterious, cheating Bill—standing in the doorway with his pregnant wife peering out from behind him.

"Yes," Mrs. Hemphill said, trying to steady her breath. "Miss Martin was just leaving." She looked pointedly at Brooke, who stood staring at the man. He met her eyes with incredulous recognition, but rather than the guilt she would have expected, he offered her a cold, amused smile that dared her to expose him.

For a moment it occurred to Brooke that doing just that to his wife and his mother would provide justice for them all.

Run this through those moral and social values of yours, Mrs. Hemphill. Your married, soon-to-be-a-father son is sleeping with my sister!

For a moment Brooke glared at him, until his grin faltered the slightest degree . . . until she could see the briefest flash of fear in his eyes. He had miscalculated her silence.

The revelation on the tip of her tongue faded, as clear thinking prevailed reminding her that she couldn't use this ammunition on the Hemphills without destroying Roxy in the process. The last thing she wanted was Mrs. Hemphill blaming her sister for his sleazy seduction. Besides, some gentler voice in her throbbing heart cried out, his wife probably didn't deserve this family she'd married into, much less the misery the news would inflict upon her. Despite her wish to put Mrs. Hemphill in her place, to repay her vindictiveness with a little of her own, Brooke couldn't be that cruel.

Slowly she tore her eyes from Bill and turned back to the woman waiting for her to walk through the door. "You know, Mrs. Hemphill, if I were you I'd make sure my own house was clean before I started trying to clean up the town."

Then she left the woman standing there, as bewildered as if Brooke had just insulted her housekeeping. Hurrying to her car, Brooke realized that she felt no better than before she'd come. In fact, if anything, she felt even worse.

HER CAR FLEW with a vengeance—not to the museum where Nick would be waiting for her—but to her own home, where Roxy probably sat waiting at the smutty beck and call of that bastard.

The car screeched to a halt in the driveway, and Brooke saw that her parents' car wasn't in the driveway. Roxy's light was on, so Brooke got out, went into the house and stormed back to Roxy's room.

"How could you?" she yelled, before Roxy even knew she was there.

Her sister looked up, confusion distorting her face. "What?"

Brooke's teeth came together, and she bit out each word. "How could you...have an affair...with Mrs. Hemphill's *son*?"

Roxy came to her feet, and she threw her hands over her face. "Brooke, don't—"

"Mrs. Hemphill's son! The *married* son of the town gossip!" Brooke repeated. "Do you know what will happen if it ever gets out? Do you know what that woman will do to you?"

"You don't—" Roxy started to scream, but Brooke stormed across the room and took Roxy's wrists and pulled them down from her face, forcing her to look at her.

"Roxy, are you trying to self-destruct? Is your life so terrible that you're just trying to ruin it once and for all? Or are you just hell-bent on following in my own miserable footsteps?"

"Maybe I don't have a choice, okay?" Roxy screamed, jerking away from Brooke's grip. "Maybe I've never had a choice! Maybe because of you, I've had my life mapped out for me!"

"Don't you *dare* blame this on me!" Brooke said. "Don't you dare!"

Roxy threw herself on the bed and thrust a fist into her pillow as she glared at Brooke.

"You don't know anything about me!" she cried. "So don't come in here judging me, when you don't know what the hell you're talking about!"

Brooke looked at her, her green eyes frosty as ice, feeling as if every miserable moment in her last ten years had been compressed and packed into this one. "Why not?" she asked her sister. "You've judged me for the last ten years."

Turning her back on her sister, Brooke ran out of the house.

TIME IS RUNNING OUT, Nick thought as he sat alone in the darkness of his Duesenberg, wondering just how much time he had left with Brooke. She would leave again, he knew without a doubt. And he had choices. He could follow her this time, try to start over on her terms. But that trust he needed so desperately from her wouldn't be reinforced that way. He would always wonder how she could discard him so easily, or if Brooke's next savior would make her his wife.

He looked at the museum, dark and dormant under the cover of night, but he couldn't face going in there alone. The best work of his life could have been created there, he thought. And last night he'd enjoyed the best moments of his life there.

Something seemed to have died inside him tonight. Something important. That something that had kept him fighting all these years . . . that something within him that reminded him he had done nothing wrong, that he was of value, that he had worth.

But now Nick had to admit that he had given his family one more bit of evidence to support their belief that he would never make anything of his life. His ma's worthless artist son had lost another job.

"You be what you want to be," his grandpa had advised him so long ago, sitting at his favorite fishing hole and teaching him how to look busy while taking time to think. *"And when they chide you about it, you justa smile and nod and go on abouta your business. Soon they'll just get tired of you and finda someone else to bother."*

Nick slammed his hand on the steering wheel and uttered a curse. When would that happen? he asked himself. For most of his life Nick had fought everyone over what he'd chosen to do. He had nodded and smiled and gone on about his business. And he had done well.

But still they chipped away at him little by little, until their prophecy that he would wind up unemployed and alone was fulfilled.

He saw headlights pull into the parking lot, and Brooke's car pulled into the space next to his. She saw his shadow in the car, got out of her own and came to the passenger side. Without a word she got in next to him.

"What are you doing?" she whispered.

"Thinking." He took her hand and held it firmly in his. Idly, his thumb stroked her knuckle. "Just thinking. Stay here with me for a minute," he said quietly. "Then we'll go in."

Brooke lay her head back against the seat and closed her eyes, not wanting to add to the already tragic night by telling Nick about her visit to Abby Hemphill and her discovery that Bill was Abby's son.... The air was already too charged, and she knew that the thoughts raging through their minds were sadly, tragically, parallel. Time was running out, and neither of them could stop it.

TEARS POURED DOWN ROXY'S FACE as she paced furiously across her room. She heard a car outside and knew her parents had come home from the grocery store. Peering through her miniblinds, she surveyed their faces as they got out of the car. Had they heard yet, she wondered frantically, about the latest scandal developing in their family? And if not, how much longer would it be? It was inevitable, after all, that it would come out soon. She hadn't doubted that for a moment when the whole thing had started, and Bill had been very careful to remind her how humiliating the consequences could be.

She went to her mirror and tore a tissue out of its box, then wiped her eyes carefully. Dabbing a little makeup on her finger, she tried to touch up the red circles under her eyes.

Maybe she would just come right out and tell them, Roxy thought. Maybe she should just get the whole thing out in the open and accept whatever came of it. She was so tired of hiding. So tired of all the lies and the sneaking around. So tired of the limits it imposed on her life.

But what would they say? What would they do? Vividly, she remembered the night ten years ago when Mr. Hemphill had called her father to tell him about his fallen daughter. She hadn't known, then, what was going on, but she would never forget her father's storming across the house threatening to kill Nick Marcello. Would her dad want to kill Bill, too, or worse, Roxy, herself?

His reaction might serve to make the scandal bigger, she thought, starting to cry again. It would just be that much more to deal with.

"Hi, honey." Her mother's voice came from her doorway, and Roxy kept her face down to avoid her scrutiny. "I thought you'd be out somewhere tonight since you don't have school tomorrow."

"No, Mom," Roxy said. "I had some studying to do."

"Studying?" Her mother stepped into the room, looked around but saw no trace of school books. "I've never yet met a senior who studied during spring break."

Roxy shrugged and grabbed one of her books. "Yeah, well. I'm having a little trouble in history."

Alice Martin sat down on her daughter's bed, concern altering her expression. Roxy knew that she wasn't fooling anyone. Her mother would have to be blind not to see the remnants of tears on her red-rimmed eyes, or deaf not to hear the rasp of hoarseness in her voice. "Honey, I'm worried about you."

"Don't worry," Roxy said too brightly. "I'll pull my grades up. I'm just a borderline B."

"I'm not worried about your grades," her mother said. "I'm worried about the way you've withdrawn lately. You've been crying, haven't you?"

"No," Roxy denied, as if the thought was absurd. "Why would I be crying?"

"I don't know," her mother said, frowning. She cupped Roxy's chin and tipped her face up. "But you have. And here you are, locked in your room again, as if you're afraid to come out—"

Thankfully the phone rang just as new tears emerged in Roxy's eyes. Turning from her mother, she snatched it up. "Hello?"

"Hey, Rox. It's me, Sonny."

"Hi." She glanced back at her mother, who waited for her to finish the call so that they could continue their talk. But the prospect terrified her, for Roxy wasn't certain she could manage to keep things to herself in the face of her mother's concern.

"Listen," Sonny was saying. "I was wondering if you might want to go out for a pizza or something. Now, before you say no, let me remind you—"

"Yes," Roxy said quickly, almost desperately. "Yes, I'd like that."

"What?" Sonny asked. "Did you say yes?"

"Yes," Roxy said again. "When can you be here?"

"Fifteen minutes," Sonny said. "No, ten."

"I'll be ready," Roxy said.

She hung up the phone and turned back to her mother. "Well, looks like I have a date."

"Really?" Her mother's smile inched back over her face. "Who with?"

"Sonny Castori," she said, rushing to the dresser to finish applying her makeup. "He graduated from Hayden last year." Deliberately she neglected to tell her mother that he was Nick's cousin. All that concerned Roxy now was getting out of the house and away from her mother's probing questions, at least until the rumors that had reached Brooke somehow reached her parents, too.

If the truth didn't come out of its own accord, Roxy wasn't sure how much longer she could hold the sordid secrets tightly within herself. And she wasn't sure how much longer she wanted to try.

Her energy was almost gone, and the humiliation of having to face Brooke with the truth had already been thrust upon her. How much worse could it be for her parents to know, after all, now that the sister she loved was disgusted by her?

CHAPTER THIRTEEN

THE MUSEUM WAS an abyss of darkness when Brooke and Nick went inside for what was to be their final time. Nick flipped the switch on the wall, casting the place in a dim half-light, brighter than the one that had enveloped them last night, but lacking the magic that had wrapped them in its gossamer web. Tonight the shadows around them seemed too big to conquer, providing a mystery that neither could unravel. Together they walked to the center of the large room and looked up at the boarded windows they could have transformed into such enchanting pieces of art. It broke Brooke's heart that the town had so ignorantly denied itself that magic.

"Funny," Nick said, his soft voice echoing in the room's emptiness. "Art is supposed to be expression. It's supposed to be pure and untainted. But what it really comes down to, what really is the bottom line, is the almighty buck."

Brooke walked across the floor and lightly kicked the drop cloths lying where she and Nick had made love just the night before. Then, money hadn't been an issue. The windows had represented a sharing of their souls that night, a union, a rebirth. The windows had brought them back together, had offered them a reason to hold their heads up in the town that had knocked them down.

Nick turned to her, his eyes filled with pain and longing, and he brought his hand up and clenched it into a fist. "It could have been so good, Brooke. It could have been so... beautiful...."

His eyes misted over as his voice broke and he turned from her, inhaling a deep cleansing breath that made his shoulders rise and fall in weary defeat.

Brooke stepped up behind him, touching his back tentatively. Despite her need to comfort him, as he had never failed to comfort her, she couldn't find the right words. Somehow what had happened last night seemed negated, to some extent, by the events of tonight. They had been censured. Their work had been aborted. Their reason for being together had been snatched away. Where would that leave them now? There was no reason for her to stay in Hayden...every reason to leave. But would Nick come with her? Did she have any right at all to ask him?

He turned around and slid his arms around her, holding her against him, stroking her soft hair with a gentle hand. No words came to make the moment easier to bear. No answers sprang to life beneath the dusty beams of the building.

Finally they walked back to the workroom, to view the progress they had made, the seeds of masterpieces they had planted together. Their work, spread out on the tables and around the room, greeted them like still-hopeful children about to be abandoned.

Nick went to one pattern pinned to the table with the cartoon and working drawing beneath it. He slipped his fingertips under the edge, poised to rip it off the tacks, but Brooke reached out and stopped him. "Let's... let's just keep them together," she whispered. "We worked so hard..."

"Why?" Nick's face reddened as he brought his eyes to her, and she could hear the anger in his voice. "Why should we hold onto them?"

His hand whipped across the pages, ripping the heart out of the drawing. "We might as well just rip them *all* up!"

"No!" Brooke grabbed both his hands and held them with all her might. "Don't, Nick," she cried. "They're ours. The town can stop us from designing them for this museum, but they can't keep us from creating them somewhere else. Don't tear them up, Nick. Please."

He looked at her, then, his eyes softening. Nick regarded the torn drawing in his hands helplessly and dropped down onto a stool. "We can't do this anyplace else," he said in a metallic voice. "It wouldn't be the same. The magic would be gone."

Brooke slid her arms around the back of his shoulders, nestling her forehead against his neck. "It could be if we tried hard enough to make it that way," she whispered. "We can make that magic anywhere we want to. Let's not lose it again, Nick. We can't lose it again."

The real meaning of her words struck him full force, and he caught his breath. He took her arms and held her from him, and looked into her eyes. A question seemed to form in the crease between his brows, but it didn't reach his lips. Instead he stood up and walked slowly across the room, looking critically, more objectively, at each of the drawings in turn. "You know, a few years ago when I started painting, I was like Sonny, just doing it for fun, because I had something so vivid inside me that needed to be expressed. It never occurred to me that there could be any money involved. But now..." He raked a rough hand through his hair and shook his head. "Now, I've made so much money on my work that I *expect* to make money on it. Nothing's just for the sake of it, anymore. And when it has a price, someone can always come along and take it from you."

Brooke understood from her soul what he meant. "I know," she said, leaning her back wearily against the table and gazing off into the distance as memories gave an extra clarity to her life. "Looking back, I see that my deepest expression, my most intense work, was on the sculpture of the hands. I haven't been that absorbed in my work since then, but I've made a lot of money. And I never dreamed, at the time, that that sculpture could ever be worth a cent."

Nick set his palm down on the tabletop, staring at the pattern of the silhouette of two lovers, as if the answer lay there somewhere, in the subtle lines and the intense emotion of the panel. "My family was so down on my being an artist that I always felt I could prove my worth by putting a big dollar sign on my work. But these windows meant so...much to me." He looked at her, his sad eyes bright. "I would have done them for free, Brooke."

Brooke inclined her head and inhaled a breath that seemed weighted with the tragedy in Nick's eyes. "So would I," she admitted. "But our salaries weren't all that was in question. It costs thousands to construct windows like these."

Nick's eyes illuminated like lanterns that had suddenly been turned on to flood the night. "Do you mean it, Brooke?" he asked. "Or are you just saying it because you know it's moot now?"

"Saying what?" she asked. "That I would have done it for free? Of course, but..."

Nick was across the room in a split second, grabbing her shoulders and peering into her eyes. Startled, she allowed him to sit her down on the couch, and watched him stoop in front of her. "God knows I have no right in the world to ask you this," he whispered, breathless with brimming excitement, "but I'm going to. Would you consider—even consider—staying here and finishing this project without pay...if we could come up with the money somehow?"

"*How*?" Brooke asked. "We can't get our hands on that kind of money."

"*If* we could, would you stay?" he asked again. "If somehow the money just appeared for the supplies, would you help me finish the job?"

Something in the intensity of his voice told her that the money would appear from somewhere...that the magic of the windows hadn't yet died. A smile sparked to slow life in her eyes at the prospect, and she brought her hands to Nick's face. "Yes, I'll stay," she whispered. "I'll help you finish the windows."

"We'll get the money," he promised. "Do you believe that? Do you trust me?"

"I trust you," she whispered. "Those windows are too important to give up on. And if they don't have a price tag, then no one can take them from us."

His lips captured hers with the fervor of their vow, sealing it with a fragile bond. He splayed his hands over her face with an artist's probing touch. "If you trust me..." he whispered, his words forming against her lips, "...that's all that matters. I love you, Brooke. I love you."

"I love you." Her declaration came on a thin wisp of breath that was swept into the depths of his kiss, swallowed and nestled close to his heart. His lips were gentle, like the intimate drops of summer rain on bare skin; his lips were soft, like a cool breeze whispering through her hair; his lips were hot, like the midday rays of sun beating on burning flesh.

His tongue marauded in a rhythm growing more savage with each labored breath, searing to her core, as he lowered her head back to the deep cushions of the couch, his weight crushing her with poignant possession.

There was a sweet power play in his kiss, but he bestowed that power on her... a subtle exchange of control for that transitory moment of love. Brooke was left limp and helpless, whimpering out his name in an urgent plea.

Clothes fell away like enchanted accomplices in a ritual as old as the night, until Nick and Brooke came together, uniting without hesitancy, without thought, without shame.

Iridescent waves of lightning-charged emotion undulated over them as they climbed to the apex of ecstasy. They clung to each other as the control they had nurtured flew into the stars like long-confined birds at last set free.

They drifted back to earth in a whispered descent, breath finding a steadier rhythm as they lay tangled in each other's embrace, basking in and savoring the love that had no price.

And as Brooke lay on the couch beside him, watching the pink flush of Nick's skin with eyes that saw love in every line of his face, Brooke knew that she had all the pay she needed for the work she had agreed to do. For no amount of money could match the wealth of Nick Marcello's love.

IT WAS AFTER MIDNIGHT when Brooke and Nick said goodnight. She came home, the soft pleasure Nick had invoked fading with the reality that she would be forced to confront Roxy again. Instead of her sister, though, Brooke found that her mother was waiting up.

Brooke went inside the dimly lit room and set her things on the telephone table. "Mom, you didn't have to wait up for me," she said quietly, the late hour dictating her tone.

"I heard about the decision of the town council tonight," her mother said, regarding Brooke with a little apprehension. Along with that apprehension was an unmistakable, if subtle, note of relief. "I wanted to see how you took it."

Brooke sat down next to her mother. "Well, we've decided not to roll over and play dead. As a matter of fact, Nick and I are going to try to get the money on our own and do the project without pay. So I won't be leaving just yet."

"Oh?" Her mother brought her hand to the collar of her robe, idly stroking the velour. "Brooke, won't that be a lot of money? You aren't going to borrow it, I hope."

Brooke almost laughed, but the subject was far from funny. "Borrow it? You've got to be kidding. Not a bank in this country would loan money for something like this. It isn't like there's any kind of return on our investment. No, whatever we put into it, we have no hope of getting back. At least, not monetarily."

Brooke could see her mother bristling as she stood up and paced across the room, struggling to keep her mouth shut despite her reservations. "Then how?" she finally asked. "You don't have that kind of money, do you?"

"No," Brooke said. "But we'll get it from somewhere. I know we will."

Her mother turned around slowly, regarding Brooke as if she'd lost all good sense. But for the first time in her life, Brooke realized that it didn't matter whether her mother understood or not. "I know I said that I wouldn't nag," her mother said, trying to keep her tone even. "But honey, I'm worried about you. I don't want to see you mortgage your business or sell your car, or do something stupid in the name of...of..."

"Love, mother?" Brooke provided quietly.

The word seemed to bring her mother's spirits down further. "Oh, Brooke," she said.

Brooke swallowed and decided it was time to be honest with her mother, as she'd finally been honest with herself. "That's right, Mom. I'm in love with Nick. That's why I'm going through with finishing those windows. It means a lot to him . . . and it means a lot to me. But you don't have to worry. My car isn't worth nearly enough, and I rent my shop in Tallahassee, so there's nothing to mortgage. Even if I sold all my tools and inventory, it wouldn't begin to get us started.''

"But Brooke, if you don't have the money, how can you—?''

"The money will come from somewhere,'' she cut in before her mother's negative words could weaken her faith. "It has to.''

With a sigh her mother dropped into a chair across the room. Her face was as strained as if she carried the weight of the galaxy on her shoulders.

"Has Roxy heard the decision?'' Brooke asked quietly to change the subject.

Her mother shook her head. "No. Roxy had gone out before I got the call.''

"Out?'' Brooke asked, her face burning in sudden anger. Had Roxy actually gone out with Bill tonight, after Brooke had confronted her? Had *he* actually had the nerve to see her, knowing that Brooke knew?

"Yes,'' her mother said absently. "With a boy named Sonny. I met him when he picked her up. I was a little worried about the motorcycle, but he brought her a helmet. He seemed like a nice boy.''

Relief stole the fury from Brooke's eyes. "I know Sonny,'' she said. "He is a nice boy. Very nice.''

Brooke's mother just looked at her, wanting, but not daring, to ask more questions about her decision with Nick, wanting to probe more into the reasons for their choice. Finally, knowing that more conversation would only wind up in argument, Brooke kissed her distraught mother goodnight and went to her room.

Her room was already aglow with the little lamp in the corner, lighting *Infinity* like a halo. Brooke stepped into her room and closed the door behind her. She picked up the hands, held them against her heart and lay down on her bed. Stroking them like a living thing she held sacred, she thought of how Nick's real touch was even more poignant than the one she had portrayed here years ago.

She had sculpted it selflessly, out of love and not for recognition, and Nick had helped her, with no thought of payment or reward. They could do it again, she thought. Somehow they'd find the way to make that magic happen again.

"Helena at the gallery offered me twenty-five thousand for it."

Nick's words came back to her, reminding her that there was something she could sell to get the money. Something worth far more to her than mere dollars.

"Why didn't you sell it?"

"Because it wasn't mine..."

Now, holding the sculpture in her hands, Brooke wondered if *Infinity* was really hers to sell. Wasn't it really theirs? Hadn't she created it as a symbol for that nameless bond between them ten years ago that had changed the course of their lives and led them right back to where they'd started?

No, she couldn't sell it, she told herself. There must be another way.

But if there wasn't, she thought, what would happen? Would she be able to put the job off long enough, perhaps, to do some expensive panels for her best clients in Tallahassee, long enough to save that impossible sum of money?

Brooke set the sculpture down and heaved a great sigh, realizing that since she'd been here, she hadn't even called her machine at home once to see if anything pressing had come up. Deciding it was time, since she might have to rely on her business sooner than she thought, she strolled barefoot into Roxy's dark room, picked up her extension and dialed her home phone number in Tallahassee.

Her own voice greeted her, the voice of someone she hardly remembered, someone empty, someone lonely, someone running as fast as her memories could chase her. She pressed out her code on the push-button dial, and heard the beep that followed.

A shiver coursed through her as she recognized the gravelly voice instantly. "Uh . . . it's Nick. I called the hotel and you'd checked out." She sat up straighter, listening to the message she realized must have been recorded the night she'd checked into the Bluejay Inn. "I hope you haven't gone home, Brooke. It's too important to give up on that easily . . . the windows, I mean. Don't give up, Brooke. It's worth whatever it takes to see it through." There was an eloquent pause, and finally he said again, "I really hope you haven't gone home."

She hung up the phone without even listening for the rest of her messages and sat in the dark, letting the warmth of Nick's voice envelope her, making her decision more clear.

Slowly she went back into her room and looked down at the sculpture, knowing finally that Nick had given her the strength to do what was necessary.

"It's worth whatever it takes to see it through."

He was right, she thought. It *was* worth it. She and Nick had had two beginnings. Tomorrow she would sell the sculpture to buy her chance at an ending . . . an ending that would offer them infinity.

SONNY AND ROXY WALKED along the courtyard outside the little strip of restaurants where they'd eaten. A fountain played in the center, spraying up and cascading down, frivolous and frothy. "I tried to hide it from them," he was saying, "but when they found what I'd been working on, I realized that it was stupid, pretending that I don't care about it. I'm a grown man. I don't have to have permission to do anything."

"Why don't they want you to paint?" Roxy asked. She had been disinterestedly quiet when Sonny first picked her up, but over the course of the evening she found him so comfortable to be with that he had coaxed her out of her shell. Now she found herself able to talk to him freely. And, even more surprisingly, she found herself actually interested in what he was saying.

"They think I'll be worthless. Nick's had to put up with it all his life. They've really given him a hard time about it." He laughed, looking toward the fountain. "My great-grandfather was the only one in the family who ever encouraged him. I hardly knew him, but he's the one who left Nick that car. The way Nick treats it, you'd think Grandpa's spirit was sewn into the upholstery or something." He shrugged, picked up a pebble from the side of the fountain and tossed it in. "I guess, in a way, Nick is doing for me what Grandpa did for him."

"Nick?" Roxy asked. "What is he doing?"

Sonny shrugged. "He believes in me," he said. "He's the only one who thinks I've got something."

Roxy sat on the fountain's edge, looking down at her feet with listless eyes. "Sometimes maybe it's best not to encourage talent, if it's only going to wind up defeating you."

"Hey." Sonny leaned over her, touching her nose with a fingertip. "It can't defeat you if you don't let it."

"Sometimes people don't have a choice," Roxy said. "Sometimes life has a way of just dragging you along by the throat."

Sonny chuckled, making her despair seem thinner and less significant. "I don't know who you've been hanging out with, Rox, but it doesn't have to be that way." He took her hand, pulling her to her feet. She couldn't help looking at him.

"Have you ever had a dream?" he asked. "Or a talent that you just had to pursue, no matter what anyone else said?"

Roxy's smile was almost too subtle to see. "I'm no artist, if that's what you mean."

"Something else, then," he said. "Hey, I'll bet you can sing. Go ahead, hum a few bars."

Roxy laughed for the first time, she realized, in months. "No, I can't sing. And I can't play an instrument. And I can't act." She smiled up at him, saw that he wasn't relenting and, almost embarrassed, dropped her face to study her feet. "But . . . a long time ago . . . I used to like to dance. Once, I wanted to be a ballerina. It was just a silly thing."

"A ballerina?" he said, inclining his head in awe. "Have you studied ballet?"

"Until a couple of years ago," Roxy said. "But my teacher kept making me dance solo in the recitals . . ." Her smile faded as the memory came back to her of a man cornering her backstage, telling her she'd "turned him on," and demanding that she dance for him in private when he saw her again. "I was always really self-conscious about all those people looking at me . . . so I quit."

"You *quit*?" Sonny asked, astounded. "Just because of that?"

She lifted a delicate shoulder and dropped it. "It was a big thing to me."

Sonny leaned against the brick wall, a poignant smile on his lips. "Do you ever dance anymore? When you're alone, I mean?"

Roxy grinned at him self-consciously, wondering how he'd managed to make the awkwardness pass. "You'll laugh."

"No, I won't. I swear," Sonny said. "If you do, we have more in common than I thought. I paint alone in my room. Because, you know, you don't have to have someone's approval to be good. All you need is your own judgment." He pushed away from the wall, and took her hands out of her pocket, held one over her head in a crude ballerina pose. "Dance for me, Roxy," he entreated on a whisper, not making fun of her, and not diminishing the art she so loved. "I'll bet you're a beautiful dancer."

Roxy laughed nervously, shook her head. "I can't . . . really. It's been a long time. . . ."

"Come on, just a few steps," he coaxed. "I'll show you my painting if you do."

Roxy wet her lips, looked up at him, and realized that the bars and chains she had felt weighing her down before she'd come out with Sonny tonight didn't seem to be dragging her down anymore. She felt light with him, easy, and for a moment she was able to forget fear and shame and guilt and heartache. For a moment she just wanted to dance.

Roxy stepped back, stood on her toes, and did a soft pirouette, bent into a *plié*, then ended in a delicate curtsy.

Sonny threw both hands over his heart and stepped back, grinning with delight. "Oh, Rox, you've got to start dancing again. That's too nice to waste."

Roxy bit her lip, wondering why she didn't feel embarrassed. "Thank you," she whispered. "Now you have to keep your part of the bargain and show me your painting."

"Okay," Sonny said. "But my moves aren't nearly as graceful as yours."

They rode his motorcycle back to Sonny's garage apartment, and Roxy knew he could feel her hand shaking as he held it and led her in. Something in her head warned her that she could be walking into trouble...that men could not be trusted...that they were all ruled by rampant hormones instead of the heart. But somewhere, deep inside, some distant instinct told her that Sonny was, indeed, different, and that he could be trusted.

He turned on the light, robbing the room of its mystery, and closed the door behind him. "Ain't much," he said, "but it's mine. At least, until my parents kick me out."

Roxy smiled. "So, where's the painting?"

Sonny lifted the spread on his bed, slid out the canvas lying face up on the floor beneath it. He held it up, its back to her, and assessed it himself one last time. Finally, reluctantly, he turned it around to show her.

Roxy stepped closer, surveying the detail of the house depicted there. There was a Norman Rockwell poignancy in the faces of the people around it, emotion in every stroke. "It's got so much," she whispered. "So many stories in this one little canvas. So many feelings." She looked up at him, surprise in her eyes as she regarded him in a new light. "Sonny, have your parents seen this? I mean, really looked at it?"

"No, not really," he said. "I mean, they saw it long enough to get mad, like I'd been growing pot in my bathroom or something. But I don't think they took the time to *see* it."

"They *have* to," Roxy said. "Sonny, you have to make them. It's...it's wonderful. It reminds me of...family. When the family is young and colorful and bright. Before everything turns gray."

Sonny set the painting down on his bed and stepped toward her, gratitude evident on his face. She looked up at him, saw the intention in his eyes and wet her lips.

Slowly his mouth descended to hers, while his hand made a gentle journey over the shape of her face. The kiss was chaste, innocent, tentative and only lasted a moment. Just long enough to taste the sweet fruit of temptation.

He took a deep, shaky breath. "I'd better take you home," he whispered with an affected grin. "I don't know how long I can be trusted up here alone with you."

Roxy looked at him, wide-eyed, surprised that he wouldn't at least try to take advantage of the situation. The respect in his choice filled her with relief. "Yeah," she whispered. "I'd better go home."

MORNING LIGHT SHONE through the windows in Brooke's room the next morning, offering new hope and an exhilarated feeling that something good was about to happen. Fully dressed and ready to set out in pursuit of the finances needed to finish the windows, Brooke took the sculpture and sat down on her bed, holding it in her lap and stroking the smooth lines, quietly absorbing the feel of it for the last time.

She heard a knock, and looked up to see Roxy standing in her doorway. "Hi," she said.

"Hi." The exchange was stiff, awkward, in light of the fight they'd had the night before. It weighed on Brooke's heart, making her regret that she had ever confronted her sister.

"Mom just told me about the council's decision," Roxy said. "I'm really sorry. I know how hard you worked on those windows."

Brooke's eyes dropped to the sculpture. "We'll pay you for the work you've done," she said. "They did agree to compensate us for what we've already done."

Roxy crossed her arms and looked at the floor. "I don't need it," she said. "Just keep it."

A moment of silence passed, but Roxy still lingered on the threshold of Brooke's room. "Did Mom also tell you that we're going ahead with the project?" Brooke asked. "Without pay?"

"Yeah," Roxy said. "But I don't understand how you plan to raise the money."

Brooke touched the fingertips of the man's hand in the sculpture, placed her own hand over the woman's. The thought of letting the piece go made her heart ache. "He said someone had offered him twenty-five thousand dollars for this," she whispered. "That'll go a long way on the windows."

"What?" Roxy exclaimed, stepping into the room. "Why would you sell that for this stupid town's museum? You'll never get the money back, and the sculpture will go into strange hands, and the townspeople probably won't even care."

Tears emerged in Brooke's eyes, and she looked up. "What else can I do?" she asked, her voice wobbly. "Those windows mean so much to Nick. To both of us. We deserve them, Roxy. If we abandon them now, where will that leave us? Right back where we were ten years ago—with everything taken away from us."

She set the sculpture down carefully and ambled to the window. The morning sunlight was shining on her parents' back lawn. "I might as well admit it, Roxy, so you can take the same shots at me that I took at you last night," she said. "I'm in love with him. And if we don't have these windows to do, I don't know what will happen to us. I can't stay here and make a living, and I don't know if he'll leave." She turned around, faced her sister, bracing herself for her reproach, her disgust, her judgment. But this time there was none. "The windows are like some kind of door we can go through to right all the wrongs," she went on. "If we let that door close on us again...I just don't know if we can ever open it again."

Roxy simply stood looking at her, a frown forming between her thin brows—a frown of deep concern—not of angry disapproval. "But, Brooke," she whispered, "isn't the sculpture just as important? He kept it all these years. He could have sold it himself."

Brooke went back to the sculpture, picked it up and held it as if it were alive. "These hands represent the beginning," she said. "But I want more than just another beginning. If I have to sell this to get a future, a life, a history with Nick Marcello, then I'll do it." She looked up at her sister, her mouth twitching in pain as she lifted her brows decisively. "And I'm going to do it today."

Roxy swallowed, and her face softened, her expression as unguarded and sympathetic as Brooke had seen since she'd come home. "Can I come with you?" she asked.

Brooke tried to laugh, but her effort ended in a sob. "I'd really appreciate that," she said, "because this is going to be one of the hardest things I've ever had to do."

In that moment it seemed as if Roxy had grown up, and she erased the distance between them and hugged Brooke in a way that she hadn't done in ten years. Suddenly all the regrets and injustices and condemnations between them fell away, leaving just two sisters who desperately needed each other's love.

CHAPTER FOURTEEN

As IF SHE HAD to witness Brooke's sacrifice to believe it, Roxy went with Brooke that day to the gallery where Nick's work was exhibited. Helena, the owner, was busy with a client when they first arrived, so while they waited, Brooke led Roxy to the wall where Nick's work hung.

"He's good, isn't he?" Brooke whispered, holding the wrapped sculpture against her like a newborn baby.

Roxy hadn't yet surrendered her grudge against Nick completely, so she nodded without saying a word.

Brooke leaned back against a corner of the wall and gazed at her sister's sad eyes. "Roxy, I know you don't like him," she whispered, "because you think that directly or indirectly he's responsible for a lot of things in both our lives. But what you have to understand is that Nick was as much a victim as I was."

Roxy settled her eyes on one painting, and Brooke could see that she made an honest effort to see, to feel the pain and poignancy Nick had captured there. "I know about being a victim, Brooke," she whispered.

"I know you do," Brooke said quietly. "You've been a victim of my scandal, and now, whether you want to talk about it or not, you're also a victim of a married man who has probably promised you the moon and the stars. But he's married, Roxy, and no matter how you add that up, you come out shortchanged."

Roxy's gaze hardened, and she turned back to Brooke. "I don't want to talk about it."

Brooke watched Roxy step away, arms crossed defensively as she glanced at other pieces displayed in that portion of the gallery. "Just remember something," Brooke said. "There's someone out there for you, who has the same dreams, the same imagination, the same kind of soul. When you meet him, you'll find that he fills all the empty parts inside of you, and you'll know in your heart that you fill the emptiness in him, too. When you find that person, Roxy, you'll understand how hollow this relationship is now."

Roxy's gaze fell to the floor, and a soul-deep sadness glistened in her eyes. "And that's what you have with Nick?" she asked.

"That's what I have with Nick," Brooke said. "That's what I felt for him when I was your age, and that's why my life hasn't quite worked out since. Because you can't just *settle* for something. Life's too important to compromise."

Roxy looked toward the gallery owner, who was walking her clients to the door, then moved her focus back to Brooke. A shred of a smile glimmered in her eyes. "Sonny's nice," she whispered.

"Yeah, Sonny's real nice."

Brooke smiled at her sister, praying that the enchantment she saw on her face meant that Roxy was allowing herself another chance to find the happiness she deserved.

But before Roxy said more, Helena was free and heading toward them.

"Sorry, darling," she said, her voice loud now that they were alone in the gallery. "That was one of my best clients. Didn't find anything she wanted this trip, though. Darn

that Nick. I could sure use some new paintings from him.
Is he working on anything?''

"A few things," Brooke said, not wanting to disappoint
the anxious woman. "The stained-glass windows are his
main priority right now, though." She felt her heart
pounding painfully, like that of a mother offering a child
for adoption, at the moment of surrender. Slowly, she un-
covered *Infinity*. "He—" her voice faltered, and she swallowed "—he told me you like this. That you had made an
offer on it."

Helena's face lit up as she drew in a deep, reverent breath.
Carefully she took the sculpture from Brooke and turned
it over in her hands as if she knew its value vividly. "The
sculpture he wouldn't sell me!" she said. "I *begged* him for
it." She looked at Brooke, her eyes filled with a new respect. "You wouldn't be the sculptor, would you?"

Brooke nodded and wondered if her face looked as pale
and lifeless as it felt. "Yes, I am."

"I see." Helena inclined her head and offered her a
knowing smile. "The last time you two were in, darling, I
figured out that you were the woman in Nick's past. Now,
I understand why he wouldn't part with the sculpture. I
thought his attachment to it was a little unusual. Especially when it wasn't his own work. And honey, I offered
him a *lot* of money."

Brooke tried to ignore the comments regarding their relationship and seized the opportunity. "Does the offer still
stand?" she asked, her voice suddenly hoarse.

"Does it ever!" Helena said. "I can write you a check
right now."

Brooke looked down at the sculpture and realized that it
could fall into a stranger's hands, someone who didn't
know the history, the pain, the heartache associated with

those hands, who'd set it on their mantel somewhere and forget to dust it.

"Do...do you plan to keep it...for yourself? Or do you plan to sell it?" The question came out as broken and wavering as her heartbeat.

Helena set a gentle hand on Brooke's shoulder. "I'm keeping it for myself, of course. I've been wanting it for months. But if an offer comes along that I can't refuse..." She took the sculpture and let out a low, long breath. "Oh, but it would have to be *some* offer." She looked into Brooke's eyes. "Are you sure you're ready to part with it, darling?"

Brooke's mouth went cotton dry, but still she managed to speak. "I'm sure," she said. "It's all yours."

"I CAN'T BELIEVE you did it," Roxy said two hours later, after Brooke had opened a bank account for the stained-glass windows expenses and deposited the twenty-five thousand.

"I can't believe I did, either," Brooke whispered, aware that the color had still not returned completely to her face. She had gone through the transactions that morning in a zombielike daze, doing what she had to do, but refusing to dwell on the pain throbbing through her. "But I have to concentrate on what it will mean in the long run. We'll have the chance to do the windows. It'll make Nick happy, and that'll make me happy." She breathed a deep sigh and tried to smile. "I'll drop you off at home before I go to the museum."

Roxy looked out the window, her expression pensive as she chose her words. Finally she looked at her sister. "You know, Brooke, I think this is really unselfish, what you're doing. And if you still need me, I'd like to keep working at the museum. You don't have to pay me."

"Really?" Brooke asked, taking her eyes off the road long enough to gape at Roxy. "You'd do that?"

"Yeah. I'm out of school the rest of this week, and then I can help weekends and after work sometimes."

The sweet, forgiving invitation was like an injection of positive energy that made Brooke's smile more genuine. "All right, Roxy. You can work today, if you want."

For the first time since she could remember, Roxy answered her smile. They drove to the museum in silence as a sense of wellbeing washed over Brooke. She had the money to get a substantial start on the stained-glass windows. Already, in her mind's eye, she could see the surprise and delight in Nick's eyes when she told him.

And that, she realized, was worth ten *Infinities*.

"YOU SAID YOU WEREN'T firing us," Nick reminded Horace Anderson as they sat in the museum office, figures and projected cost estimates spread out on the table. "If we come up with the money ourselves, we can go ahead with it, right?"

Horace rubbed his loose jaw and straightened his heavy glasses. "I don't like it," he said gruffly. "It doesn't seem fair. You and Brooke don't have that kind of money to throw away."

Nick leaned forward, anxious to get his point across. His eyes were lively with conviction. "Horace, we're going to get the money. Now, are you with us, or not?"

A grin snaked across Horace's face. "Well, hell yes, I'm with you. If you're willing to put yourself on the line like that, not even Abby Hemphill can stop you!" he said, chuckling.

Nick took Horace's hand and shook it heartily. "You're a good man, Horace."

"And you, my friend, are a devoted artist."

A knock sounded on the office door, and Nick leaned over and opened it, laughter still on his voice as he greeted Brooke and Roxy. "Great news," he sang out before either of them could speak. "Horace gave us the go-ahead."

Before Brooke had the chance to react, Nick threw his arms around her waist and swung her around.

"Then we're in business!" she cried with glee. "I just made a deposit this morning."

Nick set her back on her feet, his breath heavy with elation. "What? A deposit?" His smiled began to waver as she brandished the bankbook she clutched in her hand. He took it, opened it and read the amount. "Twenty-five thousand? Brooke—"

Brooke stemmed his questions with an outstretched hand. "Don't worry," she said, laughing and winking at Horace. "I didn't do anything illegal."

"But Brooke—"

Brooke cut him off and turned back to Horace.

"So, I guess we have enough to get a good start on the windows, anyway."

Horace let out a boisterous laugh and punched at the air. "That ought to show Abby. That old biddy never counted on dedication to get in her way, did she?"

Brooke laughed—a bit overbrightly—then glanced toward Nick, who still gazed at her with stunned, alarmed eyes. "Brooke, I have to know where you got this money," he said, his tone taking on a sharpness even he didn't understand.

Brooke's smile vanished. "We'll talk in a minute," she said, restoring her smile and taking Horace's arm. "I'll walk you out, Horace. I wanted to ask you about what the other council members said about the decision last night."

Nick watched her disappear with Horace, and finally he turned his suspicious eyes on Roxy, who stood mutely just inside the door.

"What did she do, Roxy?" he whispered. "Where did she get it?"

He could see that Roxy held the secret tightly, as well, when she shook her head and said, "It should come from her. It's really none of my business."

The significance of the girl's evasion hit him boldly in the heart. "She sold it." His voice was weak, as though the truth had knocked the breath out of him. "She sold *Infinity*, didn't she?"

Roxy stood motionless, but Nick came toward her, taking her shoulders, and forcing her to answer. "Didn't she!"

"Yes!" Roxy cried, frightened. "She had to."

"The *hell* she did!" he shouted. He hurled away from her and crashed his fist on the desk. Roxy jumped. "How could she do that? How *could* she when she knew—?"

Suddenly like a man ruled by the pain in his bruised heart, he threw down the bankbook and pushed past Roxy, out into the hall and past the construction crews working inside the museum. He paced back and forth in front of the door, watching through the window until Horace drove away. The moment Brooke was alone, he joined her in the parking lot.

"You sold it!" he shouted, bolting toward her, anger in his eyes. "How could you do that?"

Immediately he saw the fear registering in her face, her defensive posture, her rigid stance.

"Nick, wait a minute," she said, stepping toward him. "I did what I had to do!"

"Didn't it mean anything to you?" he demanded, his eyes luminous with misery. "You knew what it meant to me! I've had it all these years! I thought it symbolized what we meant to each other. Is that all our relationship is? Something you can sell?"

"Nick, you aren't being rational!" she said. "I didn't sell *us*! I sold the sculpture! You said the windows meant a lot to you. We needed the money, and now we've got it! Don't you understand what—?"

"Don't tell me I'm not being rational," he said, his lips trembling in rage. "I told you that I could come up with the money. I told you to trust me. But you couldn't do that, could you, any more than you could ten years ago, when you ran away and got married!"

Tears sprang to Brooke's eyes, and she reached for him, grasping his hand. Depriving her of that small intimacy, he recoiled. "Nick, don't do this," she cried, bringing both hands up to wad her hair. "I didn't do it to hurt you."

"Well, it did," he bit out. "It sure as hell did. It tells me a lot about our relationship, Brooke. It tells me that it's a commodity that can be traded." He opened his car door, turned back to her, his face still frighteningly distorted with pain. "What was all that crap about art not having a price tag? About nobody being able to take it away from you? Was it all just talk, Brooke? Didn't you mean any of it?"

"Every word," she said. "But I thought—"

"You *thought* it wouldn't bother me," he said, nodding. "You thought it meant as little to me as it does to you and that I wouldn't mind seeing it traded for a big fat check." He slammed his hand against the unscratched, unscarred body of his car, then got in. "I must be an idiot for falling into this with you again!"

Brooke started toward him, but he cranked the car and screeched out of his space before she could reach him. "Nick!" she cried.

Her cry tore through the recesses of his heart, resounding through each empty chamber, spelling out his destiny in a broken plea. And no matter how far he drove, he was helpless to escape it.

THOUGH SHE HAD TAKEN Roxy home, Brooke waited at the museum for the rest of the day for Nick to come back, but when darkness finally swallowed the old museum, intruding in the workroom and making her feel more isolated, she realized that he didn't plan to return.

His words played over in her mind, making a little piece of her die each time she heard them.

"I told you to trust me. But you couldn't do that, could you? Any more than you could ten years ago when you ran off and got married!"

Had he really been carrying that in his heart all these years? The anger, the pain, that she had betrayed him somehow, by not trusting him enough to wait for him?

She thought of going home, but couldn't bear the thought of facing her parents and opening herself up to their scrutiny and probing questions. She had called Nick's house so many times today, that she knew he wasn't home. He was punishing her, she thought. Making her feel more miserable than she had ever imagined feeling . . . before she had known the potency of his love, the intimate power of his expression.

Didn't that mean anything to him? Was a block of clay shaped into two human hands more important than what they had now?

It always came back to that sculpture, she thought. It was their magnet, but it also had the power to repel them. How could something so sweet create such bitterness?

Quietly she walked through the museum, turning off the lights, wishing . . . praying . . . that Nick would appear before she left and tell her that he understood what she had done, that the depth of her feeling was apparent in her gesture . . . not negated by it.

She heard the side door open and caught her breath as she swung around. "Nick?"

But it wasn't Nick. Instead, her ex-husband, Skip, stood there, looking as handsome and as self-assured as he had in college, when he'd been her best friend, her confidant, her husband.

"Sorry," he said with a half smile. "It's just me."

"Skip." Brooke tried to smile, but failed. Fleetingly she wondered if he could see the evidence of tears under her eyes, the shadows of worry over her face, the traces of sadness in her expression. "Hi."

"Hi." He looked around the room. "Looks like things are going pretty good around here. It's gonna be real nice."

"Yeah," she said, looking around her with haunted eyes, and wondering if the stained-glass windows would, indeed, be a part of it all. Unable to deal with the grim prospects now, she turned back to her ex-husband. "What are you doing here, Skip?"

Skip shrugged and stepped toward her. "I wanted to talk to you," he said. "We used to do that, you know. Talk?"

"I remember. That was before we messed everything up by getting married."

"Right," he said, and she could hear the soft hint of nostalgia in his tone where nothing but bitterness had once been. "You were the best confidante I ever had. That's why I wanted to come by and tell you . . . first-hand."

"Tell me what, Skip?"

He looked down at the floor, slid his hands into his pockets, and brought his eyes back to hers. "That I'm getting married again," he said. "Next month."

"Married?" Brooke asked, her lips parting in surprise. "Really?"

"Yep. To the cutest little redhead you ever saw. Her name's Cinda. She's the tennis coach at the school."

"Cinda," Brooke repeated. "That's pretty." She regarded her ex-husband for a moment, gauging him for more than he was offering. "Are you happy, Skip?"

"Oh, man," he said in affirmation. "She loves me, Brooke. Really loves me."

Brooke looked at the floor and swallowed a surge of guilt that she had offered Skip much less in their own marriage. "You deserve that," she whispered.

"Yeah," he said. "So do you." He went to a ladder pushed against the wall and sat down on a rung. "So, I guess you and Nick are probably back together by now, huh? The gossips in town are all buzzing...."

Brooke laughed and discovered that the rumors didn't even upset her anymore. But after a second her smile faded, and sadness welled up in her troubled eyes again. "I don't know," she said.

Skip saw her pain and wouldn't back off. "What's the matter?"

"I sold the sculpture," she said, surprising herself that she could confide in him again after all these years. "The one I did in high school. He's kept it all these years, even though someone offered him a lot of money for it. I sold it to get the money for the windows, but Nick didn't understand...he's furious with me, and I don't even know where he is." She felt tears springing to her eyes, and her lips quivered.

"It must have meant a lot to him," Skip said. "So what's the big deal? Just go buy it back."

"But the windows..." she said. "How will we pay for the windows?"

"There must be another way," he said, "if you both put your heads together."

"Another way," she whispered, shaking her head. "I wish I knew what it could be." She thought of last night, when they had agreed to finish the windows without pay, and he had told her to trust him, that he could get the money.

"Trust me." He'd said those words before, ten years ago, when he'd called her the night the Hemphills launched the missile that had devastated their lives. *"Trust me,"* he'd said. But she hadn't trusted him. Instead, she had run away... and ultimately married another man. Maybe that was why Nick had brought that up to her today, when it hadn't seemed at all relevant. Maybe his reaction was more of a belated response to that marriage than to her selling *Infinity.* Somehow, she would have to prove to him that she was different now.

"Buy it back," she muttered again, a smile slowly curving her lips as she brought her weary eyes back to her ex-husband. "Thanks, Skip. That's what I'll do."

"Good," he said with a laugh. "Because after all I went through with you, knowing you were in love with him, I'd sure hate to think it was all wasted and you two didn't get together, after all. There's got to be some justice in this world."

Brooke leaned over and pressed a kiss on Skip's cheek. "You're a great friend," she said.

Skip arched his brows with mock regret. "Yeah, that's me," he said. "Too bad I didn't have enough sense to settle for that ten years ago."

NICK LEANED BACK against his Duesenberg and dug his shoes in the sand, watching the waves chase the wind back from the Gulf, lapping the shore and taunting him, just as Brooke had done.

"Trust me."

The words were a mockery to him, empty reminders of the pain in his heart ten years ago, pain that had endured throughout all the lonely years since. She hadn't trusted him then, just as she hadn't trusted him today.

As if he were sitting beside him, Nick heard his grandfather's laughter. *"That'sa the thing about women,"* he had told him once. *"Just when you think you've got 'em figured, they change all the rules."*

Nick shook the voice out of his head and drank from the bottle of liquor he'd brought with him. The taste was too sour, too potent, too unsatisfying. Getting drunk wouldn't solve his problems tonight. He just wanted to think, make some sense of it all. He just wanted to understand....

But it was impossible to understand the heart of a woman who could love him one minute and marry someone else the next. It was hard to understand the heart of someone who could create such magnificent beauty, bestow such a profound gift, then sell it for cold hard cash....

He turned the bottle upside down and watched it pour out on the sand. When it was empty, he threw it into the water, watched the waves possess it, then take it out to sea.

Who would find it? he wondered idly. Some other lonely soul with a mixed-up heart?

He stood up and looked at the car that had been his main source of pride for as long as he'd been able to drive. He could see his grandfather in every detail, from the gold-plated wheel covers, to the leather seats. His grandpa, who had believed in him and shown him what was real, despite the pain it cost. His grandpa, who'd had dreams of his own that were never quite fulfilled.

Nick's eyes misted over, and he realized he'd give every day he'd had as an artist for one more day with his grandpa. He could use some advice right now, he thought. He could use a little help.

The night grew more opaque as clouds billowed over-head from the Gulf, and a chill wind crept around him, re-minding him that he was a couple of hours from home. But he had no intention of going back there tonight. Not until he had sorted some things out, he thought. Not until he had set some things right.

It was clear in his mind what he had to do. He only wished it had been as clear in Brooke's.

BROOKE WAS UP AT DAWN the next morning, pacing in front of the telephone until a decent hour when she could call the gallery and plead with Helena to let her buy back the sculpture. Her parents came in for breakfast and appre-hensively noted the anxiety in her face, the tremor in her hands. Before long Roxy came in, as well, and all of them sat quietly as Brooke dialed the gallery. She let the phone ring ten or twelve times and finally gave up until she could try again.

"What is it with that statue?" her father asked, irritated by her persistence.

"It's important, Daddy," Brooke said, not in the mood to go into her relationship with Nick. "It was a mistake to sell it."

"If you ask me, you made the mistake holding onto it all this time," he said, picking up the paper and flipping to the sports section. "How much did they give you for it, any-way? Fifty, sixty?"

"Twenty-five," Brooke said absently, flipping through the phone book for Helena's last name as it had appeared on her check, desperately hoping to catch her at home.

"Then what's the big deal?" her father asked. "I could have loaned you that."

Roxy's sudden burst of laughter surprised both parents. "Thousand, Daddy. Twenty-five thousand."

George dropped the newspaper with a sharp intake of breath. *"Twenty-five thousand dollars!"* he bellowed. "They paid you twenty-five thousand for a lump of clay, and you think you made a mistake?"

Oblivious to her parents' shock, Brooke eyed the clock on the wall, and saw that it wasn't yet eight. "Maybe they open at eight," she muttered. "Maybe I ought to just go there." She turned back to Roxy, ignoring her father's and mother's incredulous stares. "Roxy, do you think I should just go there?"

"It wouldn't hurt," Roxy said. "You'll have to go to pick it up, anyway."

Her mother bolted out of her seat. "You're going to give that money back? Are you crazy?"

"Yes, Mom," Brooke said, grabbing her purse and heading for the door without a second look back. "I guess I am."

CHAPTER FIFTEEN

"WHAT DO YOU MEAN, you've sold it?" Brooke's voice wobbled with panic as she stood in the gallery, gaping at Helena.

"Last night, darling. I don't run a pawn shop, you know. I didn't expect you to want it back."

A wave of dizzy disbelief washed over Brooke, and she lowered herself onto a white leather chair. "But you...you said you'd bought it for yourself...that you would keep it!"

Alarmed at Brooke's near-wild state, Helena sat down next to her, lowering her voice to a calming pitch. "Darling, I said I'd keep it unless someone made me an offer I couldn't refuse. I meant that, but that offer came last night."

Ignoring the tears inhibiting her speech, Brooke dug into her purse for a pen and a piece of paper. "All right. Who did you sell it to?" she asked. "I'll go directly to them and buy it back."

Helena shook her head slowly, and set a kind hand on Brooke's shoulder. "First of all, darling, you couldn't buy it back for twenty-five. The deal I made last night was for considerably more. I am in business to make a profit, you understand."

"More?" Brooke cried, feeling more helpless the darker things looked. "How *much* more?"

"Love, it isn't practical for me to disclose that to you," Helena said. "Besides, I couldn't in good conscience disclose that client's name to you and let you show up with that wild look in your eyes. It's just not . . . professional."

Brooke dropped her face into her hands and tried to catch her breath. After a moment she looked up, her pallid complexion contrasting with the redness in her eyes. "Helena, look," she tried again. "I know you hardly know me at all. But if you've ever cared about Nick, please help me. It means so much to him. I want it back for him."

Helena shook her head resolutely, but her face was not without sympathy. "I'm sorry, love. It's out of the question."

Brooke's shoulders drooped as if this final refusal punctured her determination once and for all. "I can't believe this," she whispered. "I thought I was doing the right thing. And now I can't even afford my own work, and I have no idea where Nick is." She came to her feet, almost dazed, and started for the door.

Helena followed her. "He's a complex man. It shows in his work." She stopped as Brooke opened the door. "If he's that upset about the sculpture, darling, it isn't really about the sculpture. It's about something else."

"I know," Brooke whispered. "I know."

She bade Helena goodbye, then got in her car and sat for a moment. It was gone, she told herself. The sculpture she had made for him, *sold* for him, was gone. And so was he.

She started her car and vacantly drove back to Hayden. Tears rolled down her face—tears of regret, tears of guilt, tears of waste. *Infinity* was gone, handed over to a perfect stranger who hadn't a clue that it meant so much to two such vulnerable souls. She would never see it again. *Where are you, Nick?* her heart cried out as she drove. *Help me to cope with what I've done. Don't you condemn me, too . . .*

But he did condemn her, she knew. That was a fact, just as vivid as the loneliness of her past ten years. They all condemned her.

But if there was an up side to the constant judgment she'd suffered, it was that she had become conditioned to living with it, accepting it, and even forgiving it. For that reason she drove to Nick's house, praying the two of them would have one more chance to forgive each other.

When she arrived at his house, she saw that the garage was open and his car was gone. Still, she went to the door and knocked. There was no answer. Grasping at some way to reach him, she left a note pleading for him to call her.

Immediately Brooke headed back for the museum, praying that she would find Nick there, hard at work. Maybe he'd put yesterday's fight behind them and he'd be willing to pull her into his arms and give her another chance to trust him.

His car wasn't there, but undaunted, and as determined to find him as she'd ever been in her life, Brooke went into the museum, stalked past the workers, and checked his office and the workroom.

"Your lover's not here."

Brooke spun around and saw the construction worker who had confronted her that first day on the job with his lewd comments about "getting to know her better." Strangely his remark today hardly fazed her at all.

"Has he been here? Have you seen him at all?"

"Not today." He grinned. "Hey, you look a little desperate. I have a lunch hour coming up soon. We could slide over to the No Tell Motel—"

Brooke grabbed the collar of his sweaty T-shirt and jerked him toward her, glaring up into his dusty face. "I'm in a lousy mood right now," she bit out, "and I think it's only fair that I warn you that if you ever come on to me again I'll find a new use for those vice grips of yours. *That's* how desperate I am.''

She let him go, and the man stumbled back, surprise striking him speechless as she pushed past him and headed back out to her car.

Brooke sat there a moment, setting aside the satisfaction her threat had brought her and racking her brain for some clue, some memory, to lead her in the right direction.

Nick's family lived in town. Maybe they would know where he could be reached. Maybe he was with them.

Quickly she drove to a pay phone, looked up the name Marcello and didn't find a listing. She remembered that Sonny's last name was Castori, so she flipped over to the Cs. There was no listing.

Maybe Roxy will know where they live, she thought suddenly, hope rising in her heart.

Brooke pulled away from the museum and headed across town to City Hall, praying that she would find Roxy there.

The parking lot at city hall was cluttered with everything from buses to pickup trucks, but Brooke found Roxy's car and pulled into a space nearby. A fleeting doubt passed through her mind about disturbing her sister at work, but she told herself this visit couldn't wait. She had to find Nick and convince him that she loved him, that he was wrong about her, before he'd written her off once and for all.

She went up the stairs to the building and stepped aside as a small wedding party came out of the justice of the peace's office. The young bride, adorned in a white lace minidress with a spray of baby's breath tucked into her French twist, laughed melodically as she tossed the bouquet toward the half dozen well-wishers surrounding her. The groom eyed his new bride possessively, proudly, and not a soul present could mistake the urgency in his eyes—he wanted to sweep her away from the crowd and have her all to himself.

Such was the stuff of which fairy tales—and stained-glass windows—were made, Brooke thought as sadness weighed down her heart. But what of real life? Were things really ever that simple, that uncomplicated?

What was it about the Martin girls, she thought, that such happiness could never belong to them?

She went to the office marked Records where Roxy worked, and lacking the presence of mind to knock, pushed open the door. The sound of hushed voices coming from the corner of the room behind a row of file cabinets stopped her.

"No, Bill," Roxy was saying, her voice somberly low. "It's over. That's it."

Realizing she had walked into something private, Brooke started to back out of the office and leave them alone, when she heard something slam against the file cabinet. "Oh, no, you don't," the man said viciously. "I'm warning you. I call the shots here, not you. And you're not finished with me until I say you are."

Alarmed, Brooke leaned around a cabinet enough to see that Bill Hemphill had braced an arm on each side of Roxy, trapping her. "Please, Bill," Roxy said, her voice raspy with emotion. "I can't take this anymore."

"Well, you're going to," he told her in a syrupy sweet voice. "I've arranged to meet you tonight at the Bluejay Inn. Room 413. If you don't show up this time, ready to cooperate, then you can kiss this job goodbye."

"Fine!" Roxy pushed him away and twisted out of his reach. "I'm sick of this job, anyway. And I'm tired of fighting you off...."

Bill's laugh was calculatingly intimidating. "Do you think that's all there is to it, babe? That your job is all that's at stake? If that was all I had hanging over your head, I wouldn't have gotten *this* far with you."

Brooke stepped back out of sight, covered her mouth with her hand and held her breath in horror as the truth—much worse than she had feared—reared its ugly head.

"You're sick!" Roxy cried. "I hope your wife finds out about this! I hope she throws you out!"

Though she couldn't see him, Brooke could hear Bill chuckle. "Do you really think that anyone would blame me if word did get out? I'd just say that you pursued me and seduced me, trying to ruin my marriage. Since that sort of behavior runs in your family, anyway, it wouldn't be that hard to sell."

"You shut up!" Roxy shouted. "I wouldn't sleep with you if you were the last man on earth. You make me sick!"

Brooke heard a loud noise, and she jumped, then looked around the cabinet to see that Bill was holding Roxy with brute force against the wall.

"Well, tonight I might as well be the last man on earth, baby, because that's exactly what you're going to do."

The final filament of Brooke's control snapped, and she barreled toward him, her green eyes aflame with outrage.

"Let go of her!" she demanded. "Get your slimy hands off my sister!"

Bill spun around, letting Roxy go, and Brooke realized that at that moment, had she been holding a weapon, she could have murdered him without one second's thought.

"If you want a scandal, you'll get one," Brooke said through her teeth. "Because if there's anything we Martins have learned from your family, it's how to play dirty."

As Roxy slipped behind her, Brooke took a few intimidating steps toward the tall young man, who stepped back in self-defense, as if he saw the capability for violence in her eyes. "Does the term 'jailbait' mean anything to you?" she asked, her eyes glowering with intense hatred. "Have you ever heard of 'statutory rape'? Have you ever heard of sexual harrassment?" She uttered a deep, humorless laugh. "Oh, we're talking about a lot more than family embarrassment, here. We're talking about prison!"

"Hey, wait a minute!" Bill said, holding his palms up innocently. "I didn't do anything. It was just a game. I never even slept with her."

"A game?" Brooke bit out. "A *game*? Is that some sick hobby you and your family have? Destroy the Martins if you can? Hit them while they're young? Win a Kewpie doll?"

Footsteps sounded in the doorway, and Brooke glanced back to see Mrs. Hemphill standing there, head cocked and nose indignantly thrown in the air. "What is going on here?" she demanded, addressing Brooke. "This is a government office, and you have no business here."

Brooke turned from the son and faced the mother. "I'll tell you what's going on here," she said, pointing a scathing finger at the woman. "You and your family have made your last attempt to ruin my family. And I suggest you watch the headlines very carefully tomorrow. There's going to be a story on page one that'll curl your hair. See how it feels, Mrs. Hemphill. You love scandals so much. Enjoy one of your own for a change." She reached for Roxy, then turned back to Bill as they started to leave the room. "I wouldn't wait too long to get yourself a lawyer," she warned. "You're going to need one."

Then, leaving Mrs. Hemphill and her son gaping after them in horror, she and Roxy stormed out of the office and down the steps of city hall.

When they were safe in the sanctuary of Brooke's car, Roxy leaned her head back on the seat and threw her hands over her face, as if absorbing the final release from her personal hell. ''Thank you, Brooke,'' she whispered, tears rolling down her face.

Brooke tried to catch her breath, but rage still spiraled up in her throat. ''Did he hurt you?'' she asked.

''Not physically,'' Roxy whispered, her voice coming out in a strained vibrato. ''But the intimidation...it's been going on for months now. I was so scared...'' She wiped her face, mascara smearing on her hands, and looked at her sister.

''When I first started working there he hardly knew I existed. But then one night last year, he saw me dance in a recital...'' Her voice broke and she hid her face from her sister. ''From then on he's been after me. At first I thought he was harmless, but for the past few weeks he's been making ultimatums...demands....'' She drew in a sustaining breath to help her go on. ''Brooke, that night when you picked me up at that bar? He had forced me to go to a motel with him, but when I refused to go into the room, he took me and dumped me out at that bar. He said that if I was so anxious to hold on to...my virtue...I could try holding onto it there....''

''That bastard,'' Brooke whispered murderously. ''I could kill him. I could honestly—''

''I never slept with him,'' Roxy said, setting her hand on Brooke's arm and anxiously meeting her eyes. ''But he had me so scared that I really believed that if I didn't do it soon, he was going to spread a bunch of lies about me, and there would be another scandal all over again.'' She shoved her hand through her hair, leaving it tangled and damp. ''I've run all my life from a scandal, Brooke. That's the thing I'm most afraid of, and he knew it. I just couldn't stand the idea of being involved in one.''

Brooke closed her eyes and let the truth cast some light on the darkness she had stumbled through. She had been wrong about Roxy, and the fact that she had assumed the worst shamed her. When she could finally speak again, she pulled her sister against her. Roxy hugged her just as she had when she was no more than a toddler. "I love you, Roxy," Brooke said, "and I hope you can forgive me for thinking the worst about you."

"Only if you can forgive me for thinking the worst about you," Roxy whispered, sniffing. "I'm just as guilty as you are."

Brooke reached under her seat for a box of tissues, and pulled out a handful for each of them. They cried together for a while longer, and finally Brooke leaned back against her car door, facing her sister. "Do you want to press charges against him?" she asked. "I'd love to see him in jail."

"No." Roxy's answer was firm, as if she'd already given the question some thought. "I wouldn't have much to stand on, since he never really got what he was after. And I sure don't want my name in the paper." She looked toward the front doors of city hall, contemplating her plight. "But let's not let him off the hook, just yet. Let him watch the head-lines everyday, wondering when the story will hit. Let him lose a few nights of sleep. I think he deserves at least that, don't you think?"

"Are you sure?" Brooke asked with a disappointed sigh. "Not even *one* night in jail?"

Roxy shook her head sadly. "No. He'd have the town believing that I was some kind of temptress. I'd rather let him build his own prison."

Brooke squeezed her sister's hand, knowing that this de-cision was one only Roxy could make. "All right," she said. "I guess I can live with that if you can."

"I don't know what would have happened to me if you hadn't been there," Roxy said quietly. "What were you doing there, anyway?"

Brooke remembered her mission, and if her heart had had any place lower to sink, it would have. "I came to ask you if you knew where Sonny lives. I don't think Nick's been home all night, and I don't even know where to look for him. I thought his family might know."

"He took me there the other night to show me his painting," Roxy said. "I think I can find the place again. You want me to go with you and show you?"

Brooke glanced hopefully at her sister. "Would you?" she asked. "I'm a little shaky today. I'm not in the best shape to meet the family of the man I'm in love with, but I don't know where else to turn."

"Sure I will," Roxy said. "I figure I owe you one." She looked at Brooke, thinking of all the pain she'd put her through. "I can see that the two of you have something pretty special," she said. "I hope everything works out."

"Really?" Brooke asked. "Do you mean that?"

Roxy smiled, her eyes lustrous. "I've learned a lot of lessons in the past few weeks. But the most important one is that things aren't always the way they look."

Brooke relaxed a little as a warm stirring of hope rose inside her. "We've all learned a lesson or two," she said.

Roxy directed her to Sonny's street, but she wasn't certain which house was his, for it had been too dark the night she'd been there. They drove slowly past each house, and had turned around to try again, when Sonny's motorcycle grumbled up the street toward them and pulled into a driveway.

"Bingo," Brooke said, pulling into the driveway behind him. Sonny took off his helmet, leaving his hair badly tousled, and looked back at them. A genuine smile tore across his face at the sight of Roxy.

He got off his bike and ambled back to the passenger window. "Hey, Rox. You remembered where I live," he said, bracing his arms on her rolled-down window. "I like that."

Brooke didn't have time to cultivate the mild flirtation. "Sonny, have you seen Nick? I've been looking for him all day."

"He didn't come home last night," Sonny said. "I was over there using his studio till 3:00 a.m., and he never came home."

"Where could he be?" she asked, sounding frantic.

"Beats me," Sonny said. "Did you two have a fight or something?"

"Yeah…something…" Brooke looked at him, her eyes tired and raw from weeping, and she knew that she had long ago cried all her makeup off. She was an emotional mess—in no shape for meeting Nick's family. But necessity demanded it. "Look, is your mother home? Or your grandmother? I'd like to talk to them."

"Sure," Sonny said, surprised at the request. "I'll take you inside."

"No." Brooke got out of the car and looked at him over the roof. "You just stay out here and keep Roxy company. I have to do this alone."

Leaving Sonny and Roxy at her car, Brooke went to the door and rang the bell, holding her breath as she waited. After a moment a pretty woman in her late thirties answered.

"Yes?" Nick's sister stood in the doorway, bouncing a fat baby on her hip. "Can I help you?"

"Yes." She cleared her throat, then swallowed. "I'm Brooke Martin . . . a friend of Nick's."

Anna stared at her for a moment, then took a quick step back. "Ma!" she belted out into the house. She turned back to Brooke, held out a tentative hand and muttered, "I'm Anna, his sister."

In less than a minute Nick's wiry little mother stood at the door, and Brooke noted the hint of resemblance to him on the old woman's dark Italian face.

"Ma, this is Brooke Martin," Anna said.

Nick's mother regarded her without saying a word, and then she peered out into the driveway. "Where's Nicholas?" she asked.

"I . . . I don't know," Brooke said, recognizing the chill surrounding her. "That's sort of what I wanted to talk to you about. I don't think he went home at all last night. I thought you might know of some place—"

"Come in." Without ceremony Mrs. Marcello took her arm and pulled her into the living room. She gestured toward an old, worn-out chair. "Sit," she ordered.

"No...thank you," Brooke said. She took a deep breath and decided to be as honest with the two women as she could. At this point she had nothing to lose. "Look, I know that you two probably feel the same way about me as my parents feel about Nick. The gossip that follows us is . . . well, it's pretty overpowering. I don't blame you for anything you think about me, but at the moment that isn't my concern. I'm worried about Nick, Mrs. Marcello. Do you have any idea where he could be?"

Mrs. Marcello took the baby from her daughter. "He wouldn't tell us. We had words."

"About me?" Brooke asked. She recognized their reluctance to answer and tried again. "He told me that you consider me still married in the eyes of God, but Mrs. Marcello, my ex-husband told me last night that he's remarrying. Our marriage was a bad mistake. If I'd followed my heart, I would never have left town ten years ago. And maybe I would have married Nick instead of Skip. Maybe that's what God intended all along.''

''You were a child!'' Nick's mother shouted, shaking a finger at her so hard that the baby began to cry. ''He has no right influencing children. You, Sonny...'' She tried to lower her voice, bounced the baby a moment, then handed her back to Anna. Two other children ran past, one in hot pursuit of the other, and Anna dashed out to intervene, leaving the two women to face each other alone. ''He has no right influencing children,'' Nick's mother repeated.

Brooke stepped across the living room to view a collection of family photographs assembled on a shelf. Her eyes scanned them until she found a young man she was sure was Nick, standing beside an old man and his Duesenberg. Instinctively she knew the old man was his beloved grandfather.

He would have liked you, Nick had said. If that was true, she thought, maybe Nick's mother wasn't a lost cause. She turned back to the brittle old woman, who was glaring at her. ''Mrs. Marcello, Nick always acted in the most appropriate manner when I was in high school,'' she said. ''He isn't big on self-defense, so maybe he's never told you. Nothing happened between us until I had already graduated. And then it was only an innocent kiss.''

''That's not what the newspapers said!''

''They were lies,'' Brooke said. ''How could you know Nick, really know him, and not realize that?'' In spite of her efforts to curb her tears, Brooke's eyes filled again and she willed her lips to stop shaking. Anna came back into the room, her steps slower as she witnessed Brooke's impending breakdown. ''Nick is the most honorable, gentle man that I have ever known,'' Brooke went on. ''He would never hurt anyone, but things hurt him so deeply. He's out there somewhere hurting right now, because of something I did, but also because of all the hurts that have built up in him over the past few years."

Mrs. Marcello's forehead wrinkled in grudging concern, but she didn't speak.

"Maybe she's right, Ma," Anna whispered. "Maybe we were too hard on him."

Nick's mother turned to his sister, gaping at her, incredulous, as if her very words were paramount to familial betrayal. "You could say that, Anna, after what he did to Sonny? Teaching him to paint, making him want to waste his life loafing like Nick has done all these years?"

Brooke had heard all she could stand, and of their own accord, her words tumbled out. "Loaf?" she cried. "Mrs. Marcello, do you know what it's like to work twenty hours a day on a job that you may or may not get paid for? Do you know what it's like to believe in your work so much that you'd be willing to live on *nothing* for months at a time while you finished it, for a town that would never be grateful? Do you know what it's like to have to find self-respect deep within, because no one else can give it to you? Nick Marcello doesn't *loaf*, Mrs. Marcello, any more than his father did, or his brother-in-law, or either of you!" She covered her mouth with her hand, sucked in a sob and went on. "No wonder he misses his grandfather so much," she said. "He was the only one who could see how special your son really is."

Mrs. Marcello glared at her, stunned silence holding her in its grip, and Anna only looked at the floor. Brooke brought her shaky hand higher and covered her eyes, thinking how much she was going to regret having said these things to his family.

"Excuse me," she said finally, going toward the door. "I have to go find him." She was about to leave when Nick's mother touched her arm to stop her.

"Do you think he's all right?" she asked in a feeble voice.

Brooke turned around and saw that the anger had drained from the old woman's face. Her own expression altered as she inclined her head, and she felt her complexion growing hot. "I don't know...if I could just...find him..." She felt herself breaking, wilting, and suddenly the old woman's arms were around her, pulling her back inside the house, leading her to the couch, making her sit down.

"Now, you sit," she said more gently. "When Nick comes home, we'll make things right." She pulled a handkerchief out of her pocket, and began dabbing the tears from Brooke's face. "And we'll tell him there are worse things he could do than to marry the girl who cries over him."

Brooke laughed in spite of herself, but the pain in her heart chased that laughter away, making her sobs more racking...more intense. And she knew that nothing would really make things right until Nick was in her arms again.

OUT IN THE CAR Sonny finally summoned the courage to say what he'd been thinking since they had pulled into his driveway. "You've been crying. Why?"

Roxy dug deep inside herself and found a weak smile for him. "I've had a bad day," she said. "I sort of lost my job."

"Really?" Sonny couldn't help grinning. "Does that mean I'll be seeing you at the museum more?"

"I'll be there," she said, "but I didn't think *you* would. They can't pay us, you know."

Sonny took her hand, turned it up, and began to trace the sensitive center of her palm. "The company there is a hell of a lot better than minimum wage, anyway," he said. "Heck, I'd pay them to let me hang around you."

Roxy grinned and bit her lip. "You're crazy."

Sonny smiled. "Out of my head. Ever since I saw you dance."

Something about the way he said it didn't seem offensive. It didn't cast her as a seductress using her body to create fantasies. Instead, his soft-spoken words made her feel beautiful. "That wasn't dancing," she said. "That was just a couple of steps."

"It was magic," Sonny whispered, cupping her chin. "And if you don't use some of your unemployed time to study dancing again, then I'm going to swear off art for the rest of my life. Think about it."

Roxy laughed aloud. "Oh, no. I couldn't have that on my conscience."

"Then you'll dance again? On stage and everything?"

Her smile faded into an expression of peaceful contemplation, and she looked down at her skirt, following the texture of one pleat with her index finger. "How can I turn down an ultimatum like that?" she asked.

"Hey," he said. "I must be getting harder to say no to. While I'm on a roll, I know this great little Italian restaurant that's not very busy this time of the week. They have tables outside and music playing and—" he offered a self-deprecating laugh "—and I can afford it."

Roxy's smile found a warm place in his eyes. "Like you said," she whispered. "You're on a roll. How can I say no?"

"You can't." He dropped a kiss on her lips. "Now all I have to do is ask the right questions."

His flirtatious promise didn't frighten Roxy at all, for she'd heard sexual come-ons before. This didn't feel like one of them. She could sense the honor in the gentle, cautious way he touched her and in the sweet, patient graze of his lips over hers.

There was no hurry for either of them, she told herself. For they would have plenty more time together.

THE TEN-YEAR-OLD PONTIAC shook as Nick reached the speed of fifty-five the next night, so he dropped back to fifty miles an hour and made a mental note to get the front end aligned as soon as he had the chance. This car was going to have to last him a long time.

He looked down on the seat next to him, and in the darkness, he could see the check with all those zeroes staring up at him. He wondered if his grandpa would have approved of what he had done. *"Women anda money. The two damnedest driving forces in the world. Don'ta let 'em get their grips in you, Nicky."*

But it wasn't that simple, Nick realized, as he passed the sign that said Hayden—Next Exit. Love and dedication were his driving forces...though he doubted they led him into making the wisest choices. Maybe his mother was right. Maybe he had wasted his life. And maybe this last thing with the windows, and with Brooke, was the biggest waste of all.

"But how do you just stop loving someone, Grandpa?"

The little boy's words played in his mind, as if it were yesterday that he had uttered them, sitting beside his grandpa's bed and begging him not to die.

"You don't stop loving them, my boy. Not ever. You remember them in a million different ways."

"But I don't want to remember you, Grandpa. I want you to be right here. With me."

"I wish that could be so, my boy. But I'ma tired..."

He had wept that night when his mother had drawn him from his grandfather's bedside. And later that night, when the man he loved most in the world had passed into another world, he had felt it as a cold jolt in his soul.

Later he had discovered that his grandfather had left him more than a memory. He had left him his car, the most treasured possession he had, even though Nick was years away from driving age.

Tears filled Nick's eyes as he took the Hayden exit, and he blinked them back, determined not to cry over his grandpa again. He had done what he had to do to give himself and Brooke another chance... at their careers, at their self-worth, at their love.

He only wished Brooke had loved him enough to trust him to do the right thing. He wished she had understood that it was time he focused his life on the living—not on the dead—and that he had the means to give them both what they needed.

The car was gone now, he reminded himself, but his grandpa was not. He was still here, with him, in his head and his heart. His voice would never die, just as his memory would linger on.

"Happiness has a heavy price, my boy. And it takes a big man to recognize its value."

Tonight Nick had paid the price. But he wasn't sure of its value yet. The pain of ten years' sorrow hadn't gone away just yet. The sting of mistrust and betrayal still pulsated through him. Maybe that was part of the price, he thought.

He navigated the dark streets of Hayden and pulled into his neighborhood. The lights and lines and shadows looked different from the perspective of this different car... more dismal... more opaque. He reached his house, saw that he had left the garage open, so that he could pull the Duesenberg right in to shelter it from harm, as if his grandfather's very soul resided there trusting in his protection. But the Duesenberg was now a part of a grand collection of classic cars.

He pulled his Pontiac into the garage, cut off the engine and sat in the dark for a moment. How long had he been gone? Two days? Three? Had Brooke been looking for him, or had she given up and gone back to Tallahassee to forget about him and the windows. Had she found another bozo to marry? Was she lining the sides of her garbage cans with the drawings they had done together, as easily as she had sold the sculpture?

He picked up the check and the box on the seat next to him, got out of the car and went to the door, finding that it was unlocked. Damn, he thought. Had he forgotten to lock up when he'd left?

He went into the kitchen and set down the box and the check on the counter, flipped on the light and looked around to see if everything was still in place. The studio was intact, though it looked as if someone had been there. He stepped into the living room, flipped on the lamp and noted that all of his works in progress were still in place. He started to turn to the bedroom, but just as he did, his eye caught on something on his couch...a blanket...a woman...

Brooke's eyes opened, and she sat up in the half darkness, groggy as she looked up at him. She wore not a stitch of makeup, and her eyes were red as if she'd been on constant crying jags for the last several days. Her hair framed her face in neglectful tangles. "Nick," she said, her voice hoarse. "You came back. Are you...are you all right?"

His heart made its thundering presence known to him, nagging at him to reach out and take her in his arms. But his anger and disappointment were too strong, so he stood stiffly back. "I'm fine," he said, not disguising the ambivalence he felt at seeing her. "How did you get in?"

"Sonny let me in," she said. "I didn't know where to look for you. I was so... worried."

"You shouldn't have been," he said in a metallic voice. "I just needed some time."

"To do what?"

"To think," Nick said, his eyes hard beneath the shadows cast by the lamp. "About you and us and the pattern that keeps repeating itself." He slid his fingertips into his pockets and took a few somber steps closer. "About how important what people think is to you, and how trust is something that you couldn't conceive of if someone paid you twenty-five grand to do it."

He saw the tears forming in her eyes, penetrating the shield in which he'd cloaked himself. "Nick, I tried to get the sculpture back," she said. "I went back to the gallery and begged Helena, but she had sold it. She wouldn't give me the name of the person who had bought it, and there was nothing I could do...."

He felt mottled patches of anger bruising his cheeks, and he tightened his lips. "So you have to live with it, right? You made a mistake, but that's the way life is, huh? Just the way you made a mistake when you married Skip Nelson, and *stayed* married to him for three freakin' years!"

Brooke came to her feet and grabbed Nick's arms, but he shook her off. "Nick, why do you keep equating what I did with the sculpture to my marriage with Skip? It doesn't make any sense!"

"Oh, it makes sense," he said, going into the kitchen. She followed behind him miserably. "It makes sense because this whole lousy era of my life started with that sculpture. Everything I've felt in the deepest part of me for the last decade of my life has had something to do with that sculpture. If not for that sculpture, I may have never fallen in love with you. And we wouldn't have been caught in each others' arms that night, and you wouldn't have run away like a scared little girl, refusing to trust me. And you wouldn't have married *him*...."

"Nick, that's crazy!" she cried. "The sculpture wasn't some magical thing that manipulated fate for us. *We* made mistakes, and we paid dearly for them. But it's like you said earlier, Nick. It's time to stop paying."

Nick leaned toward her, gesturing with his hands as if he couldn't find the right words to express himself. "You will *never* understand, will you? The reason I could never sell that sculpture was that it meant so much to me. It holds the very spirit of what you mean to me. The innocence, the gentleness, the passion..." His voice broke, and he turned around with his back to her.

"Nick," she whispered on a shredded sob, touching his back with a cautious hand. "You mean so much more to me than a piece of clay. I only sold it so that we could go on with our work. So that I could stay in Hayden with you."

Nick went rigid and turned around, shaking his head. His eyes were wild as he gazed down at her. "So now we go from the sculpture to the windows? There's always something that has to bind us together, isn't it, Brooke? What will it be after that? Is what we have so fragile that it can fall apart if our project does?" His eyes were wild as he gazed down at her.

"No," she cried, unable to make him listen anymore. "That's not what I meant."

She watched as, with trembling hands, he grabbed the box he had brought in with him and pulled out the sculpture, held it up to her as if daring her to harm it. She caught her breath in staggering relief. "You bought it back! You were the one who bought it!"

"Yeah, I bought it."

"How?" she asked, reaching for it, but he held it out of her grasp. "Where... where did the money come from?"

"I sold my car!" Nick shouted, his eyes two raging black sapphires. "Like I planned to do all along. Like I wanted to do for us. But you didn't trust me, just like you didn't ten years ago, so it wound up being a lousy little gesture for a lousy little reason."

"You... sold your car?" Her words wobbled on a faint wisp of breath, and she dropped her hands to her sides. A gentle hope stirred inside her, hope that his gesture was rooted in the same love hers was. "Oh, Nick. Don't you see? You did it for the same reason that I did. Because in some way, we *are* both afraid that if we lose the project, we'll lose each other. But if you could do that for me, and I could do what I did for you, don't you think that we have something binding? Something that can't be taken from us like a car or a sculpture?"

Her words only served to make Nick angrier, for the pain in his heart was too acute to be explained away so simply. "I don't know," he said through gritted teeth as he held *Infinity* in his hands. "Why don't we find out how binding it is?"

Without warning he hurled the sculpture to the ground with a bone-chilling crash.

Brooke cried out and fell to her knees, but it was too late. *Infinity* had shattered into a million pieces, each shard a glaring mockery of the sculpture itself. Hands shivering, she began to pick up the pieces, cupping them in her palm. "How could you?" she asked on a broken whisper. "Nick, how could you?"

He stood motionless, as shocked as she by what he had done, so stunned by his own actions that he couldn't find his voice.

Brooke got to her feet, holding the broken pieces of the sculpture in her hands like a wounded bird. There was no hope left in her eyes, only a dull, exhausted glimmer of tears.

"You're right," she said through tight lips. "I guess we can't survive it."

Then, still cradling the broken pieces in her hand, Brooke walked out of Nick's house, leaving him to clean up the rest of the mess himself.

CHAPTER SIXTEEN

ABBY HEMPHILL STOOD in her Victorian gown at the front window of her living room, staring out through the vertical blinds and the wrought-iron webbing to the houses up and down the street. Had they heard yet? she wondered with panic. Did they know that her son had sexually harassed a minor?

She turned away from the window, hands shaking, and went to the sofa to fluff the pillows there. Things could never be too neat, she told herself. Never too ordered. If they were to come here—the police, the photographers—at least they would see that her house was immaculate, that her own life was without reproach, that she had tried to keep things sterile and secure.

Her mind drifted away from the room again, and she sat down and stared at the portrait of her son on the wall amid those of her other children. That morning, when his name hadn't appeared in the newspaper, he'd considered himself off the hook. It hadn't seemed to faze him that Brooke Martin and her sister had every reason to press charges and spread the news all over the front page. Hadn't she hurt the girl and her family in that exact way more than once? Wasn't this their perfect opportunity for revenge?

Abby stood up and drifted into the dining room and, with the hem of her gown, polished a smudge off of the table. It came off, but it left a dull spot in the finish. Maybe she could have it redone, she thought. It would cost a lot, but it would be worth it, for then no one would know that it had once had a stain.

Would the news come out in the paper tomorrow? she asked herself, hysterical panic rising in her throat. Would that be the day that the police snapped cuffs on her son and dragged him to jail in front of the entire town of Hayden? Would that be the day that her life was ruined?

She went into the study, to the little drawer where she kept her private things, and sifted through the articles there that she had been particularly proud of. Her son's valedictory speech. Her husband's educator's award. The newspaper article condemning Nick Marcello and Brooke Martin.

She unfolded the yellowed article now, and reread the headlines as they had appeared ten years ago: "Teacher Fired after Affair With Student."

Pretty cut and dry, Abby mused. Didn't leave much room for doubt. But she knew now, as she had known then, that it wasn't *exactly* the truth. And she had done nothing to correct it.

She went back to the window in the living room and wondered if the papers would have a field day with her son. Would they, too, take the story a little further for drama's sake, and allege that her son had actually slept with a seventeen-year-old girl, that he had raped her?

The back of her neck prickled with a thin sheen of perspiration, and she released the top button of her gown and tried to take a deep breath. This must be how Brooke Martin felt the night before her story had broken, she thought. The feeling of being trapped in a steel box with no air and no escape. It was a miserable feeling. Worse than torture.

Vaguely she wondered if she could stop it all, by forcing her son to apologize to Roxy... she could even go so far as apologizing to Brooke herself. Maybe she could even reconsider the budget for the museum. Maybe she could find a way to bring the matter to a vote again.

Feeling a tiny bit better as she stood on the edge of decision, Abby went to the phone and dialed her son's house. His wife answered, her kind, gentle voice oblivious to the turmoil in her marriage, oblivious to the humiliation she might soon suffer. But Bill had been adamant about not warning her... for the sake of the baby, he'd said. Instead, "for the sake of the baby," he was going to wait and let his wife discover the truth in the paper. The thought sent a jolt of anger through Abby. Bill still didn't see that there were wages for his sins, she thought. He still didn't believe the Martin girls would expose him.

"Let me speak to Bill," Abby said.

"He's not here," her daughter-in-law said. "He had to go back to the office to take care of some things."

"The office?" Abby repeated. Instantly she knew that Bill had lied, for city employees rarely had to work at night. Where could he have gone? What could he be up to now?

"Yes," his wife said. "I'll get him to call you when he gets back."

"Do that," Abby said and slammed down the phone.

Tears came to Abby's eyes as she turned back to the window and stared out between the flat bars of the vertical blinds, into the night again. The waste of it all filled her heart, and she began to wonder if it was too late to change. It had all been futile. All the years of doing the right thing, the appropriate thing. All the sacrifices of heart and soul to make things neat and organized. All the loneliness and hollow memories, in the name of propriety.

And now it had come down to a thoughtless son, who in one fell swoop could wipe out all the years of work and care, and make her heart weep for that one mistake in her past, the one wrong choice, the other road she should have taken.

She closed her eyes and cupped her hand over her mouth, and tried to muffle the sobs of despair. But it didn't matter that she didn't succeed, for her husband didn't hear. He was already in bed, sleeping soundly, oblivious that anything in his life wasn't absolutely perfect.

NICK STOOPED DOWN to the floor and swept up the rest of the fragments of the sculpture and trying to hold back the painful sting in his eyes and the misery swelling in his heart. He couldn't believe he had thrown the artwork down, the sculpture that he had loved so much, that he had displayed in his house for ten years, that he had associated with one of the two unconditionally loving relationships he'd ever had in his life.

And now it was destroyed, and so was the love he had with Brooke. He fell back against the counter and set his elbows on his knees, realizing that he was destined to be alone. He didn't know if he still had the strength to endure it.

The phone rang, and he decided not to answer. It wasn't Brooke, he told himself, because she hadn't had time to get home yet, and when she did, he'd be the last one she'd want to speak to. And before he could talk to anyone else, he had things to sort out.

But the phone continued to ring, and finally, out of frustration and mounting anger, he answered. "Yeah," he said.

"Nicholas? Is that you?" His mother's voice came across the line on a sigh of relief.

"Yes, Ma. It's me."

"We were worried!" she cried. "What's the matter with you, disappearing like that without telling anyone? How were we to know that you weren't lying in a ditch somewhere? Where were you?"

Nick rolled his eyes and wished he'd never answered the phone. "I was out of town," he said. "I took the Duesenberg to a collector and sold it." There, he thought. That ought to give her something to bash him with.

"You did what?" his mother shouted. "You sold the Duesenberg? My father's Duesenberg?"

Nick gripped the phone in his fist and considered throwing it against the wall. "Ma, I really don't want to talk about this right now," he said. "I've got a lot on my mind."

"Well, I should say so," his mother lectured. "First running out on that sweet girl and now selling the car. Have you gone crazy in the head?"

Nick squinted and shook his head hard, struggling to make some sense of his mother's words. "What sweet girl? Ma, what are you talking about?"

"I'm talking about Brooke Martin, that's who. She came over looking for you, and we had a nice little visit. She was crying for you. Now, I'd like for you to tell me what is taking you so long. Why haven't you snapped her up by now? Why isn't there a ring on her finger?"

Nick flung himself back against the wall and admitted to himself that he never expected this argument to come out of his mother's mouth. He closed his eyes and tried to picture Brooke breaking down enough to go to his mother in tears. The image was incongruous with the young girl who had run away without looking back. "I thought you didn't approve of her, Ma," he said in a weary, husky voice. "You told me, just the other day, that it was wrong, my relationship with her."

"Well, maybe I was the one who was wrong," his mother muttered in a quieter voice, as if she couldn't let any other family members hear her admit that. "When a woman stands before me with tears in her eyes and defends my son as the most honorable, gentle man she's ever known, what else can I do but believe her?"

Nick looked down at the fragments of the sculpture still in his dustpan. He pinched the bridge of his nose and closed his eyes. "Yeah, well, maybe your first instincts were the right ones, Ma."

"Don't you say that, Nicholas," his mother shouted, and he could almost see her wagging her finger at him. "You marry that girl, Nicky, and finish those windows. And I'll tell everyone that my boy, the artist, was the one who made them."

Nick smiled softly, but his eyes filled with misty sadness as he realized that her blessing may have come a little too late. "Thanks, Ma," he whispered. "I'll do my best."

He hung up the phone and looked down again at the spot on his floor where he had smashed the sculpture and wondered if it was, indeed, too late to put the pieces back together.

IT'S NOT TOO LATE, Roxy thought with a smile as she pulled out of the parking lot at Madame Zouvier's Dance Studio. She'd just informed her dance coach that she was coming back. The woman had embraced her with absolute joy and asked her if she would dance in the June recital.

Roxy nibbled on her lip and asked herself if she was really up to dancing in front of an audience again. Wouldn't she feel just as self-conscious, just as paranoid, as she had the last few times she'd performed? Wouldn't she sense their whispers about her being the sister of the girl who slept with her teacher? Wouldn't she wonder about the lewd fantasies she might provoke in a perverted mind? And now, because of her trouble with Bill Hemphill, there was a chance they could have even more to gossip about.

Her heart told her no, that it wouldn't matter as much anymore. Now she knew Nick, and she knew Brooke, and she knew the relationship that was meant to be. It wasn't dirty and troublesome to her anymore, so somehow, now, she could deal with it. It was more than a story passed around town. It was reality.

Just as Sonny was reality. And he wanted to see her dance.

She smiled and glanced in her rearview mirror and noticed that a pair of headlights followed her too closely. She'd had that same feeling—that someone was tailing her—on her way to the studio tonight.

Beginning to worry, she turned off the street she was on and noticed that the car turned with her. Quickly she reached across the passenger seat to lock the door, while she released the wheel long enough to lock the one closest to her. She made another turn and watched in her mirror as the car followed. As its headlights were briefly diverted, she saw the color and make of the car.

Bill! she thought, panic-stricken. He'd figured out that she wasn't going to report him, and now he was going to make her pay for her bluff.

She stepped on her accelerator and flew home, praying that her father would be there and that she could get safely into the house before Bill caught up with her. Roxy's hands trembled as she raced through town, fearing that he would find some way to keep her from getting there and attack her on a dark street where no one could hear.

Her car skidded to a halt in front of her house, but Brooke's and her parents' cars blocked the driveway, so she had no choice but to park on the street. As fast as she could, Roxy threw it into park and got out.

But Bill was faster than she was. He had grabbed her before she got halfway across the yard, and the potent smell of Scotch on his breath assaulted her as he threw his hand over her mouth and dragged her to the side of the house.

"I'll teach you to threaten me," he said as she struggled to break free. "I'll make you regret that you didn't do this the easy way."

She tried to scream, but her cry became no more than a muffled sound as his hand crushed harder against her mouth.

Bill flung her against the side of the garage and ripped her shirt open, wrestling her fighting arms with his free hand. "Shut up and do what I tell you," he said, "or every neighbor on this street will be out here in thirty seconds flat. I may go down because of you, sweetheart, but you're going down with me. And when it's all over with, it'll be worth it."

Roxy squeezed her eyes shut and fought with all her might as his free hand tore at her clothes.

NICK DROVE ONTO BROOKE'S STREET and saw that there was no place to park, either in front of her house or in the drive. He frowned with dread, wondering if her family had company. *That was all he needed,* he thought. To be cordial as his heart burst to get her alone. Pulling to the curb at the house next door, he took mental inventory of the cars and realized that there was only one there that didn't belong to the family.

Nick parked in front of the house next door and swallowed as he got out, praying that Brooke would agree to talk to him. He didn't know why she would, after what he'd done. But if he could just talk to her . . . calmer . . . more rationally, maybe he could make her understand the fragile state of his heart. Maybe he could make her forgive him.

He closed his car door and started toward her yard, when he heard the broken, muffled cries on the side of the garage.

"Stop . . . please . . No!"

He broke into a run and followed Roxy's voice around the house until he came upon Bill grappling with her against the wall, tearing viciously at her clothes as she wrestled him with all her might.

Something inside Nick snapped, and all the anger and pain and heartache and frustration burst into an explosion of adrenaline as he lunged forward. His fist made shattering contact with Bill's jaw, hurling him to the ground, and Roxy clutched her blouse around her and screamed.

Bill struggled to his feet when he heard the front door of the Martin house open. Nick grabbed his collar and shoved him against the wall, his face inches from Bill's. Unaware that Brooke and her parents had run out of the house at the sound of Roxy's scream and were huddling around the terrified, trembling girl, Nick grabbed Bill's throat. "If you *ever* lay a hand on that girl again, I'll kill you," he promised.

"That's pretty noble coming from you," Bill spat out, his lip dribbling blood. "You know, you and I aren't so different. You liked them young, too, if I remember."

Nick jolted the man's skull against the wall again and jerked his face up so that Bill couldn't avoid seeing the fire and murder in Nick's eyes. "There's a vital difference between you and me," he said through his teeth. "I loved Brooke too much to have ever compromised either her reputation or her self-respect when she was a teenager. And despite the lies that have managed to keep us apart for ten years, we're going to be together for a long time. So if you ever come near Roxy Martin again, I'll know. And I'll be here to carry out my promise."

He threw Bill to his knees, and the man crawled to his feet and smeared the blood across his face. He turned around to see Roxy's father coming toward him with his own murderous intentions obvious in his eyes.

"Call the police, Alice!" George shouted. "Tell them to throw this bastard in jail."

Bill barreled past them toward his car, his eyes luminous. George started after him, but Roxy stopped both him and her mother. "It's over, Daddy," she said, her sobs punctuating her words. "I don't want everyone to know about this. They'll tell more lies, and it'll get out of hand, and we'll spend the next ten years fighting them."

"He won't come back," Nick said, his shoulders rising and falling with each heavy breath. His eyes met Brooke's across the dark expanse of the lawn. "I meant every word I said to him, and he knows it."

Brooke took a tentative step toward him. "Thank God you were here," she whispered.

Nick set his hands on his hips and looked down at his feet, his heart swelling with regret. "Brooke...I'm so sorry...for breaking the sculpture," he said softly. He covered his head with both hands, shook it, dropped his hands to his sides. "I don't know what's gotten into me lately. All I know is that I can't live without you. I need you."

Brooke was in his arms before he even saw her coming toward him, and Nick closed his eyes and held her with the intensity of ten years' love. For a moment it was just the two of them in a world of their own, a world that no one could either penetrate nor destroy.

Then suddenly George Martin tapped Nick's shoulder, and they broke their embrace. Nick let Brooke go and faced the man who had believed for a decade that he'd stolen his daughter's virtue as shamelessly as Bill had tried to steal Roxy's. Holding Roxy protectively under one arm, George extended his right hand to Nick. "I think I've been wrong about a few things," he said quietly. "I owe you an—"

"You don't owe me anything," Nick cut in, his eyes misting with emotion. "You don't even know me."

"Well, maybe it's time we changed that," Brooke's father said.

Brooke's eyes filled with tears as Nick took her father's hand and shook it in both his own. When her family had gone back inside, Nick wilted against the side of the house and raked both hands through his hair. He looked at Brooke, the moonlight casting curved slivers of light in his weary eyes. "What can I say?" he whispered. "I'm a crazy man. Crazy in love. I guess I just don't know how to deal with it."

"I'll teach you," she whispered, stepping toward him and framing his face with her hands, "because you've taught me." Brooke stood on the tips of her toes and pressed her lips against his. "Ten years ago I should have stayed."

"Ten years ago I should have followed." Nick closed his eyes, allowing her lips to trace the lines and angles of his face. "Things could have been so different. Tell me you won't leave me again," he whispered. "Tell me that when we finish the windows, and we aren't bound by this project, that you'll stay no matter what they say about us."

"I'll be wherever you are," she whispered. "I'm not going anywhere."

He blinked the tears from his eyes, gazing up at the moon. "Sometimes loving you makes me so miserable." His arms closed around her, and he pulled her so close that they were one single silhouette against the moonlight. "Put me out of my misery, Brooke," he said, his mouth against her hair. "Marry me and put me out of my misery."

Brooke pressed her forehead against his mouth and closed her eyes, savoring the words she had longed so many times to hear. "What if I marry you, and you're still miserable?" she asked. "What if, in your heart, you never really trust me to trust you, and you question every gesture I make and misinterpret it and read things into it that just aren't there?"

Nick's fingers threaded through her hair, and he tilted her face up to his. "It won't happen again," he said. "It's just that I find it so hard to believe that you could really love me...I couldn't see that you had sold the sculpture for me *because* you love me—that it didn't destroy what we had any more than my selling the Duesenberg destroyed my grandfather's memory. I see that now."

Brooke nodded, and he wiped the tears from her face. "Just like I see that you only broke *Infinity* because you love me, and you were hurt."

"Not one of the brighter things I've ever done," he whispered.

"No," she said. "It wasn't. But we don't need that sculpture, Nick. We have each other. And we won't break apart as easily."

EPILOGUE

THE WHITE LIMOUSINE driven by Horace Anderson pulled to the front entrance of the Hayden Museum, parting the hundreds of townspeople who had gathered there for the unveiling of the windows.

Nick's hand tightened over Brooke's, and she looked up at him with wonder and awe in her emerald eyes. "Nick, look at all these people," she whispered. "They actually came...."

"They came as much out of gratitude as curiosity," the mayor, sitting across from them in the limo, said. "I've been making phone calls myself, making sure everyone in town realizes the sacrifices you two made for those windows."

Nick leaned over and gazed, awestruck, through the window at some faces he recognized. "Let's just hope they like them, or we'll be tarred and feathered by sundown."

"I've seen the windows," Horace said, chuckling. "I don't think that's likely."

A cheer rose up from the crowd as Brooke and Nick got out of the car, hands clasped tightly. They stood still for a moment, utterly amazed at the emotional welcome they received, but finally the mayor gestured for them to cut through the crowd and enter the finished museum.

They went in, shaking hands as they went, and found that the inside held even more people than outside. The room resounded with a loud roar that escalated as they made their way through to the podium.

Brooke felt a heady feeling of disbelief as she climbed the steps to the podium that was decorated in white. She glanced anxiously up at the windows, now covered in sheets that would drop to the floor at the assigned moment. Would the townspeople really like them, when they saw them? Would they understand how important they were to Nick and her?

Nick nudged her lightly and gestured toward a cluster of people standing near the platform. Brooke looked down, saw Roxy and Sonny standing arm in arm, beaming proudly up at them, and her parents, puffed up with pride that all the hooplah was over something their daughter had done. And then she saw Mrs. Marcello and the Castori clan, all waving at Nick as if to show everyone in the room that he was cut from their cloth.

The mayor stepped to the podium and quieted the crowd, and they saw the captive, anxious faces turn to listen. He began to speak about the reasons for the renovation, the steps involved in reconstructing the museum, the expected tourism it would generate. Brooke's mind wandered, and she glanced over the proud faces, one by one, and asked herself if these had, indeed, been the same people who had condemned her and run her out of town? Had they been the ones who had gossiped for weeks after she and Nick eloped? Had they been the ones who had continued to deny her the money, even after Mrs. Hemphill backed down?

Her eyes found the woman she had once detested so, standing among the other council members, that familiar pinched, strained look on her face. Brooke almost felt sorry for her now. So much had gone wrong in Mrs. Hemphill's life in the past year. Bill, her son, had wound up in jail after his baby was born, when he'd driven drunk and rammed his car into the glass front of a gas station, injuring the young woman in the car with him—the young woman who wasn't his wife. The scandal had created an uncrossable fissure in Mrs. Hemphill's family, and she had ultimately left her husband and her immaculate house and taken an apartment in a middle-class section of town.

"But these two weren't daunted by the lack of funds available for a project they so believed in," the mayor was saying, and she moved her gaze back to him. "They made supreme gestures of sacrifice to get the money to build the windows for a town who has been less than gracious to them. I consider this a real act of love for the town of Hayden. But in gratitude for that love, the town of Hayden has a love offering to give to them in return. A belated wedding gift, if they want to consider it that."

Brooke looked up at Nick, who seemed as confused as she as the crowd roared with delight, and she wondered if everyone else in Hayden had been let in on the secret. The mayor stepped toward them and offered them a small envelope.

Nick's hand trembled slightly as he released Brooke's to open it. He caught his breath as he pulled it out. "A check," he whispered.

Brooke gasped at the sight of the amount that more than made up for what they had spent on the windows. She threw her hand over her mouth and looked up at the mayor.

"The town council agreed to match whatever the townspeople themselves could raise," the mayor said, laughing with delight at the shock on their faces. "And boy, did they come up with it."

Tears filled Brooke's eyes, and she turned back to the crowd as another wave of applause swept over the audience. Nick drew her against him, his own poignant, eloquent expression touching her heart as he pulled Brooke with him to the microphone. "Thank you," he said, his voice cracking with emotion. "But there wasn't anything short of blowing us up that would have kept us from finishing those windows."

He waited a moment as the laughter died down, and finally he swallowed and nodded to Brooke that the moment of truth had come. "So now, if you're ready, I guess it's time to see what all the fuss is about."

He leaned over and cupped Brooke's chin and dropped a kiss on her lips. "I love you," he whispered.

"I love you," she said, trust and adoration glistening in her eyes. "Now, let's do it."

Together they reached for the single rope that would release the veils all the way around the museum, and the crowd grew still in anticipation.

They pulled, and the sheets billowed to the ground, revealing a lifetime of color and emotions, events and milestones.

For a moment no one, of all the hundreds of people present, made a sound as they gazed up, their eyes circling the room, quietly experiencing the poetry of the windows.

Brooke's mouth went dry, and she shot Nick a panicked look. His frown told her he was as bewildered as she by the absolute silence.

Then suddenly, near the podium, someone began to clap slowly. Brooke and Nick turned to see Abby Hemphill, standing with tears in her eyes, clapping fervently as her gaze moved around the room.

Then everyone was clapping, and Brooke saw other faces wet with tears and children laughing at panels that portrayed their own antics and lovers embracing and elderly people nodding in affirmation that, yes, they had captured the whole span of life. And it seemed that each person present embraced the windows as if they had been put there to speak directly to them.

Nick pulled Brooke into his arms and kissed her before God and the world, beneath the halo of beauty they had created with their own hands. And as he held her close, Brooke knew that the rest of her life with Nick would be as intense as the work they produced together, as emotional as the visions they shared, as all-encompassing as the windows that skirted the ceiling of the museum for all the world to celebrate.

And she knew that *Infinity* would forever define the strength and limitlessness of their love.

Harlequin Superromance®

COMING NEXT MONTH

#382 THE CLOSER WE GET • Ruth Glick
A mining accident had left Stephen Gallagher
confined to a wheelchair. He couldn't marry Elena
Castille under such circumstances . . . no matter how
much he loved her. But he'd underestimated Elena's
ability to overcome any obstacle thrown in her path.

#383 BLUE MOON • Dawn Stewardson
In 1862, a gold miner lugged a beautiful, strangely
dressed woman into Dr. Henry Lockhart's office.
The woman—Erica James—was unconscious, but
Hank reckoned there wasn't much wrong with her.
Then she came to and started muttering nonsense
about being from the future. From 1989, to
be exact. . . .

#384 TO WEAVE TOMORROW • Debbi Bedford
Jamie Forrester had come to the Texas-Mexican
border to teach immigrant children about life in the
land of opportunity. Unfortunately, even her
classroom wasn't a refuge from "*La Migra*"—
border guard Daniel Salinas. Despite their
conflicting loyalties, Jamie fell in love. But love
knows no boundaries and there was a wall wider than
the Rio Grande around Daniel's heart. . . .

#385 CROSS TIDES • Elaine K. Stirling
Talia Gibrian was fiery, dark, exotic—a striking
contrast to Matt Lehtonen's blond good looks and
gentle disposition. And while Matt had been busy
farming and raising his two kids, Talia had been
overthrowing a government. Matt was convinced
that *he* was about to be her next coup!

HARLEQUIN Temptation

Montana Man
BARBARA DELINSKY

When you think of Harlequin Temptation, it's hard not to think of Barbara Delinsky. She was there from the start to help establish Temptation as a fresh, exciting line featuring extremely talented storytellers. The title of her very first Temptation—*A Special Something*—describes what Barbara has continued to bring to you over the years.

We thought it was high time to officially recognize Barbara Delinsky's contribution to Harlequin. And by happy coincidence, she gave us *Montana Man* for publication in December. We couldn't have hoped for a better book to carry Harlequin's Award of Excellence or a better gift to give *you* during the holiday season.

It's tempting to say that, of Barbara's eighteen Temptations, *Montana Man* is the most moving, most satisfying, most wonderful story she's ever written. But each of her books evokes that response. We'll let you be the judge in December....

AE-MM-1

Have You Ever Wondered If You Could Write A Harlequin Novel?

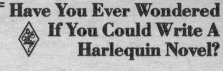

Here's great news—Harlequin is offering a series of cassette tapes to help you do just that. Written by Harlequin editors, these tapes give practical advice on how to make your characters—and your story—come alive. There's a tape for each contemporary romance series Harlequin publishes.

Mail order only

All sales final
